# SWORDS
# &
# SORCERIES

## Tales
## of
## Heroic Fantasy
### Volume 4

# SWORDS

# &

# SORCERIES

## Tales of Heroic Fantasy
### Volume 4
### Presented by

# David A. Riley

# Jim Pitts

**PARALLEL UNIVERSE PUBLICATIONS**

First Published in the UK in 2022
Copyright © 2022
Cover & interior artwork © 2022 Jim Pitts
*In the Iron Woods* © 2022 Dev Agarwal
*My People Were Fair and Wore Stars in Their Hair* © 2022
Andrew Darlington
*At Sea* © 2022 Geoff Hart
*The Flesh of Man* © 2022 Frank Sawielijew
*City at the Mouth of Chaos* © 2022 Adrian Cole
*In the Belly of the Beast* © 2022 Edward Ahern
*The Tracks of the Pi Nereske* © 2019 Wendy Nikel
First published in *Epic Fantasy*, Flame Tree Press
*Slaves of the Monolith* © 2022 Paul D. Batteiger
*The Green Wood* © 2022 David Dubrow
*Demonic* © 2022 Phil Emery
*The Whips of Malmac* © 2022 H. R. Laurence

**ISBN: 978-1-7398326-7-4**

**Parallel Universe Publications, 130 Union Road, Oswaldtwistle, Lancashire, BB5 3DR, UK**

Dedicated as always to the memory
of writer, editor,
and publisher,
Charles Black
who inspired this anthology series

# CONTENTS

 # INTRODUCTION

Welcome to our fourth volume of swords and sorcery stories, which sees the welcome return of some writers from previous volumes and an introduction to many new ones. We have increased the number of stories and the page count. Of the eleven writers in this volume six have never been published by us before (Frank Sawielijew, Edward Ahern, Wendy Nikel, Paul D. Batteiger, David Dubrow, and H. R. Laurence), though we also welcome the return of Dev Adarwal, Andrew Darlington, Geoff Hart, Adrian Cole, and Phil Emery.

Opening this time is Dev Agarwal whose story *Stone Snake* appeared in volume 2. Dev is a science fiction and fantasy writer. His fiction has been published online and in magazines including *Albedo One, Aoife's Kiss, Aeon* and, forthcoming, in *Mithila Review*. His non-fiction has been published online and in a variety of magazines.

Dev has been editing non-fiction for a number of years and is non-fiction editor for the magazine *Khoreo*. He is also the editor of *Focus*, the magazine for genre writers produced by the British Science Fiction Association.

His fantasy often draws on historical events. His story *In the Iron Woods* is a sequel to *Stone Snake*.

Regular contributor Andrew Darlington tells me he bought the very first edition of *2000AD*, and also bought the latest issue of the Galaxy's Greatest comic.

"My latest book is *On Track: The Hollies, Every Album, Every Song* (SonicBond Publishing), and I regularly write about music for glossy bi-monthly *RnR* - most recently interviewing Kiki Dee and Suzi Quatro, as well as lots of people you've probably never heard of!"

Andrew's website is:

*http://andrewdarlington.blogspot.co.uk/*

Geoff Hart last appeared in volume 1, with a witty take on the Fafhrd and Gary Mouser stories. His story, *Chain of Command,* was an affectionate homage to Fritz Leiber's disreputable heroes, but "with gender swapped protagonists and a more modern sensibility."

This time he has written a humorous homage to Asterix and Obelix, though again with "gender swapped protagonists".

Geoff works as a scientific editor, specialising in helping scientists who have English as their second language publish their research. He's the author of the popular *Effective Onscreen Editing* and *Write Faster With Your Processor.* He also writes fiction in his spare time, and has sold 54 stories thus far. He has had stories in two of Darrell Schweitzer's Lovecraft anthologies: *Mountains of Madness Revealed* and *Shadows Out of Time,* and in *Andromeda Spaceways Inflight Magazine* and elsewhere. Visit him online at:

*www.geoff-hart.com*

*The Flesh of Man* is Frank Sawielijew's first story in *Swords & Sorceries: Tales of Heroic Fantasy.* His story follows the adventures of Thurzo, a barbarian who seeks to hunt and slay a dread-lizard, whose heart can heal his father's ailment. His way leads him into the mighty Karthan Range, and the woman who acts as his guide warns him of the savage harpies that dwell there…

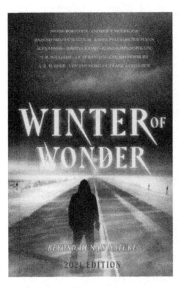

An "eccentric" Russo-German author with Bulgarian roots, Frank Sawielijew loves to forge fantastic tales set in strange, imaginative worlds. Due to his love for the pulp classics, he often combines fantasy and science fiction in unorthodox ways. He writes in both English and German and has had a handful of his short stories in various anthologies since 2015. He has also written profess-ionally for the video game industry. When he's not working on anything, he wastes his time watching campy 1980s barbarian films, taking long

walks through nature and playing *Thief*, "the best game ever".

Adrian Cole has the distinction of having been in all three previous volumes of *Swords & Sorceries: Tales of Heroic Fantasy* and returns this time with another instalment in his popular Voidal series.

Adrian has had some two dozen novels and numerous short stories published, including e-books and audio books for nearly fifty years, writing sf, fantasy and horror. His collection *Nick Nightmare Investigates* won the British Fantasy Award for Best Collection in 2015.

A major new historical fantasy trilogy, *War on Rome*, has its first volume, *Arminius, Bane of Eagles*, published in September by DMR Books (US). Set in an alternative Romano/Celtic Europe, the trilogy continues with *Germanicus, Lord of Eagles* and *Boudica, The Savage Queen*. Adrian writes regularly for *Weirdbook, Heroic Fantasy Quarterly* and *Tales from the Magician's Skull*.

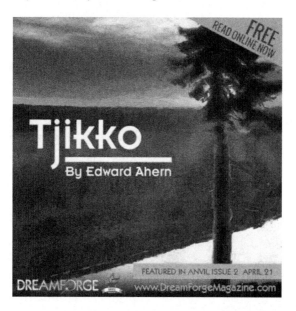

Newcomer to this series, Edward Ahern started writing fiction at sixty-seven, and poetry at seventy. He sometimes detours into literary fiction but is best known as an innovative genre writer and poet. He's tucked away several awards and honourable mentions for four hundred published short stories and poems, and six books. They've appeared 800 times in ten countries and, counting reprints, over two hundred publications. Several of his stories can be listened to through Audible.

In addition to writing, Ed's been abusing other writers for several years at *Bewildering Stories*, where he serves on the review board and manages a posse of nine review editors. Ed is an active member of several writing groups, including the Fairfield Scribes, and the Poets' Salon, where he's known for his tough-love comments. He is also lead editor for the *Fairfield Scribes Micro Fiction* journal.

He has his original wife but advises that after fifty some years together they are both out of warranty. Two children and five grandchildren serve as affection focus and money drain.

His writing began with a degree in journalism from the University of Illinois. Ed's career thereafter has been "an enjoyably demented hopscotch game." U.S. Navy officer (diver and bomb disarmer); reporter for the *Providence Journal*; intelligence officer living in Germany and Japan; international sales and marketing executive at a North American paper company (twenty-three years, seventy-four countries visited, MBA from NYU); ten more years as a sales executive for the company that also owns the New England Patriots; and retirement into writing like hell to make up for lost time.

Another newcomer to *Swords & Sorceries: Tales of*

*Heroic Fantasy,* Wendy Nikel is a speculative fiction author with a degree in elementary education, a fondness for road trips, and "a terrible habit of forgetting where" she's left her cup of tea. Her short fiction has been published by *Analog, Beneath Ceaseless Skies, Nature,* and elsewhere. Her time travel novella series, beginning with *The Continuum,* is available from World Weaver Press. For more info, visit *wendynikel.com*

Another newcomer, Paul D. Batteiger has been writing ever since he knew what it was. He has won awards, and his fiction has been published in numerous anthologies such as *Barbarian Crowns, Beauty Has Her Way, Fast Ships, Black, Sails* and others. Fantasy, SF, Adventure, and Horror fiction are all things he loves. His inspirations include Lovecraft, Dunsany, Clark Ashton Smith, and especially Robert E.  Howard. He lives and works in Tulsa, Oklahoma.

*The Green Wood* is also David Dubrow's first story in this series. David is a husband, father, and writer who lives on the west coast of Florida in the United States. His published works include the *Armageddon* trilogy of Biblical horror novels, numerous short stories, and a non-fiction book about surviving a Zombie Apocalypse. You can find him online at *davedauthor.com.*

Author of *Demonic*, Phil Emery's work has been published in the UK, USA, Europe and Canada since the seventies. His fantasy has appeared in the Rogue Blades' anthologies *Return of the Sword* and *Demons*, and *Swords & Sorceries: Tales of Heroic Fantasy Volume 2*. His book-length fantasy *The Shadow Cycles* was published by Immanion Press. His essays on S&S have appeared in *The Dark Man* journal of Robert E. Howard studies and a thesis on the subject, 'Revivifying the Ur-text' can be found online from Loughborough University.

A long-time fan of weird fiction, H. R. Laurence, another newcomer to this series, lives in London, where he works in the film industry as a cameraman and editor. His work revolves around cameras and computers, but his writing tends to focus on sword and sorcery.

His work has appeared in *Whetstone* and will feature later this year in *Rakehell* and the anthology *Samhein*

*Sorceries*. He's also the writer of an upcoming B-movie with the working title of *Viking Revenge*.

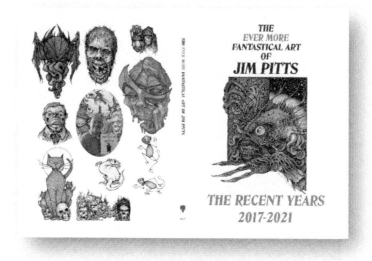

Finally, this volume is again graced with the artwork of award-winning artist Jim Pitts, whose second hardcover volume of his art has just been published by Parallel Universe Publications: *The Ever More Fantastical Art of Jim Pitts*.

David A. Riley

Oswaldtwistle. 2022

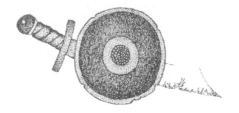

# IN THE IRON WOODS
## *Dev Agarwal*

"We go to pay homage?" Princess Irene asked Arvo. "We are imperials, not Lamian subjects."

"We pay our respects to our allies," Harry said smoothly. "No one expects us to swear fealty. But this way, we do not draw attention to you, my lady."

A wooden staircase led up to the common room of the inn. Before they ascended, Simeon said quietly, "Harry, how many soldiers do you have with you?"

"A century. And the best, Seraphim."

Simeon smiled. He knew their worth.

As Harry Arvo had promised, Sir Ned Flores held his court in the inn. His huge army was bivouacked for a mile around it. Lamian knights stood inside, drinking and planning their campaign. Scythian and Sicambri horse lords, and Galatian mercenaries lined the common room, drinking beer and wine.

Irene wrinkled her nose at the odour. Simeon smiled again. It was the familiar medley of spilled wine and vomit, horse oats, lamp oil, and salt pork.

"My lord General," Arvo said. "May I present Baron Simeon and his wife to you?"

Ned Flores was a minor Lamian lordling, but he dressed grandly in a gold and blue tunic. He was not an impressive man. Waddling and egg-shaped, he stood shorter than his serjeants and the waiting tribesmen.

"Baron Simeon," Ned Flores said, "The Stone Snake, no?"

One of the younger Scythians looked interested to hear that name.

"You are the Emperor's bodyguard?" Flores said. He took in Irene's tunic and breeches. "And with you a lady, dressed as a male rider!" Sounding delighted to see such a thing. As excited as a child.

"The Baroness Arina," Arvo said, careful to hide that Princess Irene was the daughter and heir of Emperor Flavius. The Lamians were allies but not confidants.

The Scythian stepped forward with a look so intent that it would be insulting out in the yard. "You are the Stone Snake?"

"This is Baron Simeon," Arvo said.

The Scythian said, "You will not know me. I am Rami Huskiss. But you will know my lord father, Davith Huskiss. Head of our clan."

Simeon spoke, but a fraction too late. "Of course. Davith Huskiss is well known – far beyond the Iron Woods."

The Scythian noticed that delay. A flicker of annoyance darkened his eyes. Rami Huskiss was young and well-muscled. A warrior, Simeon saw, who bore a cavalry sword.

"You hunt the Scythians, Captain-General?" Simeon asked.

"We do!" Flores' eyes shone. "A splendid business. Ten thousand men and five thousand Scythian allies. Rami is leading us, our head scout."

"We wish you success," Irene said.

"Come with us!" Flores said. His men laughed politely at this sally. "You look like a fine warrior, Baroness."

Arvo made their excuses and drew Simeon and Irene away. Outside the inn, they returned to their horses, tied off beside a wide river.

Scythian warriors stood outside drinking. Warriors from the forest, their faces were hairy, with braided and forking beards. They covered their arms with woad and swirling blue tattoos. Simeon wondered how many of these men were married into the Scythian families that Lamia hunted. How did they feel warring with their kinfolk?

On their horses, Arvo led them across a meadow beside bulging lines of oaks and fir trees.

This was the start of the Iron Woods.

"You know these woods?" Arvo asked Simeon.

"A little." The imperial highway, the Fossway, ran through their edge. He had travelled down it on his way west in his search for Princess Irene.

Irene asked, "The Lamians fight for this forest?"

Simeon said, "This is the home of the Scythians. And also their allies, the Sicambri and the Bructeri."

"And now they are at war," Arvo said. "The Scythians have foolishly attacked the Kingdom of Lamia."

Dense, tough trees, Simeon thought, trotting alongside the Iron Woods. And those woods were filled with tribesman, just as tough. Scythians, intermarried with the Sicambri and Bructeri, and with fathers sworn to sons across each tribe. The Scythians made for formidable archers and horsemen. They had fought for Irene's father, the Emperor Flavius. They also fought as sellswords for the King of Lamia.

"The last time I was at my father's Court, I had not heard of fighting in these woods," Irene said.

Arvo said, "Recent trouble. Your father sent me to Lamiae as soon as he got word. I am here as his legate and speak on his behalf. The Lamians arrived a week ago, hussars and hoplites. Commanded by Sir Ned Flores."

Simeon stretched his back. His tailbone ached from

riding. "How big a force did Flores say he has?"

"Ten thousand men. Mostly on foot." Arvo hesitated. "They are reinforced by sellswords."

"Which sellswords?" Irene asked.

Arvo grew tense. "Some are Galatian. But most are Scythian."

Ned Flores hunted Scythians with more Scythians.

That, Simeon thought, might give a man pause for thought. But that was another man, not Flores.

"This is not our fight," Simeon said.

There were many days' hard travel ahead to get Irene back to her father. Emperor Flavius waited impatiently for her return to his Court at Great Stone.

They rode beside the river. The tribesmen had placed an iron grill over the bright coals of a fire. On this they'd laid an array of forest meats – parrot, squirrel, dog and globs of blood sausage that sizzled and spattered over the coals. The acrid smell drifted on the breeze as the meat sputtered and ran with juice.

"What river is this?" Simeon asked Arvo.

"The Widow," Arvo said. "I took it as far as the Fossway. There is a bridge nearby, the Milkhouse, where the river narrows. I have a barge holding there, ready for the princess."

Simeon had not considered the water route.

Irene settled her horse, skittish and high stepping near the fire. "That roasting meat is making me quite ill. Yet I must eat." She looked at Arvo, "No dog, if it pleases you."

Simeon studied the grill as it spat. "No dog. But blood sausage?"

*

"You riled the Scythian, Rami," Irene said as they rode out of the meadow.

"I insulted Davith Huskiss' son," Simeon agreed. "He seems quick to take offence."

Irene said, "You seem to suspect that the Scythian scouts are not to be trusted. If they are false, they will not let that insult pass. Perhaps you have tested them by accident."

Simeon smiled at the princess. They had ridden for five days together. She had been closely observing him.

"Test away," Arvo said drily. "As long as any fight remains with you, Snake, and not with the man *next to you*."

Beyond the meadow they rode among goat-hide tents that spread in all directions. Arvo led them across lines of Lamian troops, organised in squadrons, and the jumble of their Scythian allies. Bearded and drunk, dicing or wrestling, the tribesmen were loud and unruly. The Lamians looked on disapprovingly.

Arvo's imperial guard, the cavalry called the Seraphim, were quartered by the river Widow. Camp followers and traders were scattered throughout the lines. But none came close to the disciplined ranks of Seraphim.

"This strike into the Iron Woods is no small endeavour," Irene said. She dismounted at a corral of Seraphim horses and a groom took her horse.

"Indeed, my lady." Arvo led them to a cooking fire with a sizzling cauldron.

"But how nimble is this army?" she asked.

Arvo and Simeon exchanged a glance.

Irene said, "What? You're amused that I have a thought in my head?"

Simeon laughed. "Ignore Harry. He's spent too long at Court and with Ned Flores. It's made him slow-witted."

Taking a bowl of soup, Irene said, "I *grew up* at Court."

"You expect courtesies from this one?" Arvo passed Simeon soup – beef and onion with crispy turnips.

They were all too hungry to argue further. And besides, Irene was right, Simeon thought. Flores' army stretched in every direction. But when it moved it would crawl, dragging noisy Scythians or inflexible with battalions of hoplites.

"And what of our Seraphim? Are our riders more nimble?" Irene asked.

"We would struggle also. That is why we go no further. We mount up at first light and ride clear." Simeon looked at Arvo. "Your duties allow your absence from Flores?"

"No. I am Emperor Flavius' legate."

Arvo had a royal charter to represent the Emperor. But Flores seemed, at best, destined to blunder through these woods hunting Scythians that he'd never find.

"Your duties to me come first," Irene said, brushing aside Arvo's concerns. "As the Baron says, we ride at first light. I want all the men as my bodyguard."

A shrewd answer, Simeon thought. Irene saw the folly in Flores' mission and the risk to Arvo remaining here. She was the Emperor's heir and she protected his courtier.

Arvo hesitated for a moment, then nodded and returned to his soup.

*

The sun began to set as Arvo changed over the watch. The cooking fires burned in the soft summer light. Mosquitoes whined about Simeon's ears as he strode past the Seraphim's tents and into the woods. Arvo had found Simeon a black bottle of chanian wine. Sweet and light on a summer's evening, he sipped it as he walked.

The woods ran for leagues, crammed with outlaws, Lamian deserters, warring tribes, and wolves. Simeon could imagine wandering in a green world that stretched out forever.

Silvery moths danced through the campfires' light. Running water was a steady pressure on his ears from the Widow snaking unseen nearby.

Gods still walked this land, Simeon thought. He was far from the Court at Great Stone. Out here, away from orders and the rules of men and emperors, he was much closer to the old gods. When he stared through the mossy backs of those trees, he expected to see the gods step out and reveal themselves . . .

The lowering sun turned the sky bloody. Like chanian wine, a fine red shade spilled across the darkening sky.

Inattentive for that moment, Simeon missed the man's approach from further in the woods. But, just as Simeon thought he'd sensed the gods within these green walls, he sensed him before he stepped any closer.

Through a spin of midges, Rami said, "Your pardon if I startle you." The younger man bowed. "I would be pleased to join you."

Simeon held out the bottle. "No cups, but make free with it."

Rami took the wine and sipped. He threw a tall shadow.

"You are out strolling, Baron? Beyond your sentries?"

"These are your woods. With your army close by. We are safe enough."

They walked together.

Rami was the man that led Ned Flores into the forest to quell the Scythian rebels. Simeon wondered at that. What loyalty Rami felt to Lamia, as he turned on the Scythians and their allies – his cousins and childhood friends?

"The Captain-General was excited by your arrival." Rami stepped over a fallen log. He glanced back at Simeon and tossed back his hair. It flowed as long as a maiden's. But Rami was far from girlish. He was younger than Simeon and probably stronger. "You have quite the reputation. The Stone Snake. Emperor Flavius' first knight."

"Too much of a reputation," Simeon said. "In truth, any reputation is too much."

"Why so?"

"Our business is fighting. That's easier done when your opponent misjudges you. A reputation gets in *your* way, not your enemy's."

"Yet your reputation grants you special favour from your emperor, no?"

Rami pushed past a weeping willow's branches. The woods smelled of wet, living things. The branches tugged as Simeon brushed by them. The oaks were squat, but the ashes and firs towered over them, forming a dark canopy.

"As well as special favour, do you also undertake special tasks for your emperor?" Rami asked.

Here it comes, Simeon thought.

"Are you on one of those special tasks now?" Rami asked.

"I am returning to the empire, travelling up the Fossway."

"And the lady you ride with? A special friend?"

"My wife," Simeon said. The lie sounded unconvincing to his own ears.

"A woman who manages to command Captain Harry Arvo. He scurries for baths and servants for her. And he readies *all* of his Seraphim to escort you to the border. Tell me, is that normal?"

Rami steadied the bottle on an oak's branch. His sable

26

cloak fell open. His sword belt carried a sabre, a cavalry officer's weapon. An old leather belt rode low on his hips, its heavy buckle was silver wrought in a tribal pattern, a honeycomb.

Simeon nodded at it. "Fine work. Scythian, is it?"

"Yes, my mother's."

"You keep the old ways, then?"

"Yes." A slight pause and Rami smiled, his teeth very white in the forest's gloom. "But I am sworn to Ned Flores. I am a duke of Lamia now."

Simeon noted the bulge of a second shorter blade on Rami's hip. He walked on, careful of the damp uneven ground. "Yet you are of the Huskiss clan still?"

Rami watched Simeon. "A man can keep two oaths."

"No man I know has managed that," Simeon said, setting his feet firmly as the ground levelled out.

"You must not know any Scythians."

"How does your clan feel about this war? About Lamians in their woods? Lamians hunting fellow Scythians?"

"My clan is led by my lord father. Davith Huskiss took an oath to the Lamians. He sent his oldest son to fight alongside them as brothers."

"Brother. Or hostage? You were Scythian royalty but looked down on by the civilised Lamians? Was that the way of it?"

Rami shook his head, a minimal movement to say no. But he no longer smiled. His lip tightened. Some memory, the slights of his time with the Lamians perhaps, played out over his face. Simeon was close enough to smell his sweat above the mulch of the forest floor. Rami's eyes darkened with irritation as they had in the inn.

"I know the Lamians. They are proud. Yet what do they

make of you? Are you Lamian, and a tribal traitor, or still Scythian, but exiled to Lamia?"

"Scythians are strong people. This dilemma you think I have, Baron," Rami said, "That would only occur if General Flores meets the Scythian rebels."

"You think he will not?"

Rami shrugged. "These are big woods."

Unsaid, but there before them, was Rami's view of Captain-General Flores. Too helpless to even find the enemy.

Simeon raised his fist in front of Rami's face and slowly extended his index finger, pointing around them. "Here, in these woods, if a traitor were to plot against Ned Flores, it could spell disaster for Lamia."

"No mission into the Iron Woods is without risk. But we are soldiers."

"And what do you think Flores' hussars would do to that person? To a so-called soldier who sought to betray them all?"

They both knew. Flaying or a crucifixion. A public death and a slow, painful one.

He read the Scythian's tension. Rami loomed in the red light of the sunset, almost rearing at Simeon.

Simeon felt those gods again, moving closer, intrigued by their tautness, by the emotions stirring between the two men.

They balanced, tipping in towards one another.

Simeon saw how much Rami wanted to fight, to test himself against the Stone Snake. But the Scythian relaxed. He stepped backwards, refusing to give in to that desire.

"Look elsewhere for your traitors and spies," Rami said. "For I am bound to Flores as my clan is bound to his great house."

Liar's words.

Rami smiled again. But he even as he did, he probed, and tried a new cut. "And you might know more than I about spying and secrets kept from Lamia, eh, my lord Baron?"

Rami handed the chanian bottle back, bowed and bid Simeon good day. "You break camp in the morning?"

Simeon had not told anyone when they would leave. But the Scythians saw everything.

"We do."

"I will see you on the morrow, then."

Rami spoke of *special tasks* and *secrets*.

He knew who Irene was. And he was not afraid to let Simeon know it.

Ned Flores, Simeon thought, watch your Scythians closely.

Rami moved nimbly through the forest, comfortable and at home.

If Rami did not lead Flores into a trap, it was a waste of a trap so readily at hand.

*

Coming back out of the woods, Simeon strode through the lines of Seraphim to Arvo's tent.

"Irene?" he asked Arvo.

"In her pavilion. I have men stationed around her –"

"Saddle up."

"My lord?" he asked, surprised.

"Break camp and get us out of here, Harry."

"By night?"

Simeon nodded.

Arvo hesitated, then said, "The Scythians?" His voice pitched lower now.

Simeon nodded. "Rami knows who Irene is. He if full

of insinuations and questions. Soon all the Scythians will know."

"They are the friends of Lamia. And Lamia is *our* ally."

"The Princess's identity must be kept secret. We cannot risk her – and I don't trust Rami. He may be playing the Lamians false – there is no reason for us to remain here to find out."

"You'll want to reach the Fossway," Arvo said.

"What's our most direct path to it?"

"Half a league. The southern tip of the Iron Woods lies between us, which will slow us, but at a cautious pace in the dark we can still reach it in hours. Then we head for the Milkhouse bridge and the crossing of the Widow."

"Your barge?"

"Held with Seraphim. It awaits your arrival."

"Good work, Harry. That's our way."

Arvo whistled for his serjeants-of-horse. "Strike camp. Quietly, lads. Send the men out, in groups of ten. Abandon the tents. Weapons and rations only. And *no women*."

His serjeants slid away to pass the word.

"We inform Irene now?" Arvo asked.

Simeon nodded. "We put Irene in the middle of our cavalry."

"Where do you fear attack?"

"In the Iron Woods? From everywhere."

*

The Seraphim slipped into the dusk. Simeon stood by the fire with Arvo. A goat roasted on a spit and one of the men turned it regularly. Everything normal, even as ten men saddled up to run their mounts. With three-foot lances in hand and their shields, the Seraphim trotted out.

Simeon watched the sky. Thunderheads crowded the horizon in the low light. "Rain for the rest of the watch," Arvo said.

Irene appeared behind them, dressed in britches and a doublet. Her hair was wet and pulled back beneath a scarf.

"Baron?" she asked, puzzled, summoned from her bath into rain and mud.

"Stay here, if you please," Arvo said. He nodded to a serjeant, ahorsed and waiting. This man wheeled and whistled like a jay. Nine men rode out with him, a little faster than the first.

"We ride?" Irene said, grasping what was happening.

"We do, my lady," Simeon said.

"It is the Scythians?"

"We are just cautious. We ride eventually, let us go now."

"Baron," Arvo said, "once we leave the Fossway we may have the advantage." The legate smiled. "The Scythians do not travel on water. They do not know the art of swimming."

Fifty Seraphim in batches of ten had left the encampment.

"You have our rear-guard," Simeon said. "Irene rides beside me."

Arvo whistled and a serjeant rode closer. "This is Jon Rutt," Arvo said to Simeon. "He will guide you well."

They mounted up and started a slow trot through the meadow. Lamian eyes watched them – and Rami would know of their departure soon enough. But he could do nothing without alerting the Lamians.

"Why do we ride at night and not tomorrow?" Irene asked, drawing her mare up beside Simeon.

"It is not safe around Davith Huskiss' son. He taunted

us. He plays games insinuating that you are the Emperor's daughter. He does not respect your father's name."

"You have us ride due to disrespect?"

Simeon smiled at that. "No respect. No *fear*. Why is he not more scared of the Empire? The Lamians demand his good conduct to us as their ally. But Rami holds his own general in contempt. You can't trust a man like that."

"You cannot *know*," she insisted.

Simeon said, "Think on this, Princess. What if I am wrong?"

"Then you insult our Lamian allies and a friendly tribe."

"I do," Simeon agreed and showed her his indifference at that.

"And if you're right, you keep me safe and you keep the Seraphim from the fight," Irene said.

"Your father demands it of me."

The long meadow gave way to broken ground, choppy gullies and grassy scrub as they lowered into the tangle of the Iron Woods. The lead serjeant called for walking pace and for one man in two to light lanterns. The mounts slowed. Simeon's bay picked its way clear, high stepping over the cluttered ground. Jon Rutt appeared beside him, bearing a lantern. The serjeant was a grey man with a face like a closed fist.

The column walked through rain-soaked trees that shivered with water. The forest spread into a great palace, green and dark by lantern light.

Thunder shook the sky, shaking the ceiling of spread branches. The rain sped up, striking his men's helmets and ringing off their shields. Irene cursed and shook rainwater from her scarf. Birds scattered above them, unseen in the darkness. Dark rivers of water tumbled across the riders.

Jon Rutt called to Simeon, "My lord."

Men came out of the sheets of rain. On foot and on shaggy ponies. Tribesmen, carrying their swords and axes openly. They had the numbers on the Seraphim. And they had archers. Armed with powerful recursive bows.

"Behind us as well, Snake," Irene said, sounding tense. Shadows fluttered through the trees, beyond range of the Seraphim's lanterns. The woods crawled with armed men.

There was no doubting the Scythians now.

Rutt swung his falchion free, the blade singing in the wind. "Stand aside," he said.

"How disappointing," a voice called from the darkness. "You are Seraphim but you do not croon sweetly." The Scythian ranks parted and their leader rode forward. A short man in armour. His breastplate ran like molten bronze in the lantern light.

Rain pattered his pot helm.

Armour, Simeon saw. Not how Scythians went to war.

"What is the meaning of this?" Arvo said, riding up the narrow trail to them.

"I come on behalf of your good friend, Rami Huskiss."

Irene squinted into the rain. "You're no Scythian."

The small man smiled. "Galatian," he said.

"A sellsword," Arvo said, displeased.

"Mercenary Captain Liam Vaniti. Master of horse for Rami Huskiss. He would speak with you once more, Stone Snake." He looked past Simeon's shoulder. "About your travelling companion. That lady."

"We are the imperial Seraphim. Household cavalry to Emperor Flavius," Arvo said. His voice shook with anger. "Stand aside. The Emperor will hear of this, *sellsword*. Our Lamian cousins will *hear* of this."

"You do not yield?" Liam Vaniti asked.

"No," Simeon said.

"As you wish." Vaniti sounded pleased. He raised his arm high. When he dropped it, the rain filled with the snoring sound of arrows in flight. The darts burst from between the trees and the night split open with the screams of men. Their horses reared, scared and confused.

"Shields!" Simeon shouted. His bay danced back, also scared, but Simeon had his shield up, pulling at Irene's arm with his free hand. Steel and stone-tipped arrows rained down. Painted tribesmen ran out to meet the imperial riders, shrieking battle cries.

Arvo kicked his horse and shouted to his men. "To me! To me!"

Simeon's horse reared, and its hoof cracked a tribesmen in the head, even as Simeon drew his falchion and struck left and right through the darkness. He forced his horse about, trying to block the tribesmen from Princess Irene as they fell on them from all sides. The tribesmen were ghosts, darting and jabbing with their spears.

The sellsword, Vaniti, popped out of the darkness beside Simeon. He called out, "No harm to the woman. Or the Stone Snake."

Simeon leaned out over his bay, swinging from his hips. His falchion's heavy blade sliced hard against Vaniti's helm. The impact of the blow ran up his arm. Vaniti flew off his horse, his pothelm whipped from his head. Simeon would have killed him then, crushed his skull for him, because that mercenary captain had not liked being hit. Had not liked being knocked down, with his eyes wide in his white face. But there were Scythians everywhere. They flooded round Vaniti, slamming clubs off Simeon's shield, striking at his horse until it screamed and threw him off. Simeon tumbled, sprawling through a spilled world of lanterns and trees and rain, until he slammed the ground, losing his shield, but still holding tight to his falchion. His horse screamed as high as a woman and landed with a thud that shook the ground.

Above him, Simeon saw Jon Rutt reach Irene, blood splattering across his face as he sheared the arm off the Scythian grabbing her reins. Irene screamed, as did the maimed Scythian and then men mobbed the serjeant, dragging him into the mud and killing him with their swords.

Irene's mare shuddered and kicked, before the Scythian's heavy fists gripped her saddle. Arvo was there, hacking them back with his sword. Simeon ran to join him. Something heavy landed hard between his shoulders – perhaps a mace – and staggered him. He spun without looking and struck flesh with his sword. Something dense as lead struck his thigh and his leg folded. On one knee, a Scythian took hold of his sword arm, wrestling with him. The muddy ground rose up and smacked his face.

Rainwater smothered his nose and mouth.

"Simeon Stone Snake," a voice said, deeply satisfied. "The druids will want this one." Then something struck his head with dizzying force and the world spun with light.

*

Simeon floated through the forest. The Iron Woods flowed by silently. Mud, horses' hooves, lush grass. Dimly, he realised that he was slung over his horse, jolting with the animal's trot. His head hummed with a distant pain, as if he'd drunk too much good wine.

He listened to drumming hoofbeats, the clash of swords and the scream of war cries. Lamians shouted to form up or fall back as their Scythian allies turned on them.

Liam Vaniti's riders formed a river of steel and painted men, a river that flowed back through the trail, across the Iron Woods and out again, into the meadow and the Lamian camp of hussars and hoplites. Moonlight and torches turned their faces ghostly and their steel weapons into silver, until they could be elves, striding down a mountaintop bearing ghostly flames to scorch the hapless humans with...

Arrows hissed into the darkness. The Scythians and Galatian mercenaries laughed. They knew already what this was: victory. Dead Lamians and Seraphim lay scattered behind them.

As he lolled across his saddle, Simeon sensed another presence. A woman. She slid through the moonlight to keep pace with his horse. She was unconcerned by Simeon's silence, his dull reactions. Content, she watched him fight to remain awake.

Not a woman, he thought, a goddess...

His head throbbed harder for a moment and his eyesight flashed with bright lights. When his vision settled, the goddess had vanished, and his horse carried him deeper into the Iron Woods.

*Irene*, he thought. *Defeat*. His mouth tasted the ashes of his failure to keep her safe. His face filled with the stench of the Lamian army burning behind him...

\*

Simeon opened his eyes on a slate-coloured sky. He struggled to swallow, his throat parched. His head thrummed with pain. Hunger warred with his headache. His hands were bound tightly behind him, his fingers numb from loss of sensation. He lay in a campsite. Scythians wandered through the camp, perhaps fifty of them. Some drunk, some injured, grumbling, kicking at sleeping sentries and stray dogs.

Around Simeon lay the remnants of the defeated army. Gilded hussars and hoplites, concussed and bloody, slumped across an L-shaped clearing.

Simeon had no weapons, but the Scythians had not taken his spurs. Slowly, he rolled to his side to see what happened. No one stopped him, no tribesman manhandled him. He remained lying still for a stretch. Then he bent his knees and brought his heels up to his bound wrists. They'd used tightly woven hemp. He waited again, then stroked the rope with the spinning rowel of the spurs.

The rowel dragged on the hemp, catching, then breaking free. Inching forward and back, Simeon cut into the strands of hemp. He left just enough thread to make them appear bound, then he lay still once more. No weapons, and he was alone – the other prisoners stank of defeat and were not likely to rise up with him. But he had whatever advantage he had just made for himself.

By dawn his headache had dulled, though his throat remained swollen. Perhaps two hours later Liam Vaniti came for him.

"Up," Vaniti said. Simeon did so, slower than he needed to.

A burly Scythian with a bulging gut stood behind Vaniti, cleaning a long knife with a leather cloth.

"I regret we did not fight longer, Stone Snake. I know of your prowess. I would like to have bested you with my own blade."

"Find me a sword," Simeon said. "You can do so now."

Vaniti laughed at that.

"The Scythians have won?"

"A great victory. They call it the Battle at the Widow.

The Lamians were slaughtered. The survivors are in chains within the Iron Woods, or are scattered." Vaniti smiled.

"And Captain-General Flores?"

"Sadly dead. He and his officers all fell together at the Widow." His eyes shone, as if he'd commanded this victory.

"Your kind are common enough," Simeon said. "Battlefields are full of you. Arriving after the watch is stood down and the campaign ended. You fill brothels and regale whores and stay-behinds with your heroic tales. You're a small man, Liam. And quite yellow."

Liam Vaniti did not like hearing any of that. He stiffened within his doublet and his hand drifted to his gilt sword. But his hand stopped. Just for show, it looked like to Simeon.

"The Scythians follow forest gods," Vaniti said. "Their druids have special rites. They want you, Snake. They want to put you in a wicker cage and slowly burn you."

"No sword, then?" Simeon said, still pricking Vaniti's ego. "We can both use yours, yellow man."

"Take him to Long Meg," Vaniti snapped. The burly Scythian, not drunk like his brothers, tossed his rag aside and shoved Simeon forward. The other Scythians nearby laughed at the imperial Baron stumbling along a worn mud trail. But no one stopped to inspect Simeon's bonds.

*

A fireball flowered in the darkness of the woods. Huge and soundless and beautiful till the roar of heat and burning reached her. The heat burned Irene's face like scalding water and her horse screamed in terror. She fought to steady it as the Scythians bellowed and surged forward.

The fight was a blur, too bright with fire arrows striking into faces and bodies around her – too dim as lanterns were smashed and the moonlight fled behind the Iron Woods' trees.

As Simeon was knocked down and overrun by the Scythians, Arvo reached her. He shoved her horse, forcing the mare's head to the left.

"*The river,*" she shouted, and Arvo nodded. His eyes were wide with urgency. Then she kicked her horse across the trail and down to the Widow. Their mounts stumbled over the rough ground between the firs that lined the bank. When the trees crowded too tightly for their horses, Arvo shouted, "Off!" and she slid from the saddle. She glanced back at the fight before they ran through the trees. Her father's men tried to form up, locking their shields together, their lance points shining in the firelight. There were no battle lines, only a swirling chaos. Dead men and dying horses lay everywhere. More and more Scythians attacked. Men in costumes and in pelts, even men naked save for their blue tattoos.

She slipped in the mud. Arvo stepped over a fallen oak and took her hand, pulling her into a bower of nettles and cold moss.

"The river, my lady. Use it as your guide. Go east, reach the Milkhouse bridge. Take ship to the Empire. Confide in no one. Trust no one."

"Can we make it?"

Arvo pressed a stiletto into her hands, still in its scabbard. "You shall."

Screams rang through the night air. Light bloomed and crackled where fire arrows caught hold of tinder. Beyond the woods, a dozen Seraphim wheeled and charged the Scythians. Outnumbered, the imperial troops still refused to run. Laughing, the Scythians and Galatians met them, plucking riders off their horses with their spears.

She heard the crash of iron axe heads on oak shields and the terrified braying of a maimed horse.

Arvo gripped her forearm. "Now, my lady. *Go.*"

He turned back the way they'd come.

*Wait,* she wanted to say. *Don't do it.* But Irene knew better than to beg him to come with her. He was her father's man, as Simeon had been.

The night carried the Scythian's laughter to her as they combed the forest. Arvo ran from the fallen tree, cutting to the right. He shouted to the Scythians, drawing them to him. He struck the first tribesmen to reach him in the face. But the second and third attacked on either side, slashing with bright swords and spears. As more Scythians and Sicambri came at him, Irene slipped away.

She was ashamed to run as she pushed through brambles and fallen branches. She heard the moans of fallen men from the trail down to the muddy bank of the river. Her stomach clenched and she forced her gorge back down at the sight of bloody and butchered corpses.

Her gut clenched with fear and she stumbled to the river.

*

Long Meg, Simeon learned, was neither woman nor man. It was a hollow in the forest, set within a ring of monoliths. The trail to reach it wound and angled sharply. Soon both he and Vaniti had to drive their boots in to climb the steep incline. The burly Scythian behind them moved more slowly, struggling to lift his own bulk.

Below and quite distant, Simeon heard the Scythians in their camp, singing and fighting, drunk and restless.

Simeon worked his fingers, bringing the sensation back now that he'd frayed his bonds. His headache beat more fiercely, from the axe blow last night and his thirst and dizziness now.

Ignore it, he commanded himself. Vaniti's head would similarly be ringing from where Simeon struck him off his horse.

The path narrowed, crammed beside the hard bark of evergreens and an old slate wall. Then they halted, facing a wall of old granite. Or rather the wall was two monoliths with a crack for an opening.

Vaniti called a greeting and waited, glancing back at Simeon to be sure of his whereabouts.

"Sacred ground, Snake. We do not enter without old Cocheen's blessing." Vaniti smiled impishly, amused by Scythian ways, perhaps. His earlier irritation with Simeon had vanished.

A reedy voice called out from beyond the monolith. Vaniti edged through the gap, watching Simeon still. Simeon waited until the voice called again and the Scythian warrior shoved Simeon forward. Simeon stumbled at the stones, almost ripping his frayed ropes open. Then he stepped through the tight gap.

More monoliths ran to the left and right, forming a ring. The stones were ancient, moss-backed and slanted. The ground inside their ring had been cleared save for another granite slab, this one tipped over as an altar.

Cocheen, waiting for them, stood like he'd been here as long as his stone circle. The man was thin as a rake and looked eighty years old, his bald skull wizened and scarred, his beard flowing snow white down his black robe.

Wicker cages stood tied off to four pine trees at each compass point, with fires smouldering beneath them.

The ground was mud with only tufts of grass remaining. Fist-sized rocks lay in flowing patterns across the mud, up to the monoliths and across the altar stone. They had been painted an intense white and formed the triquetras and serpentine shapes of tribal embroidery.

It was almost peaceful – certainly quiet. In the silence, Simeon felt the forest god again. Her breath whispered through the trees, rustling leaves against branches, and made the hair on his nape stand up.

Their goddess would be drawn here to this place of sacrifice.

The Scythian warrior had not crossed the entrance. It looked like a tight fit for him through the gap in the stones. He stayed without, watching closely.

"Burning, or the knife. Old Cocheen will decide," Vaniti said, sounding satisfied.

Simeon noted where Cocheen and Vaniti stood. He looked back at the overweight Scythian through the gap in the monoliths.

The druid spoke to Vaniti, muttering in a thick tribal dialect. Vaniti squinted, then nodded and said to Simeon: "The priest asks me, where is the woman? Where did you send her?"

"My wife?"

"Don't test me, you fool." Vaniti's tone soured. "We know she is of high value to you. We will ransom her if you help us find her."

Simeon took another look round the stones. The forest burst beyond their shoulders, towering and thick. But no Scythians watched and waited. This was a secluded holy place.

"Well?" Vaniti said.

"So you do not have her." Simeon smiled.

In one movement he stooped, flexed his arms and tore his frayed ropes apart. He straightened with a heavy white-painted stone in either fist. The first one caught the Scythian sentry in the middle of his face, just about his mouth as he gaped in surprise. He staggered back, his nose thick with blood.

Simeon stepped fast to his right and grabbed a fistful of Liam Vaniti's doublet. He jerked the smaller man forward and slammed the second rock hard on his temple, just below the pot helm. The stone made a loud hard crack. Vaniti had his sword half drawn. But that blow staggered him, and forced his eyes shut. In that instant, Simeon hit him again, the stone landing with a thicker knocking sound. Vaniti groaned and slumped within Simeon's grip. He sagged with a sleeping man's weight and ripped the stitching from his doublet.

Simeon drew the sword out of Vaniti's scabbard.

Cocheen glared at Simeon, at this reversal of fortunes. He was perhaps ten paces away. The Scythian behind them swayed into the narrow gap, his head hanging like a drunk pup's. Simeon ran at Cocheen in long strides. The druid had time to draw breath to shout the alarm before Simeon came down upon him. And Simeon, thinking how the druid had a fire going and a wicker cage ready slammed the sharp edge of Vaniti's sword into the man's face and smashed through his jaw. There was no alarm, only the sickening crunch of the old man's jaw breaking loose.

He had shared Vaniti's sword after all, Simeon thought.

Then he ran on, vaulting the murder stone into the wall of greenery beyond. Undisturbed, drunken singing reached him, drifting up from the Scythian camp down the trail.

And beyond that, too far away for Simeon to place, he heard a woman's trickling laughter. The forest god grew merry at his mortal antics, even as her own druid was cheated of his death.

*

Simeon ran from Long Meg through brambles and wild roses and back into the thicket. Behind him, he heard a lowing hunting horn. He kept running, dizzy and tired, through the endless green world.

Irene. Her father had commanded Simeon to bring her safely home. He would not leave her now in the hands of these tribesmen.

Along a game trail, he discovered a palfrey, nervous and bloody down one flank. Its rider's blood, Simeon found once he'd calmed the beast and stroked its neck. He mounted up, the palfrey happy enough with this new rider. There was even a quiver of arrows on the horse's saddle and, mercifully, spring water in a canteen. Simeon turned the horse and set a steady pace along the trail. The palfrey stepped over fallen men and around dead horses.

If Irene lived, she was hiding or running. Either way, Simeon would not leave these woods until he'd found her. It would go better for Davith Huskiss' son if Irene lived.

*

Irene lay still throughout the night. She had crawled into a bog to hide in marshland too spongy to hold a man's weight. Nearby, fallen knights and men-at-arms fouled the firmer ground with their bodies. Irene spent the dark hours shivering in foul smelling muck. The Scythians did not wish to wade through filth, even to harvest the dead of their gold and iron.

She had learned about life in the Iron Woods. The forest was often lightless, crowded and oppressive where the treetops hunched together. In those moments, the tallest trees canted in and cut out the sky as surely as any pavilion roof might. The Scythians, hunting her and the remains of Ned Flores' army, wandered through a permanent twilight, regardless of the hour of day.

When dawn's light finally trickled through the canopy, Scythian women and broods of children came to the forest. The morning began with shiny blades and laughter in the deep shadows as they cut soldiers' fingers away for their rings, or ears for the fun of it.

By the breakfast hour, the tribesmen quartered the woods again. They struck down any Lamians who tried to stand and fight. Swords against axes and dying men's screams rang through the forest. Later, the Scythians took prisoners in chains, bowed in defeat, across the forest. She heard chanting voices. Priests, she guessed. Irene had been told tales of the gods that the Scythians followed. She knew of their burnings and foul blood sacrifice.

She sank deeper into the marsh, her face smeared and obscured by moss and mud. But the children didn't linger. Past dawn they moved to the banks of the river. The Widow bubbled beside her, silvery sounds that kept her company as she shivered with the cold. Still she waited. She could smell cooking as the Scythians gathered at their firesides for porridge and to tell tales of the slaughter. Only then did Irene draw herself from the marsh, fighting its sliding embrace, its sucking grip on her mud-filled boots. Her body felt leaden after her freezing, terror-filled night. She crept through bracken and ferns, her arms scoured by brambles. But always, she kept Harry Arvo's stiletto tight in her fist.

The river would take her home. She hurried towards it. Arvo had died for her. A century of Seraphim had died, and the Stone Snake was lost. She would not add to her father's misery by failing to come home.

She slid down a slanted bank to the Widow. Moving warmed her and soon she was sweating again.

More bodies lay here, horribly smashed and destroyed. Arrows peppered their flesh, their faces twisted in lasting agonies. Men her father's age and grooms no older than boys. She gagged with the latrine stench of bodies bloated in the day's heat. She saw few Scythian dead, just tides of Lamian bodies. It was Lamia that had lost here. The dead Seraphim were incidental. Sick with rage and nausea, Irene bent over and heaved up her empty stomach.

Closer to the river, she found a boat. A skiff, with an intact sail. A fishing boat, she thought, beached in the mud. She took a last look around – and saw children and a mother coming through the firs behind her. Then, before she could hesitate, Irene marched forward in her stained clothes, as if she belonged here. Was meant to be pushing the boat into the shallows.

She heard shouting behind her, but by then she had waded up to her waist and the boat was free, bobbing and feeling light on the water. She dropped the stiletto inside the wooden bottom and boosted herself inside. River water swirled with mud behind her, washing her legs clean.

When she sat in the boat, the children ran along the bank, the mother shouting back into the Iron Woods to the warriors. Irene pushed the oars through their locks and started rowing. The boat turned in the wind and the sail snapped with the breeze. It moved, catching the current.

I'm free, she thought for an instant, before the Scythian horsemen trotted out of the Iron Woods. Not many, but she saw at their head a man that she recognised. Rami Huskiss. The traitor to Lamia. Meeting her eyes, he tossed his long hair back and smiled. He looked satisfied and very unconcerned at her escape.

*

Simeon recalled that Irene had ridden with them from the camp when Harry Arvo repeated their route from the Iron Woods. The river. She had asked him about the Milkhouse bridge over the Widow. She might be there – *if* she remembered and if no Scythian stumbled upon her. But Simeon at least knew that Rami and Vaniti had not taken her last night.

He reached the river and ran the horse alongside. The palfrey moved more eagerly by the bank. Eager enough with the Iron Woods now only one side, rather than hemming in close on both.

Finding Irene felt like a fool's errand with enemies scouring the woods, but Simeon was sworn to try. What kind of friend would fail to do everything to find Flavius' daughter? And more than that, he could not imagine losing Irene this way.

Simeon rode down the left bank of the wide river, riding in rough sand, looking further still to his left, into the depths of the woods. Game trails and wider turns led among the towering trees, but he ignored them. He slowed to a trot, giving Irene more chance to see him. But he also painted a roundel on his back, inviting every archer in the Scythian army to make his mark.

He saw no one, not even stragglers. Occasionally sounds of steel on steel drifted out of the woods. The river bank lay empty. He rode past a skiff, lodged in the mud. Simeon considered stopping. The boat looked seaworthy, and had its oars shipped and ready. But there was no benefit to him waiting here or giving his palfrey over for a skiff.

He heard shouting once. Glancing back he saw a Scythian staggering after him, naked except for a tribal shirt and a Lamian helmet sliding off his head. The man, very drunk, waved a short sword at Simeon, then sagged forward, too winded to follow.

Simeon rode on past fires and dead bodies, stopping only to take up a fallen recurved bow and a throwing axe from the hands of dead tribesmen. By late morning, sweating in the heat, Simeon reached the Milkhouse crossing. The river turned rightwards, a grey watery snake.

The bridge was as Harry Arvo had described it. Lamian built. New-sawn logs tied off with rope supports crossed the river's narrowest point. The further bank was still hundreds of feet away for the river was very wide.

The Scythians had fired the bridge, of course.

The stench of the blackened wood hung heavy in the morning. The bridge meant civilisation and an intrusion into their world. The Scythians would want nothing left standing. Better the Iron Woods never benefited from Lamian bridges or imperial roads than the Scythians allowed Lamia to give the tribes a taste of civilisation.

He stopped his mount and turned in the saddle. The woods stared back at him, a heavy cascade of every shade of green and brown.

Too vast, he thought. Too full of murderous Scythians.

Simeon could only blunder inside after Irene.

That was hopeless, he knew.

On this side of the Widow the bank rose twenty feet higher than the river. The drop became sharp falls of loose white sand. The river was snarled with flotsam and burned planks and corpses.

More dead men lay on the trail around him. Seraphim – the men Arvo had left with his barge, and what looked like Lamian civilians. Their bodies stank and ran with coatings of shiny black insects.

He dismounted and hobbled the palfrey inside the woods. It protested inside the green walls of the forest until it found it could rest and chew on long grass. Simeon found a point of land, sandy but well covered by the edge of the forest. With the axe, his falchion, the bow and its arrows, he settled down to wait, tucked into the greenery behind him. He carefully nudged his shiny weapons into the tall grass. A dead Lamian, dressed in a green surcoat and bloated and stinking, lay beside Simeon. Good masking, he left the corpse alone, paying the smell no mind.

Settled, he watched the Widow and the length of bank that he'd travelled. They both led back to the fighting. Irene would have to come this way to meet him. She had to get out before he could help her.

That, he thought, was a heavy burden to place on a princess closeted at Court. But he could wait. He could see what happened.

He ignored his belly's complaints and the chafing from his wrists. He sipped warm water from the palfrey's canteen. The grey river trickled by him, keeping him company as he watched.

*

He saw the same skiff, growing larger on the river. The breeze filled out its sail.

Still just a boat, Simeon thought. Even if it was the one he'd seen that morning.

He remained watchful, expecting nothing.

As it grew, seven riders cantered ahead of it up the side of the bank.

The men halted in a billow of dust and the clink of harnesses and bits and bridles. They'd run their horses hard, slathering them with sweat. The lead roan's eyes rolled as it fought its bit. Simeon would have taken Rami Huskiss for a gentler horseman.

However, Rami sat his horse, indifferent to the beast's winded breathing.

The men spoke among themselves in Scythian – even the two in Galatian steel breastplates – as they watched the skiff. Simeon heard them say Irene's name. He tensed, imagining that she rode on the skiff.

Simeon heard *Flavius* too and knew that the riders either recognised her as the Emperor's daughter or knew he would value her.

Good. If he failed here, they must not treat her roughly.

The riders glanced about them, back into the woods and at the burned-out bridge. Simeon remained still and their eyes passed indifferently over him and the nearby corpse.

The skiff came slowly, the oars worked by a single rower.

Irene. He saw her now, struggling and wavering the line of the boat through the water. She was unused to this work.

The two Galatians dismounted, tossing their reins to other men. They left their broadswords on their saddle bows and shrugged off their metal armour. The Galatians had the swimmer's art. They retreated along the pathway, reaching the water where the land flattened out.

Simeon waited till they had waded into the river and begun swimming, then he rose from beside the dead Lamian. He carried the falchion and the axe. He made his feet soft, as if walking on the finest paper. Stepping up to the first rider in line, he slashed the horse's flank till it screamed and fell off the bank with its rider. The other men reacted, shouting and turning in unison. He swung the axe hard into the next Scythian's spine, and kicked the neighbouring horse in the flank. That lost its footing and went over the side of the drop.

Rami turned with his sabre raised high. Simeon blocked Rami's downward cut with his falchion. With his other hand, Simeon had Rami's foot out of the stirrup and flipped him over his horse. Rami fell awkwardly on one shoulder, his other foot still trapped in the stirrup. The lathered horse reared back, eyes wide, and lost its footing. It tumbled, screaming and legs kicking, as it took Rami spinning away into the waters below.

The last man had to swing and lean past his skittish horse to strike. Simeon faded back and stepped in in one long step, bringing his hand to grip the man's head and drive him down onto the point of Vaniti's sword with a *crack* of his sternum breaking. The man spasmed in Simeon's hands, stiff as oak. Then he shuddered and relaxed as death took him.

The swimming Galatians called to one another, trying to decide where to go, back to the bank or on to their prize.

Simeon drew the sword out of the dead Scythian and faced the remaining warrior. The man sat flat on the ground, his legs splayed before him, Simeon's axe still embedded in his back. He raised his head. His stare was as shallow and weak as an old hound's. Then he sighed and swooned sideways, sagging and dying.

The remaining men shouted below, struggling and panicked, or swimming on to Irene's boat. Irene, watching closely, started pulling on the oars, angling away.

Simeon set the falchion down and took up the curved bow. Standing with the arrows scattered at his feet, he knocked an arrow and aimed downwards. Three heads below him and two swimming after Irene. He straightened the bow, kept his elbows soft and breath shallow. The arrows flicked out. He fell into a pattern, bending for an arrow, knocking and shooting. He paid little attention after the release, busy reaching for the next arrow and aiming again. He heard solid *thunks* of fire-hardened points embedding in flesh or scoring off bone. Then a bellow of rage from a man's throat. With the last arrow knocked he surveyed his handiwork. Both Galatians at Irene's boat bobbed in the water, pricked with arrows. In the shallows near the bank, two Scythian warriors lay twisted and caught by more arrows, bloody and wobbling with the current.

Irene had stopped rowing. Her shoulders shook with exertion. But she looked up and waved to Simeon. Perhaps she smiled.

Simeon aimed down on the remaining man below. Rami, up to his knees in water, stared back at Simeon. He held his long cavalry blade in his hand. He glared upwards, red-faced and helpless, twenty yards apart.

"There is a reason," Simeon said, "that this river is named the Widow."

Rami's face purpled with even greater rage.

That made Simeon smile. Though it risked everything and made no sense, he set the bow carefully aside. No need to damage its fine wood. He lifted Vaniti's falchion and tested its weight again.

"Find the bank, Rami," Simeon called down to him. He would not kill Davith Huskiss' son from afar.

"You have my thanks for that and nought else."

To Irene, Simeon called, "Princess. If I fall, pass by the Milkhouse bridge. Keep going, you'll reach Imperial country."

"*When you fall,*" Rami said, loud enough for Irene to hear. He strode out of the river, casting off his sodden cloak.

Confident, Simeon saw, even after six of his men died and he tumbled from his horse. Confident of his own reputation, Simeon thought. He even warned Rami of that.

Rami spat river water and tossed his long hair back. But he could not resist one more sally. "Fair warning, Snake. This is a blood matter. I do not fight like one of your courtly knights."

Simeon smiled. "Good lad – neither do I."

Beware his knife. Simeon saw it again, tied low on the belt Rami's mother had made for him.

The water shone, the grey surface metal-bright in the midday sun. Irene, on the wobbling skiff, shouted. A Galatian, with Simeon's arrow buried in his shoulder blade, surged out of the water, swinging a footlong dagger at the princess's face.

Simeon froze in place, helpless with his bow set aside.

Rami roared with pleasure and pounced.

Simeon met his downstroke with Vaniti's falchion. Swinging overhand and advancing each time, Rami came and came at Simeon. His steel flashed as he struck. Rami swung and backhanded, stepping forward each time. Testing, probing for weakness as Simeon retreated, diverted by Irene. With each strike, Rami changed his angle, pressing Simeon up the slope. The still air rang with their steel.

Behind Rami, Simeon saw the Galatian, sprawling over the gunwale, dragging himself out of the Widow...

In that moment of distraction, Rami struck with his dagger, coming unseen from his left side to Simeon's right. Simeon felt the blade slice through muscle and snick into the bone of his forearm. Rami laughed. "Scythian fighting, Baron."

Simeon ignored the bright slice of pain, the tugging of the hooked blade and he shoved his palm hard into Rami's chest and kicked him in the knee to occupy him. He grabbed Rami's sword arm with his left hand and pulled him in close, as if they were dancing. Simeon dragged his right arm back, bringing the dagger tearing with him, and stabbed his falchion into Rami, driving the needle point of its great blade into the Scythian's side.

On the water, the Galatian caught Irene's ankle, dragging her to him...

Rami twisted away, but he was hooked on the falchion's curved tip. Locked together, spattered with blood, they wrestled like lovers. The dagger split Simeon's forearm, burning like fire. His falchion pierced Rami's body. Simeon held Rami's sword arm at the wrist all the while. He levered the falchion and snapped two ribs like sticks in Rami's side.

Irene, relaxing in the Galatian's grip, slid down the boat to him. She closed so fast he had no time for surprise. She met his throat with the point of the stiletto in her fist, pinning him to the hull...

As she did so, Simeon drove his sword to the hilt into Davith Huskiss' son and killed him.

"No." Rami's eyes bulged and he blew out a huge breath. "*Simeon*..."

"Call me Snake," Simeon told him and let the proud Scythian slide off his falchion and to his knees.

Then, dizzy with nausea, Simeon also sank forward beside the dead man. His forearm screamed when he pried Rami's knife free. Blood ran over his fist and his hand cramped hard on his sword's grip. He stayed bent over till he was sure he could move. Irene called to him and started rowing to the bank. Simeon waved to her to show he could move.

He cut Rami's cloak into pieces and bound his forearm. It felt a little better after that. He set the palfrey free, then stripped and tied his boots around his neck. His right arm worked well enough for that, but he could only lift the fine tribal bow above his head with his left arm as he swam out to Irene on the boat. Blood swirled through the grey water as he approached.

Irene shoved the Scythian corpse off the skiff.

"Thank the gods," she said. She looked teary, perhaps with relief.

Simeon felt the god's touch again. Not angry, not amused. She was behind him, hidden in the green towers of the Iron Woods. She accepted that he had escaped the forest – this time. He even felt the goddess smile. Her mouth was bloody from sipping at his wound and the far richer Lamian tribute she had gorged on. Still amused, she gifted Simeon more wind to push him across the water. A boon that he accepted gratefully, even as he recognised that it built a debt for another day.

Simeon knew that gods always claimed their due.

# MY PEOPLE WERE FAIR AND WORE STARS IN THEIR HAIR

## *Andrew Darlington*

The day Otranto Muretta was killed was drab and dismal, after which things only got worse.

He remembered the assault on necromancer Gandala's stronghold. The cries of the maimed and dying, the pennants of doomed battalions curling in the smoky air beneath the haunted tower on the gaunt crag, circling dirigibles erupting in sudden detonations of vivid flame, tongues of green fire spitting death into the massed besiegers. Otranto was part of a group of mercenary freebooters climbing a steep escarpment that promised access to the fortress's lower levels when their progress was barred by monstrous elementals in golden armour. Unable to advance, with his retreat blocked by pressure from the rear, the halberd took him through the stomach just below his ribs. He could feel its cold insinuating chill before the pain of impalement sucked all strength from his limbs. The last thing he saw before darkness flooded him was the impassive visor of his assailant glint bronze in the sky-glare of the setting sun.

Then he inhaled with such a convulsion that his whole body trembled in spasms of aftershock. A disturbed land-crab skittered out from behind the cage of his ribs, dropped to the dust and scuttled away to seek concealment within cracks in the hard shoulder of stone behind him. There was a woman of indeterminate age squatting on the far side of a small flickering campfire, watching his revival with close scrutiny. A little older than he, perhaps, but with the subtle beguilement of wisdom. The climbing sparks caught up in strands of faint smoke confuse the night sky constellations as they ascend. The hard tang of its aroma burns into his head.

"I have no nose," he said, his fingers fumbling to define the contours of his face. "And yet I smell."

She laughs, not unkindly. "You've been dead a thousand years or more, it's hardly surprising your corpse smells. There are sand-mites and fire-ants that nibble and gnaw. There are rats who enjoy rotting carrion. You remain remarkably intact despite their endeavours."

"I have no ears, yet I hear your voice."

"You hear my thoughts. That is not exactly the same thing."

His tunic had rotted away to scraps and fragments. The sword suspended at his waist was rusted. "I have no penis."

"From what I ascertain from your memories you scarce used it for anything other than pissing."

"Nevertheless, we were attached. We had a connection." The bitter laugh rumbles and echoes in his empty chest.

She is Amaro Palmarina, gifted with subtle magics. He feels gauche and ugly in her presence. A little resentful of her interference.

Next he was aware of dawn flushing night away. The campfire was reduced to smouldering grey ash. There were buzzards circling the copper coin of the sun high above them. He stands unsteadily on skeletal legs, in order that he can look around him. If this was still the place he'd been killed, the necromancer's stronghold seemed to have been levelled. Not, he suspects, as a result of the warfare in which he'd played an incidental part. More the effect of the slow erosion of centuries. There were still struts and mounds that suggest the collapse of architecture, bitten-off walls that enclose only desolation, the stubs of towers snapped-off as if by the tantrum of a malevolent child.

"What have you done to me?" wails Otranto, his voice a melancholy wheeze of dry air from his lipless mouth. An echo of the despairing breeze that soughs through the ruins.

"We have need of each other," snaps Palmarina. "This debris was once the domicile of magus Gandala. A necromancer who boasted extraordinary skills in the transmigration of souls. You are dead. I have given you the temporary gift of life. The least you can do is demonstrate a little gratitude."

He paces warily, unsteadily, in an exploratory way, uncertain of his returning strengths. "They're all gone. My comrades. My tribe. My parents." He reaches out with arms of leathery skin, fragile with dusty flakes. "My entire world is gone."

"Stop whinging. At least you can see this world. I gave you that gift."

When she walks, for want of an alternative, he follows. They climb a slow incline, a winding path, meandering as though worn by beasts rather than people. At intervals he could pause to gaze out over the valley below, green with forest, threaded by sparkling streams feeding into the shimmer of lakes where flocks of waterfowl rise and fall in organic choreography. Yes, to be alive at this moment is good, even in such a shambling guise as this.

"But this post-life is temporary?"

"All is transient." Her dark eyes seem uncertain, on the brink of venturing more. Her long deluge of midnight hair is braided with silver, decorated with luminous stars. "You want more, you must seek it. You were here when this ruin was a living thing. You were a besieger, predatory for loot. You must have seen military floorplans of the stronghold in preparation for your assault?"

A sudden burst of memory, a storm of unbidden images, as though she's ransacking his mind. The glow of the tavern, blurred by the pleasing sway of wine, where mercenaries gather, attracted by the lure of plunder. He'd voyaged in a brigantine from a far isle, drawn by rumours of war. He could taste the salt on his tongue, even though he no longer has a tongue. He could hear the gulls although he has no eardrums. He could feel the intoxication of wild adventure roaring in his veins. The sweet anticipation of gain.

By now they'd emerged on a high plateau of vast desolation. There are pits that fall away to the very core of the world. And a solid flight of curving stairs that lead upwards to nowhere. Pockets of weed blaze with yellow sun-blossoms woven into tangles of briar that crawl over shattered masonry. A haze of insects dance on the air above stink-holes of slime.

Yes, he'd seen maps, detailed plans. That was how they'd calculated the steep escarpment that promised access to the fortress's lower levels. To where he'd met death at the thrust of a halberd. He shudders involuntarily at the piercing horror of the memory.

"Think. Magus Gandala had basement laboratories in subterranean chambers, where he practised the forbidden arts of thaumaturgy. Where he perfected the secret transmigration of souls from one body to another. Concentrate. Think."

"I wasn't motivated by magic tricks. I thirsted instead for his hoard of gems," he muttered truculently. Yet despite his denials Palmarina was inside his head, ransacking memories, throwing them up and extinguishing them in her haste.

She has a theodolite, or maybe it's a sextant? Where she's produced it from he never knew. She lines up planes of perspective across the rock-strewn surface, using the truncated staircase as a focal point. This angle of alignment, then another, making micro-adjustments to fine threads and screws. Indicating yes, this way. A collapse of stone forms the deep mouth of a pit. A hazardous descent where cascades of rubble slip away underfoot. They descend, one step at a time. Otranto reaches out to assist her. Palmarina supports and helps him over uneven barriers of fallen marble columns. The circle of sky above them seems to darken. There's the unseen dripping of water. The scuttling of horned bugs as big as the palm of a hand, that retreat defensively into tight crevasses. Luminescent plants, with barbed tendrils flicker in dark shadows.

The opening of a paved corridor slants downwards. He's aware of the weight of ancient ruins pressing down from above. She leads the way without hesitation. He limps after her. Is the fatigue he feels natural, or the onset of renewed death? This borrowed life is transient. She told him as much. It will not last. Is he feeling symptoms of terminal close-down already? Or do his thousand-year-old limbs simply ache through centuries of neglect? The legacy of stiffness from while he was lying dead beneath mounds of gritty debris. He scrats an irritation on his shoulder. Flakes of dead skin rupture and float free.

There's a circle of seven sealed doors, each with a configuration of devices etched into the surface. She stands back, glances across at him questioningly. He shrugs, but already she's inside his head, ripping away at memories, bringing them into sharper focus with a painful intensity. He can still feel pain. That, in itself, is reassuring. He sees sketches, specifications, line diagrams that swim and merge, overlapping into each other. Door five. It must be. Against his own volition he steps forward. She's controlling his every action. His fingers move across the shadows of worn sigils embedded in the door. Pressing in the sequence specified by texts he'd merely glanced at a hundred centuries ago.

There's the grating sound of ancient mechanisms. A cascade of dust. The door shudders once. It raises by slight degrees, and halts. It lifts no further. They squat, and crawl, wriggling beneath the portal. A sudden moment of terror, as if the precarious balance is about to fail, and the door slam back down in a lethal descent. Yet they squirm free on the far side, first her, then him.

The air is sour inside the subterranean chamber. The twilight is stale within the secret basement laboratory of magus Gandala. Amaro Palmarina looks around in an awed sense of wonder. Otranto Muretta slouches, as though drained of energies. There are interlocking clockwork devices of great complexity smothered in a soft furring of dust and filmy spider's webs. She scrubs her hand across a row of chambers. Behind crystal there are frozen forms. A huge black bear. An aviary of stilled birds. A monstrous reptile. And naked human figures, male and female, paused as if in death. Experimental subjects preserved in perfect suspension. In induced sleep. Ancient devices. Yet still with the pulse of function. Energies that flicker undimmed by time.

Palmarina takes time scrutinising each chamber, selecting. Then turns to face him. The theodolite is gone. Instead, she holds a jewelled scimitar. "All is transient." Her dark eyes are no longer uncertain. "Your life is finite. Already it draws to a close."

Otranto watches her, waiting. He sees her fingers dance in rapid sequence across a symbol-display set into the chamber rim. A spell. An ensorcellment. "Me too," she explains over her shoulder. As if loath to meet his eyes. "We are alike in that condition. I have a double-tumour that grows in my brain. My own rebellious cells multiply and attack me. I sought out the greatest living magicians and surgeons, but a cure is beyond even their powers. So I began questing into arcane tomes and the wisdoms of antiquity. Skills and alchemical techniques that have now been lost and forgotten. It was those tales that brought me here. I want to live. I wish to be reborn into a new untainted body."

She takes a step forward, towards him. "I needed your memories. I thank you for that. Now your usefulness is done." She lifts the scimitar, lunges, in a single sweep that amputates his legs. He teeters. Then falls. His face crashes into the stone paving of the floor. The twin columns of his skeletal legs are ludicrously standing, side by side. He can see them through a blurring haze. There is no longer any pain. There's no blood. He was not alive, simply a reanimation. Yet he feels the outflow of his temporary life eking away.

She has dropped the scimitar in her haste. The once-sealed chamber is open, an empty shell with a drift of white gas congealing into a frost around its rim. He's aware of movement around him. He uses his fists, impacted into the stone, lifting his torso sufficient to see. Her discarded body lies beside the empty chamber. She has a new body, infused with the transmigration of her soul. New life.

He uses his hands as claws, to drag himself across the floor. He supposes it is cold, although he has no sensation of cold. His fingers snap and break free. He leaves them where they lie, and crawls. He has the scimitar. He uses it against the nearest random chamber. He can crawl no further. He knows the spell. She extracted the ensorcellment from his own memories. The rapid sequence-dance across a symbol-display set into the chamber rim is still an open wound in his awareness. No need even to think. No need to concentrate. Just a fall into repetition.

Then he inhales with such a violent convulsion that his body trembles in spasms of aftershock. The sweet inoculation of pain, a kick that betrays the presence of an active nervous system.

He struts. Preens. Stretches his wings. Cocks his head this way and that.

He's perched on a crumbling cadaver that he'd once inhabited.

He takes flight. Beneath the stilled portal door. Along the slow incline of the corridor. Flying above Amaro Palmerina in her new body. She glances up in wonderment. No recognition in her ocean-blue gold-flecked eyes. He emerges into the collapsed pit, and soars, higher, ever higher.

In the euphoria of freedom the crow climbs the sky. His powerful wing-beat arrows him over a valley that is green with forest, threaded by sparkling streams feeding into the shimmer of lakes where flocks of waterfowl rise and fall in organic choreography.

Otranto Muretta targets the horizon, and flies towards the copper coin of the sun that is setting in the east.

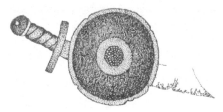

# AT SEA
## *Geoffrey Hart*

"Man overboard, four points off the port-bow!" came the cry from the crow's nest. "About a bowshot distant."

The crew who weren't otherwise occupied rushed to the bow and looked over the side, some bearing ropes, others bearing flotation devices. "*There!*" cried one, pointing, and all eyes turned in that direction. Each time the swell pushed the ship higher, they saw what appeared to be a very large man swimming towards them. As the swimmer approached, the lump on his back resolved into what appeared to be a child perched, cross-legged, squarely between broad shoulders. The child held a long bundle wrapped in what appeared to be sailcloth carefully above the water.

"Heave to!" called the First Officer, and sails slackened, spilling the wind and letting the ship coast under its own momentum, wallowing between the swells.

The captain removed his elegantly plumed hat, and mopped his brow before perching it once more at a rakish angle on his head. "Ahoy there!" he called as the pair drew closer.

The large swimmer paused and began treading water, causing some scrambling from his burden, who managed to maintain their burden above the water. "Ahoy yourself." To the captain's surprise, it was a woman. She looked up at the dark faces lining the rails, her skin pink from the strong sunlight.

The captain exchanged startled glances with his First Officer. Taken aback, he cleared his throat. "Might one be permitted to wonder why you're out for a casual swim, a day's sail from shore? With a child on your back?" His voice was deep and rich, with the lilting accent of the tropical islands.

The big woman continued treading water, but frowning. "One might certainly be *expected* to wonder."

"But one might not be expected to mistake one for a child," the second figure added, somewhat acerbically. She threw back her hood and revealed the face of a mature, if tiny, woman.

The captain shook his head as if to clear it. Then he smiled ferociously down at the duo. "One might then be expected to wonder whether the answer to one's question should persuade one to pause in one's journey rather than simply continuing along one's former course and leaving the definitively not a child and her steed to ponder the wisdom of a courteous reply. Rather than, say, accepting the other one's offer to effect a rescue."

The small one replied, an equally fierce smile on her face. "I'd be just as happy to continue our relaxing mid-ocean swim, should one grow too insistent."

The large woman snorted. "Easy for you to say. You're not the one who's doing all the swimming."

The captain cleared his throat. "If I might try again? What in the name of the Kraken are you doing swimming in the gods-be-damned middle of the ocean?"

"*Swimming*, as you so astutely remarked."

"Hold your tongue, small one, or we'll leave you to taste the depths with it in the hope you might learn a less confrontational style of discourse."

The small woman frowned, but it was the large one who replied. "Your ship seems to be blocking our way, and as we have a long way to go, we'd be grateful if you moved your ship aside and reduced, however slightly, the length of our travel."

The captain snorted. "Are you *mad*, woman? It's more than a day's sail—several days' swim—from shore. Somewhat longer," he added, "when you're swimming the wrong way."

"*Trust the barbarian*," grumbled the big one.

"In fairness," replied the small one, "this trackless waste provides none of the clues a proper barbarian needs to orient herself."

"And yet…"

The captain cleared his throat. "First Officer? Prepare to set sail and move from their path. It would be ungentlemanly to delay them further."

"Not so fast," rejoined the big swimmer. "If we tell you why we're up to our teats in saltwater, will you bring us aboard?"

The captain reflected a moment. "If your answer satisfies me you're no threat to my ship or crew."

The small one replied. "We were sailing for Losthaven when our ship encountered pirates. We were holding our own until the treacherous bastards produced a wizard who blew a hole in our ship, thereby flinging us into the ocean. We alone survived." She shook her head. "It defies comprehension that so few sailors learn to swim."

"It defies comprehension that a *barbarian* never learned to swim," the large one replied.

"In fairness, there are precious few bodies of water where I come from in which it would be desirable, not to say safe, to swim. The prudent barbarian therefore avoided such activities."

The large one spat a mouthful of seawater in reply.

The captain called up to the crow's nest. "Any other ships?"

There was a moment's hesitation as the lookout swept the horizon with her eyeglass. "Nary a one, captain."

He returned his gaze to the swimmers. "And yet, there's no ship to be seen."

"We were following the pirates in the hope they'd lead us to port."

"Or to board them and secure passage," added the tall one.

The captain closed his jaw, which had fallen open. "*You were going to board them*?"

"If we could swim fast enough to catch them."

"If *I* could swim fast enough, you mean."

"I acknowledge your point. Shall we board *this* ship, Freya?"

"Wait!" called the captain. "You're that savage barbarian named Freya?"

"No, I'm the savage *city dweller*. The little one—"

"Mouse?"

"—is the savage barbarian. It's a common mistake."

"If half the stories they tell are true, we'd be happy to offer you a berth. On the condition you swear to do my crew no harm, and to defend us against the pirates should they cross our path."

"We so swear," called Mouse.

"One more thing," the First Officer chimed in. "What's in the bag?"

"Why, our weapons, of course." The small one shook the bag, which clanked.

"Which are now sworn to your service," the large one added.

"Then welcome aboard!" The captain nodded to the First Officer, who gestured to a seaman, who tied a rope ladder to the rail and flung it overboard. The two women climbed the ladder, the large one moving distinctly slower than the small one. Once on deck, they shook hands with the captain.

"Freya," said the larger, grasping the captain's hand in a crushing grip.

"Mouse," said the smaller, grasping the captain's hand less firmly, having noted his alacrity in withdrawing it from her friend's grip.

Shaking his head, the captain replied. "Lars Svenson. Welcome aboard *Trickster's Wager*. Bound for Losthaven with a hold full of island rum."

"That explains the accent," Freya murmured.

"A cargo worthy of our protection," her companion replied.

"Would you join me in my quarters to restore yourselves with a sample of our cargo?"

The women exchanged glances. "We have our weapons to care for first," said Freya.

"Leave them with my arms master." He gestured to a tall woman with a scar that made a pale slash across one dark cheek, who joined them and held out her hands.

Mouse hesitated. "We'd be disarming ourselves."

The captain laughed. "Two swords and a handful of knives against a whole ship?"

Mouse laughed, with less warmth. "You have a point. We're somewhat over-armed." But she handed over the sailcloth.

The captain's eyes widened, and Freya shook her head. "Ignore the small one. She has violent thoughts."

He shook himself. "Can we take your clothes too?"

"I didn't think that was part of our employment contract," Freya observed.

The captain gaped a moment, then burst out laughing.

"Nay! I meant only that I'll have the cabin boy wash the salt from them." He briefly admired Freya's impressive bosom, then thought the better of antagonizing her. "Get us under way," he said to the First Officer. Then he led them to the rear of the ship, where a cabin stood with windows open to the breeze, and held the door as they entered. He rang a bell, and a small brown child appeared out of nowhere.

"Holger, my lad: fetch clothing for our guests." Then he examined Freya more closely. "My apologies, lass, but there's none on board large enough to clothe you." He looked back at the cabin boy. "Fetch a blanket for our large guest. A *large* blanket."

The child, who bore a distinct resemblance to the captain, knuckled his forehead, and without a word, darted out the door. While they waited, the women inspected the cabin. It was bare of decoration, save for a brace of cutlasses with gem-encrusted guards, crossed and hung from the wall across from a large liquor cabinet, bolted to the floor and filled with an intriguing assortment of bottles, and an intricately worked brasswork that hung from the wall catercorner to the swords. Closer inspection revealed the tableau of a multi-armed sea creature, its long, ropelike limbs wrapped about and crushing a three-masted ship.

"The Kraken," Svenson explained. "A creature that infests the sea along our small island. It's said we learned the manufacture of our rum because the creature loves that drink more than any living man or woman, and is only propitiated by hurling a keg of rum into the sea before a ship leaves port. The Kraken comes, drinks down the keg, and then retreats to the depths to sleep it off. While it does, ships can safely leave port."

"And yet you reveal this secret to anyone you pluck from the sea?"

The captain's eyes twinkled. "Perhaps the actual solution is somewhat more complex than I alluded to, Mouse."

"Have you never thought of poisoning the beast?"

The captain frowned. "Nay. Its presence also means that no armada can attack us if they don't know the secret of our defence."

The cabin boy returned bearing clothing for Mouse and a large blanket, and Svenson rose from the table. "I've duties to attend to. Dress yourself" – he glanced at Freya – "or cover yourselves as best you can, then give your clothes to the boy. Lad, clean their garments of salt and return them when you're done." With that, he left, pulling the cabin boy behind him.

*

When the door closed, the friends removed their salt-crusted clothing and boots. Mouse's clothing was too large, but not unsuitable, whereas Freya managed to drape her blanket sufficiently artfully to provide a modicum of dignity. As she finished adjusting the blanket, she noted the smile on Mouse's face.

"What?"

"A clever ploy on your part. Our captain friend will undoubtedly be distracted by your garb when we dicker over the price of our services."

Freya snorted. "Then I shall perforce have to help him focus."

"I wish you luck," Mouse smirked, and pushed the door open. "Boy! Here are our clothes." She left the door open and cast a critical eye across the deck, where sailors moved about their cryptic nautical duties.

The captain returned and urged them to sit at his table, an impressive slab of dense blonde wood bolted to the cabin's floor. He hung his hat on a coat rack, revealing a large, bald spot from forehead to the dome of his skull, and opened the liquor cabinet. In a moment, three silver mugs appeared in one hand and a squat brown-glass bottle in the other. Returning to the table, he poured them each a large serving, then sat.

"Confusion to our enemies!" he announced, raising his mug, then took a hearty swallow.

Mouse echoed him, then began coughing. "Whoosh! Strong brew indeed."

Freya sipped more delicately at her rum. "Tasty. I can see this would be a valuable cargo."

Svenson swallowed a more judicious amount. "Yes. Fortunately, the crew is large and experienced. The pirates test our resolution at their peril!"

"And yet..."

"Yet?"

"Their sorcerer blew our ship to flinders with a single spell."

"They'd not try that with *Wager*. They'd lose the cargo."

Freya nodded. "Aye. But that might not dissuade them. If they turn that magic on the crew, the battle may not end as you hope."

Svenson took a bigger swallow. "You never said what you were doing aboard the sunken ship."

"To be honest?"

"Honesty would, I feel, place our relationship on a more secure footing."

"We were hired to guard the cargo," Mouse said.

"We didn't succeed. But of course, nobody warned us there'd be a sorcerer."

The captain nodded. "Life's sometimes inconvenient that way."

"I like this one," Mouse observed, hooking her thumb at the captain.

Freya ignored her. "Still, forewarned's forearmed. I've been pondering how we might be better prepared the next time."

"You fear a next time?"

Freya grinned. "Pirates. Rum. How could there *not* be a next time?"

"You've a point," the captain conceded, and drained his mug.

"But all's not lost."

"You can provide your own sorcerer? Perhaps the small one?"

Mouse snorted and drained her mug. "Return my sword and I'll teach you a thing or two about magic."

Svenson held up a hand, palm outward. "Peace, Mouse. 'twas but a jest."

Mouse sat back, snagging the bottle of rum as she did. "Perhaps you'd best listen to *the large one*. She's cleverer than you'd guess from her looks."

Freya nodded. "In both relative and absolute terms. Nonetheless, my pondering may lead us somewhere profitable." She sipped her rum, winced, and pushed back the mug. "Have you long chains aboard?"

"Obviously. For the anchors."

Freya nodded. "That should suffice. Have you any silver?"

The captain's eyes narrowed and he met her gaze a long moment. Then he sighed and relaxed. "Aye, we've silver aplenty."

Freya smiled. "Then I have a plan." And she leaned

across the table and spoke conspiratorially to the captain, who, once he understood what she was proposing, grinned.

"The two of you may prove worth your weight in gold!"

"Speaking of gold..." Mouse hinted.

"Aye," the captain laughed. "I thought you might be tempted to renegotiate the terms of your employment once your feet were dry. Very well: save us from the sorcerer and you'll each have ten silver once we've sold our cargo."

"Twenty," Mouse suggested.

"A dozen."

"Fifteen."

"Done!" He spat into his hand. "Have we a deal?"

Mouse spat in her palm. "Deal." And she clasped the captain's callused hand firmly enough that he winced.

*

Freya descended a stairway steep as a ladder into the bowels of the ship, with the skill gained from her previous, though brief, nautical employment. There, she was obliged to stoop lest she strike her head on the ceiling. She had a word with the ship's carpenter, a stocky woman who had a word with the captain, who had a word with the purser, who produced a chest of clinking coins and handed them to the carpenter, who retired below deck.

The captain doffed his cap and scratched his bald spot. "If the pirates don't appear, and we've wasted all that coin..."

"Never fear," Freya winked. "You can deduct it from our pay."

Smoke soon billowed from the forge, then after a time, stopped. Shortly thereafter, there came a prolonged screech of metal on metal that went on long enough most crew members gritted their teeth and began muttering threats of violence. Eventually, the noise ended and the carpenter came on deck with a spool of silver wire.

Sometime later, a handful of crewmen went below and returned, groaning under the weight of a spare anchor chain. Once on deck, they secured it under a tarpaulin at the foot of the mainmast. By then, the women's clothing was dry, and when the cabin boy brought it to them, they retired to the captain's cabin and hastened to dress. Shortly after they returned to the main deck, the arms master arrived with their weapons. They'd been scrupulously cleaned, and their edges were razor sharp. Both women complimented her work. Before she'd vanished below deck, they'd buckled on their weapons.

"*That* feels better," Freya observed.

"Now, should one of our gentlemen shipmates venture an impropriety, you'll have the tools at hand to correct his etiquette."

Freya snorted. "I'll be called on to protect them against your depredations, more like."

Mouse grinned. "Poor helpless men. They'll be fortunate to have your protection."

Freya shook her head ruefully. "Will you join me at the bow?"

"With much joy."

Together, they walked to the bow.

*

Though Captain Svenson ran a tight ship, with the decks scrubbed immaculately, the brightwork polished to a blinding gleam, and all loose objects stowed securely, there was only so much that could be done about conditions belowdecks. Even with hatches opened to admit the breeze, the smell was... bracing. Exchanging glances, the two women chose to sleep on deck, wrapped in blankets against the cold, humid night air. They were woken in the morning by a piercing whistle from the crow's nest, followed by the sound of running feet as the crew came on deck.

Mouse poked her nose from beneath her blanket and yawned. "Bastard pirates! Couldn't wait for us to break our fast?"

Freya dropped nimbly from the rail, where she'd been standing. "No worries there. The mast's still on the horizon. It'll be hours before they arrive."

Not long after the whistle, the cook arrived on deck with a cauldron of thick oatmeal filled with small lumps of what Freya hoped was some form of dried fruit. She was wise enough not to ask Mouse's opinion, for her partner had proven on numerous occasions she'd eat anything that had stopped moving, and many things that hadn't. They ate heartily, standing at the rail and watching the pirate ship draw rapidly nearer. The *Wager* was a square rigger, with a belly full of casks of rum; in consequence, she crested the waves like a drunken sow fallen into the moat. The pirate was a sleeker design, and cut the waves like a knife; she sailed like some great predatory fish attacking a dying whale. There'd be no hope of outrunning the pirates, particularly with the gentle breeze and long, low swells that did nothing to inconvenience the smaller ship.

Before the pirates came too close, Freya took the captain aside. "It's time."

Svenson nodded, and shouted orders. Working together, his men winched one end of the chain to the top of the mast, where they fixed it in place beside one of the stays.

Then one man ascended, leaving the carpenter's spool of silver wire on the deck and threading it through the chain, link by link, as he rose. When he reached the top and wound the wire around the last link, several burly men took the deck end of the chain and ran it over the side until it dangled in the water, far enough below the surface it didn't emerge from the water when the ship rose on the swell.

Svenson came to stand beside them. "Is the chain strictly necessary?"

Freya shrugged. "The silver will catch the spell, but can't possibly hold that much energy on its own. But the iron will drain the energy into the ocean. That is," she grinned with only one side of her mouth, "if I've understood what I've read of seawater's magical properties. Sorcerers aren't known for their clarity."

Mouse patted her forearm. "If anyone could understand that gibberish, it's you."

Svenson gave them both a long look, then left to begin organizing his crew.

Freya covered her friend's hand, then turned to watch the preparations. The crew was busy spreading coarse sand on the decks. "To soak up the blood," remarked the captain as he hurried past.

Cutlasses and cudgels were being handed out. Some sailors took one, some took the other, and some took both, just to be safe. A few unwrapped and strung bows. As they watched, the pirate ship slid nimbly upwind of the trader, stealing the wind from its sails, then gliding to a halt itself as the pirates let the sails luff, maintaining just enough momentum to hold station on the *Wager*. Close enough to see the faces of its crew, who were a scarred and unpleasant group of ruffians.

"Ahoy!" bellowed a voice from the pirate ship. It came

from a large man with a beard that trailed across his chest as if he'd tried to swallow a russet badger and stopped halfway. Atop his head sat a ram's skull, complete with spiral horns; across one eye socket, a tattered patch fluttered in the breeze. "Surrender, or prepare to be blasted."

A slender figure dressed in long, flowing robes stepped to the rail beside him, withdrawing a slim wand from the depths of her cloak. "By me," she added unnecessarily, with a flamboyant courtesy to the *Wager*'s crew.

Svenson laughed and spat into the sea. "Do your worst, pirate! This isn't our first dance."

The pirate captain shouted something at the sorcerer, who raised her wand and chanted several guttural syllables. Bright crimson light flashed from the wand, spreading like an opening fan, but just before it struck the trader's crew, it veered sharply toward the anchor chain. The silver flared white, the anchor chain glowed red-hot, strange lights danced the length of the chain, and the smell of scorched wood came from where the chain passed over the rail. Below, the sea began bubbling.

The crew cheered, and hurled insults across the gap.

Frowning, the sorcerer attempted another spell, with much the same results, though this time, whisps of smoke came from the rail.

"Archers!" yelled Svenson, and a dozen men and women with crossbows pushed forward to the rail. "Fire at will!" They did, concentrating on the sorcerer without being told. Though the first volley of bolts shattered against an invisible barrier, the force of the impacts threw her back, and rather than risk a second volley, she withdrew behind her crewmates. Undeterred, the archers began firing into the crowd on the pirate ship's deck, who returned fire with slings. Sailors began falling on both decks.

The pirate captain spat orders at his crew, and the smaller ship filled sails and slid downwind, closing the gap with the trader. There came a crunch of wood, the trader swaying under the impact, then before the ships could drift apart, pirates had affixed grapples to the trader's side and bound the ships together. With a ragged shout, the pirates surged aboard.

"Who gets the captain?"

Freya held up her hand. "Best of three?"

Mouse nodded, and they each pumped a fist up and down, then held out their hand. Mouse had her hand flat, palm downwards; Freya showed a fist.

"Blanket covers baby. Again!"

Three pumps, and Mouse held her hand flat again; Freya showed a knife-edge hand. "Knife cuts blanket."

Three more pumps, and Mouse showed a fist; Freya showed the knife-hand again. "And baby grasps knife."

"You always win!"

Mouse smirked. "You always end with the knife."

"Your barbarian games bemuse me. Plus," she grinned ruefully, "I keep hoping you'll believe I've learned my lesson. Anyway, play safe." And with that, she drew her greatsword one-handed and ran at the boarders.

Mouse, sabre in hand, ran to where the pirate captain had just cut down an unfortunate trader. "Captain! Will you dance?"

The pirate took in her diminutive but shapely figure and his grin widened. "*Dance*, is it? When the killing's done, I'll make you happier than you've ever been dancing with another man." Then he licked his lips and glanced at Freya. "Or woman, for that matter." Then he flicked a backhand cut at her with his cutlass.

Mouse deflected the blow over her head and lunged, catching him in the thigh. She'd meant to take him in the belly, but had failed to account for the rise of the deck under the swell. Blood began trickling down his leg.

"Your dancing will be clumsy. But you'll dance well enough for the next few breaths." With that, she began a series of blows, alternating slashes and thrusts, driving the larger man backward as he parried frantically. He began sweating, drops cutting through the grime on his face. Each time he prepared a riposte, she pressed him just a bit harder, and she could see his frustration growing as he tried to muster breath to taunt or curse her.

"Stop playing with him," Freya called.

Mouse cast a glance at her companion, who stood by a windrow of bodies missing various extremities, including an orphaned head that rolled past her as the deck canted. As Mouse watched, Freya disarmed a second pirate and kicked a third so hard in the belly he flew backwards, folded nearly in half. Seeing what he thought was an opening, the pirate captain tried to close with her. Without missing a beat, she ducked under his wild swing and rose, ringing her sword's basket hilt off the side of his head. His blade fell to the deck, followed by its wielder, the double-thump inaudible above the din of sword on sword and cudgel on skull.

As he fell, she turned to survey the damage Freya had wrought. Her large friend had cleared a wide gap around her, none of the survivors daring approach, and she was clearly frustrated; it would be difficult to attack another pirate without pushing aside the traders, who continued to hold their own against the remaining pirates.

"Freya! Boarding time?"

Freya nodded. "Me first!"

Mouse nodded, not having forgotten the sorcerer. Freya usually had plans to deal with such inconveniences, and Mouse was happy to follow her lead. She waited a beat as Freya hurdled the rail and dropped onto the pirate ship's deck. Then she followed.

All of the pirate ship's crew, save the helmsman and a couple of men tending the sails, were on the trader, leaving the sorcerer standing alone on deck. From the set of her jaw, she was clearly more angry than worried.

The sorcerer held up her wand. "You're a brave one. But it won't save you." She pointed the wand at Freya, and crimson light flared. Freya ducked a hand into her pocket and emerged with a coil of silver wire, which she wrapped around her hand before tossing the spool behind her. Once again, the spell's energy flared in the silver. But this time, the scent of scorched flesh and hot metal filled the air, and Freya gritted her teeth. With her free hand, she cut at the sorcerer. Again, some invisible barrier saved the woman, but the strength of the blow forced her back a step, then another as the deck canted. But now the wire glowed hot enough Freya could no longer hold it, and she cast it from her.

As the sorcerer raised her wand, Mouse removed a certain knife from her sleeve. A vendor who had very good reasons not to cheat Mouse had promised it would be proof against any magic, and had demanded a correspondingly hefty price. Without pausing, she flung the knife overhand at the sorcerer—and saw it carom off the invisible barrier and fall to the deck. Mouse raised an eyebrow, then rushed the woman, hoping the barrier was only proof against weapons. And indeed, she caught the arm holding the wand and pivoted to swing the woman in a short arc behind her, where she met Freya's fist coming in the opposite direction. The sorcerer dropped to the deck like a sack of corn.

Unfortunately, she'd forgotten the wand. It struck the deck with a crash far out of proportion to its size and weight, and fell through, leaving a splinter-edged hole large enough to swallow Freya, echoed by a second crash and a third as it passed through the lower deck and then the ship's hull. Water began flooding into the ship.

The helmsman and the two men in the rigging exchanged glances, dropped their weapons, and held their hands in the air.

Silence had fallen. Looking up at the *Wager*, they saw the trader's sailors lining the rails. Seeing the mage under control, a cheer went up, and Freya bowed deeply. The hull made a desolate groaning noise, and she cast a wary eye towards the hole. The water was rushing in with increasing vigour, causing the ship to settle. Mouse retrieved her thrown knife, sheathed it, and went to stand by Freya's side.

From the rail, Captain Svenson's voice boomed down. "Well fought!"

Mouse frowned. "Too well fought. It seems we've scuttled their ship."

Svenson beamed down. "Rather inconvenient if you've no alternative means of transport—other than resuming your swim home." Seeing their faces, his smile widened. "Still, I suppose you did save us from their sorcerer. Without you and your friend, we'd have been fish food. Best get aboard quickly; that deck will soon be awash."

The trader's crew began cutting the ropes that bound the two ships together, letting the pirate ship sink faster. As the gap between the decks increased, Freya gave Mouse a hand up. Then she clambered back onto the *Wager*, whose crew were tossing the pirates, dead or alive, over the rail and onto their ship's deck, which was nearly awash. Those who could still move crawled towards the rails, trying to stay above the water. Svenson waved a cheery farewell, then turned to his crew.

"Raise sail and get us clear!" he bellowed. "Deck crew! Take the wounded to the surgeon." As the *Wager* gathered speed, he turned to his passengers.

"Traditionally, we hold a feast to celebrate a victory at sea. Fortunately, we've several kegs of wild boar we've been saving for a special occasion. They infest our island and play havoc with the crops, but they're damned tasty." He smacked his lips. "You've not lived 'til you've tasted boar marinated for several months in island rum."

Mouse glanced at Freya. "They fought well for rum-sodden sailors. I'll feast with them!"

Freya looked to the captain. "I don't suppose you have any white wine?"

Svenson's grin widened. "I'm sure I can find something suitable."

*

As night fell, the crew emerged with a strange contraption, a rectangular box the size of coffin, made of some unfamiliar dark wood. Several crew attached a spit, while others filled the box with coal. Seeing Freya's puzzled look, one explained. "It's an enchanted device that lets us cook on deck without fear the fire will spread to the ship."

Soon, a pair of boar carcasses hung from the spit over a roaring fire, fat bubbling and sizzling and a heavenly odour rising, borne on the night wind. Freya ate heartily, sipping her wine from its bottle and exchanging tall tales with the sailors. After a time, she noticed Mouse had disappeared. For a moment, she was alarmed. Then she saw that Svenson, too, was missing, and she smiled and took another pull at the bottle, followed by a mouthful of the pork crackle, melted fat running down her chin. In the darkness, she looked back at their ship's wake, limned in flickery blue light. Some magic of the sea, she imagined.

As the ship rose upon a long swell, she smiled at the darkness. Definitely better than swimming.

**Author's notes**

If this story feels like it has a hint of Asterix and Obelix exchanging pleasantries with their pirate friends, with Mouse and Freya taking on the role of the Gaulish protagonists this time, that's not a coincidence.

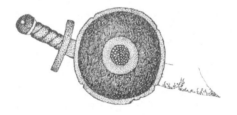

# THE FLESH OF MAN
## *Frank Sawielijew*

Thurzo watched with disgust as three armour-clad men harassed a young woman on the ground. They pulled her by the hair, kicked her between the ribs and threatened her with blade of sword against her neck.

Such were the manners of civilized men, yet they called him a barbarian. He spat on the ground and shook his head.

"What has she done?" he shouted at the men, his fingers rubbing the pommel of his sword.

The three looked up and exchanged worried glances. The barbarian's large frame was an intimidating sight. His unbound hair and long moustache waved in the wind, and his sleeveless vest proudly displayed the bulging muscles of his arms.

"She's a thief," said one of the men. "Stole a chicken off Bolon's farm in broad daylight."

"She's a savage thing," said another. "Tore the poor animal's throat out and ate it raw! We caught her in the act."

Thurzo looked at the woman. "Is that true?"

She nodded. "I was hungry. I had nothing to eat."

One of the men kicked her hard in the stomach, causing her to cough and retch. "Silence, wench! We'll drag you to the dungeon, there you can feast on stale bread and the mould on the walls!"

They seized her by the hair and tried to pull her to her feet, but she struggled against their grasp, beating against their mailed arms with bare fists.

"Release her," said Thurzo.

The men let go and she slumped to the ground, putting her hands over her head.

"But she's a thief! She stole one of Bolon's..."

Thurzo cut the man off. "How much was the chicken worth?"

The men exchanged uncertain glances and shrugged.

"Uh... about five silvers, maybe?" one of them wagered.

Thurzo reached into the pouch at his belt and tossed a handful of coins at the three men's feet. It was more than five silvers.

"There. Now release her."

Hesitantly, one of the men got to his knees and picked up the coins. He counted them in his fingers and nodded to the others. But they made no effort to leave – too precious was the prey cowering at their feet.

Thurzo pulled his sword halfway from its scabbard, polished steel glinting in the sunlight. They finally got the message and walked away without another word. He approached the cowering woman and helped her to her feet.

"Are you hurt bad?"

She shook her head and mouthed a silent *thank you*.

He allowed her a moment to gather herself before he asked, "Do you know your way around the mountains?"

She looked into his steel-blue eyes. Her own were a sulphuric yellow, a colour he had never seen in human eyes before.

She averted her face before she spoke. "Mountains? You mean the Karthan Range?"

"Yes."

"I know them well. They used to be my home."

He put a finger underneath her chin and gently moved her face towards him. "You don't have to look away when you talk to me. I won't hurt you."

But she pushed his hand away and averted her face again. "What interest have you in the mountains?"

"They hold something that I seek, but I am not familiar with the terrain. I need a guide."

She shook her head, a look of apprehension in her eyes. "Not me. I left the Karthans for a reason and have no desire to return."

He held her chin with three fingers and looked deep into her yellow eyes. "I bought your freedom. You owe me, woman."

She held his gaze for a while. There was defiance in her stare, and the look of a woman too proud to be made slave.

"Very well, stay if you wish. I'm sure the guards would love to keep you."

She let out a frustrated sigh and resigned herself to her fate. "Alright, I'll guide you through the mountains. But it won't be a pleasant journey."

"I'm not heading there for pleasure."

He took her by the wrist and marched along the ragged dirt road leading away from the town and towards the majestic Karthan Range, a ridge of orange sandstone cliffs whose tall, pillar-shaped peaks reached far into the sky.

She pulled loose from his grasp and went ahead, keeping him at some distance behind her.

The girl didn't seem to be very sociable. But Thurzo didn't care – as long as she led him to his destination, he would share his provisions and protect her from any danger that lurked at the peaks.

All he needed was her guidance – he could handle the slaying of the dread-lizard on his own.

*

The guards' accusation of savagery had not been unfounded. When Thurzo brought a young boar to their camp, she immediately cut off a haunch with her knife and tore into the raw meat. He carved the rest of the animal into smaller parts and hung them from the wooden frame he had constructed over the fireplace.

As the meat cooked, he watched the woman devour her raw leg of boar. Blood ran down her chin in rivulets and dripped upon her brown linen tunic, staining it red.

"Don't you want to wait until it's cooked?" he asked.

She put the raw boar leg down and wiped the blood from her mouth with the back of her hand.

"I'm sorry. I was hungry."

This was the first time she had spoken to him without averting her face. When she opened her mouth, he saw that her teeth were sharp as a wolf's.

"You ate the chicken raw, too. Seems like you like raw meat."

She looked into the fire, the flames reflecting in her yellow eyes.

"It's how we eat in the mountains. There is not much wood for fires."

"They're a treacherous place, so I have heard. That's why I need a guide who knows her way around them."

Her hands reached for the leg of boar again and she took another bite, her sharp teeth tearing effortlessly through the flesh.

"I left the mountains long ago, seeking a better life in the valley. They are no longer home to me."

Thurzo prodded a cut of boar with his sword, testing its firmness. It seemed done.

He took it from the cooking frame and ate. It had a crispy sear on the outside but was still rare and juicy within.

The woman finished her raw haunch and grabbed a cooked piece from the frame. As she reached for it, Thurzo noticed that her fingernails were sharp and black like a predator's claws. The men of the mountains seemed to be a wild breed.

"There are savage tribes up there," she said. She bit into the cooked meat, savouring the taste of seared flesh and rendered fat. It was a rare delicacy for her. After a long moment, she swallowed and added, "And harpies."

"I've heard of harpies. Winged women with eagle-like claws for their feet. But I've never seen one before."

"Then hope that you never will, for they prey on men. We must pass through their territory on our way to the peaks. What do you seek up in the Karthans, anyway?"

He skewered another piece of meat with his sword and removed it from the fire. It was steaming hot, the fat still sizzling at the edges.

"Among the peaks of the Karthan Range dwell the mighty dread-lizards. I must hunt one and harvest its heart, for my father is suffering from deadly illness and the cure requires blood from a dread-lizard's heart."

"You must be very close to your father if you are willing to hunt such a beast for him."

"Yes. He is a great man."

They sat in silence for a while, gorging themselves on the freshly cooked boar until they were full and watching the dance of the orange flames against the darkness of the night. The woman removed her boots and put her feet close to the fire for warmth. The nails on her feet were sharp and dark like those on her hands, and they had torn holes into the soft fabric of her wine-red socks, making her toes poke through.

"I ran away from my family," she said as she wiggled her toes in front of the fireplace. "It must be a beautiful thing to be close to your father."

Thurzo got to his feet and removed the last pieces of meat from the frame. By now, they were thoroughly cooked.

"It is," he said while his hands busied themselves wrapping sheets of leather around the meat to store it for transport.

"Forgive me, I have not yet told you my name. I am Oria."

"I am Thurzo, son of Thorak."

He finished packing up the meat for their journey, and they spent the next hour watching the fire turn to faintly glowing embers, allowing a comfortable silence to sit between them.

When the fire had gone out, they went to sleep under a bright full moon.

*

They broke off camp early the next morning and resumed their journey into the mountains. With each step, the majestic peaks came closer and the landscape turned from lush forest and grassland to barren rocks. Only few resilient plants grew in the vicinity of the Karthan Range, thorny bushes and short gnarly trees that barely reached the height of a man.

Thurzo chewed on an overcooked strip of boar meat as they walked. He offered one to Oria, who gratefully accepted. She wolfed it down quickly, her sharp teeth making short work of the tough meat.

Their ascending path led past oddly shaped pillars of red and yellow stone, through serpentine caverns that carved their way through imposing cliffs, and across jagged crags that cut into their palms and the soles of their boots. The higher they climbed, the sparser the vegetation grew, and soon they reached a height at which not even the misshapen little trees dared bury their roots into the cracks within the stone.

They came upon a wide plateau whose flat ground offered their legs welcome respite from the arduous climb. Many tall pillars studded the plateau, shaped into curious forms by millennia of searing winds. Even taller cliffs loomed in the distance, their steep faces pocked with yawning mouths of caves.

"The harpies make their home within those caves," Oria said in a low voice, careful not to make her echo heard across the plateau. "We must be careful."

Thurzo acknowledged her warning with a silent nod.

Oria kept her eyes fixed on the faraway caves as they walked, carelessly neglecting to watch the ground underfoot. She lost her footing and was almost swallowed by a narrow crevice within the rock, but Thurzo reacted quickly. His mighty arms closed around her waist and pulled her to safety.

"Careful! You should keep your eyes where you step."

"I must keep my eyes where they lurk."

She pointed to the caves and motioned for him to stay low. She cupped a hand around her ear and listened – her little misstep had sent a handful of rocks rolling down the crevice, and their echo rang long after they had vanished in its depths. The disturbance was heard across the plateau.

They sat motionless for a long while; Oria seemed to expect something that filled her with dread. Thurzo nervously fingered the pommel of his sword, itching for action.

Then it came: a shriek like a whetstone grinding against steel, answered by another, and another, and another. A wild cacophony of howls and screams filled the air, sending a chill down Thurzo's spine. It was the most inhuman thing he ever heard.

"They're coming," said Oria. "We must hide!"

She sought cover underneath a small overhang. Thurzo drew his sword, but lowered it back into its sheath when he realized that the sun's glare reflected on its polished surface. Crouched low, they watched the skies for movement.

Thurzo spotted a pair of leathery wings passing just above them. They belonged to a strange reptile with a long, beak-like face and elongated head. Upon it rode a woman with wild, tangled hair wielding a long spear of bone.

"Are these the savage tribes you mentioned?" he asked Oria in a whisper. "They do not strike me as harpies."

She took a deep breath and closed her eyes. "They are harpies."

Thurzo counted more and more of the winged lizards circling in the sky above. Their riders seemed to know by intuition where he and Oria were hiding, for they passed as closely by their shelter as the treacherous geography allowed them.

"Come out, Oria! I can smell you down there!" shouted one of the riders. "You have always had the stench of humanity about you, but today it is strong like that of a city-dweller! Reject the settled ways and return to your nature! Come!"

Thurzo gave her a questioning look, but she shook her head. Now was not a good time to explain.

The other riders joined in the shouts.

"Come out, come out Oria!" they yelled, accompanied by the screeching of their reptilian steeds. "Come and return to the fold!"

Oria drew her dagger, a pitiful weapon to face the airborne riders with, and came out to face them.

Thurzo followed and drew his sword, raising it to the sky. Its polished steel gleamed bright in the sunlight. He walked out into the open plateau and issued his challenge.

"Face me if you wish to take her, fiends! My sword thirsts for blood!"

"She brought a man with her! A man!"

"And what good meat he has on his body! Attack!"

One of the harpies descended upon him, her winged reptile gliding through the air with rapid speed. Her long spear was aimed at his chest, its tip a dreadful spike of hooks and jagged edges. At the last moment he jumped away and slashed his sword across the belly of her flying steed. The creature lost its bowels and screeched in pain. Its wings folded inward and it went to the ground, throwing off its rider.

Thurzo felt a sharp pain in his left shoulder. Another harpy swooped down behind him, her spear taking him in the back. The hooked tip broke off, stuck in the tough flesh beneath his shoulder blade. He stabbed his sword upward as the harpy passed above him, but his strike narrowly missed the winged reptile.

From all directions they fell upon him, spears of jagged bone stabbing at his limbs. He jumped away from their strikes until his legs burned, and his sword was soon stained red from the blood of the airborne beasts. One by one he felled, slicing through their necks, the soft flesh of their underbellies, and the thin membranes of their wings. The air was thick with the dissonant screeches of dying reptiles.

Just when he felt he was about to collapse from exhaustion, the harpies backed off. They rose into the sky and circled above him like vultures, watching him bleed from his injured shoulder and breathe with laboured breath.

But the real threat was not above, but on the ground. The riders of the beasts he felled had gotten to their feet and regrouped. Half a dozen harpies encircled him, their long spears far outclassing the reach of his sword.

Even as a barbarian himself, he found them to be the image of savagery. They were clad only in simple loincloths and thick leather wraps around their shins and wrists. The nails on their fingers and toes were sharp and black like vultures' claws and their eyes were the sickly yellow of sulphur. Sharp teeth stared at him from snarling mouths.

Suddenly, Oria broke through their ranks and threw herself at his feet. Her dagger slipped from her sweaty palm, clattering to the ground.

"Leave him! It's me you want – take me and let him go!"

One of the harpies laughed, a shrill sound that made Thurzo's skin crawl. From the colourful beads woven into her tangled hair, he judged her to be the leader.

"Our sweet Oria has made friends with a man! Come. Come here! We will not harm him if you surrender."

"Do you swear it?"

"By the sharpness of my claws I swear it. We will even treat his wound so it may heal."

Oria got to her feet but hesitated. She glanced at Thurzo, who shook his head. He was ready to die standing. These creatures could not be trusted – even if she was one of them.

She walked into their arms regardless.

The leader grabbed her by the wrists and twisted her arms behind her back. She tore a sleeve off Oria's shirt and used the strip of cloth to tie her hands together. Then, she put an elbow into her back and forced her to the ground.

"Not only are you friends with men, you dress like them, too!" the harpy shrieked. "You even hide your claws!"

She knelt down and ripped the soles off Oria's boots. When she discovered the socks underneath, she snarled in disgust. Her sharp claws reduced the soft fabric to shreds with little effort. Only when Oria's boots and socks had been reduced to legwraps of leather and cloth, leaving everything below the ankle bare, did she let go of her feet.

"You are a harpy, not a human! You are a hunter, a predator!" She grabbed Oria by the hair and yanked her to her feet. She spread her fingers in front of her face, moving her sharp claws dangerously close to Oria's eyes. "These are your source of pride. With these, you kill and slay and eat. You do not hide them. And you do not use a dagger like a soft-fingered man."

"Don't tell me what I am." Oria averted her face, throwing a defiant look towards Thurzo. "I know I am not one of yours."

The harpy's claws gently stroked Oria's chin, too lightly to break skin.

"Oh, I will make sure you become one of ours again. Harpies – take the human's sword! Tie him up and bring him to our caves!"

Oria gasped in shock. "But you promised to let him go!"

The harpy grinned a sharp-toothed smile. "I said we would not harm him, and my word I shall keep. He shall be our honoured guest tonight, and since he is your friend, I will let you enjoy his company."

*

The harpies shoved a bowl of fruit through the narrow gaps between the iron bars of their cell. Thurzo took a big red pear-shaped thing from the bowl and eyed it with suspicion.

"They are not poisoned," Oria said with a sigh. "The harpies want you strong and healthy. You would be no use to them dead."

He bit into the fruit. It was sweet, with a slightly sour aftertaste. A refreshing treat.

He finished eating it and tossed the core out of the cell before he said, "You could have told me that you're a harpy."

"I may have their claws and their teeth, but I am not one of them. I left because… because…"

She averted her gaze from Thurzo and looked to the ground. She shuffled her bare feet and scrunched her toes in a vain attempt to hide her claws. Her hands were clenched into fists, blood dripping out as her claws cut into her palms.

"You left because your soul is not as savage as their ways. I understand. But there's no need to hide from yourself. Had I known your nature, I would still have taken you as my companion."

Oria sobbed, and tears came rolling down her cheeks. "I left because I did not wish to eat the flesh of men. Harpies are hunters, Thurzo, and humans are our prey. I never liked it. I will devour any beast, but men? The thought alone makes my skin crawl. Yet they always tried to force me to partake of their feasts when they returned with a slain merchant or traveller. But I refused to eat."

Thurzo picked another fruit from the bowl and rolled it between his fingers. It was the size of a cherry but had the colour of an orange. "I always thought harpies were winged women with the bodies of birds. Yet you have not the shape of beast at all… and neither do you have the soul. There is more humanity in you than in many of the so-called civilized."

"Whether I am beast or man, you will soon see." She looked at the bowl of fruit and her lips curled back in disgust. "They feed you, but not me. We harpies are carnivores – these fruits do not nourish me. They want to starve me out until my hunger makes me fall on you. Then they will accept me back into their fold."

He put the orange fruit back into the bowl, his appetite lost. "I see. Then I hope we can find a way out before it happens."

She shuffled closer towards him and laid her hand on his, careful not to scratch him with her claws. "Don't worry, Thurzo. I would rather starve than fall upon a friend."

They sat like this for a while, without exchanging a word. The harpies' cruelty made Thurzo's blood boil, but he had nothing to release his rage on. Their cell was a dead end within a cavern, the only exit blocked by thick bars fashioned from a giant creature's bones. The strength of his arms alone was not enough to break them.

Focusing on the gentle weight of Oria's hand on his helped to calm his anger. Her struggle against the cannibalism of her race was admirable; even if the other harpies were, she was no beast.

She was the strongest woman he had ever known.

*

Days had passed without an opportunity for escape. The harpies never approached the cell too closely – when they brought Thurzo's food, they placed the bowl on the ground and pushed it into the cell with their spears from a distance. Even if he tried to grab their spears, they were too far to snatch the key from their belts.

The pain of hunger gnawed at Oria. She drummed the claws of her fingers and toes against the hard stone floor to distract herself, clacking with an irregular rhythm. She glanced at the bloodstained bandage on Thurzo's shoulder and licked her lips. The smell of old, dried blood made her salivate and her mind kept wandering into places she wished it didn't.

"I don't see a way out for us," said Thurzo, kicking against the door of bone that blocked the exit. He looked at Oria, who sat on the floor and rocked back and forth, tormented by stomach pains. It was a pitiful sight. "We'll be stuck here until the hunger takes you and you do as your sisters wish."

"I would rather slice my own throat than have you as a meal," she hissed through clenched teeth. "I will not stain my soul with the flesh of men."

Thurzo admired her resilience. With every ounce of strength, she fought the primal urge within her. He would gladly have died alongside her in a fight, calling her his battle-sister. But the harpies' cruel torture denied them such a fate.

A commotion at the mouth of the cave drew his attention. Several harpies were bickering with each other, but he couldn't make out their words from the distance. Then, a group of four approached, headed by the tribe's leader.

"See, Marra. Even as she is pained with hunger, she does not touch him," said one of them.

The leader – Marra was her name – spat at the suffering Oria through the bars of her cell. "Pathetic! She is no real harpy. A disgrace unto our tribe!"

"What shall we do with her?" asked another. "Shall we throw her into exile? Execute her at the stake?"

"No," snarled Marra. "I will make her eat, if she wants it or not. I will butcher the man myself, and when we feast upon his flesh I will force it down her throat until she learns to enjoy it. Open the door."

The harpy bowed before her leader and took a small bone key from her loincloth's thin belt. She opened the cell door and Marra stepped inside, her sharp claws raised to slaughter Thurzo with a strike at his throat.

He planted his feet on the ground and clenched his fists, ready to give her a fight.

But Marra never reached him. Oria, weakened as she was, leapt at the leader of her tribe with a savage scream on her lips. The impact knocked Marra over, and Oria pinned her to the ground with her knees against her chest. She swung her right hand down and mercilessly raked her claws across the surprised harpy's face, clawing both her eyes out.

Thurzo seized the opportunity and escaped through the open door, falling upon the three harpy guards before they could react. He punched one in the face, cutting his knuckles on her sharp teeth. The harpy went down and dropped her spear, and he snatched it out of the air before it clattered to the ground.

The other two were faster to react. They quickly lowered the tips of their spears and stabbed at Thurzo. He stepped back and parried their strikes with the shaft of his own spear. With relentless jabs, they forced him into the defensive. Dealing with two spears at once left him no opportunity for strikes of his own.

Then Oria assaulted them from the flank.

With clawed toes she kicked at one harpy's shins, tearing deep wounds into her legs. She fell to the ground, and Thurzo finished her off with his spear. The other turned to face Oria, but she was already too close to make use of her spear. Oria's clawed fingers reached for her throat and tore it out, leaving her to drown in her own blood.

Then, her bloodstained hand seized Thurzo by the arm, the sharp tips of her claws breaking his skin.

"Come, we must flee! I know where they keep the pterodactyls!"

"Pterodactyls?"

"The flying reptiles! Come!"

She broke into a run, dragging Thurzo along with her. They emerged from the cave and followed a narrow path along the edge of a cliff. Oria's footing was sure, as she had walked this path many times before, but Thurzo's was not. He tripped over a loose rock and fell, sliding down the steeply angled cliff face.

He dragged Oria down with him, even as his arm tore loose from her grasp. He rammed the soles of his boots against the cliff face and tried to grab for handholds, but his fingers slipped and he slid down further, his arms and chest painfully scraping against the jagged rock face.

Oria dug her claws into the soft sandstone and managed to hold onto the ledge. She stretched out a bare foot for Thurzo to grab and shouted, "Take my leg!"

He wrapped a hand around her ankle, but with his added weight, the piece of sandstone underneath Oria's fingers broke away. They both slid down the cliffside, their descent slowed by their bodies scraping against the rough, jagged stone.

Thurzo hit the ground first, his strong legs absorbing the impact. Oria landed on his shoulders, and his hands instinctively reached up to grab her legs and steady her.

Their muscles tensed for a moment, and then he relaxed and helped her down, careful not to drop her. They were panting with exhaustion, and Thurzo examined his bare arms. A multitude of scrapes and cuts covered his skin, but the wounds were shallow and barely drew blood. Oria's right arm, where Marra had torn away her shirt sleeve, was similarly hurt, but the fabric of her shirt had caught most of the damage on the rest of her body.

She looked at the shallow wounds on her arm and licked her lips.

"Even my own blood looks appetizing now. My stomach craves for food."

Thurzo discovered his spear not far from where they had landed. Miraculously, it had survived the fall. He picked it up and put a firm hand on Oria's shoulder, reassuring her.

"We will hunt once we get out of the harpies' lair. But I'm afraid our fall has alerted them to our escape. We should hurry."

Oria closed her eyes and shook her head to discard her ravenous thoughts. "Of course. The pterodactyl pens are not far – your clumsiness got us a shortcut!"

Thurzo laughed. "Well worth the scratches on my arms, then! Let's go!"

Oria went ahead and Thurzo followed with his spear levelled ahead. Their path led through the harpies' residential area, a village of tents made of bone frames draped with rough-cut sheets of leather. Some of them looked to be tanned from human skins.

Harpies emerged from several of the tents, hissing at the trespassers. Thurzo threatened them with his spear, but Oria shouted for him to run. He cursed under his breath and followed.

They sped through the village as fast as their legs could manage, followed by a growing horde of unarmed harpies.

More and more emerged from their tents, hissing and shrieking. Soon the entire tribe was on alert.

Oria and Thurzo dodged past many a clawed hand reaching out for them, and soon they arrived at the pterodactyl pens. Two spear-armed harpies stood guard there, instantly alerted by the commotion.

Thurzo hurled his spear at them, hitting one in the stomach. Its barbed tip buried itself deep within her guts, and she collapsed to the ground clutching her wound.

The second guard lowered her spear and braced herself. Oria charged, throwing herself at the guard with the last of her strength. The spear caught her in the side, ripping a nasty wound into her flesh, but her clawed hands tore into the guard's throat. With a gurgling scream on her lips, the guard collapsed.

Oria ignored the stinging pain in her side and mounted a pterodactyl. The creature let out a shrill shriek.

Thurzo picked up a spear from the fallen guards and seated himself behind Oria, wrapping his left arm around her waist. He felt a wetness dripping into his elbow and noticed the wound in her side.

"You need to get that bandaged," he remarked.

"Yes, once we're in the air. Go! Go!"

She jabbed her heels into the reptile's sides, urging it to take to the sky. Thurzo looked over his shoulder and saw the horde of angry harpies catching up with them.

"They're almost upon us!"

After another nudge from Oria, the pterodactyl finally flapped its wings and hopped off the ground. It caught an updraft and ascended, leaving the harpy village behind.

But the harpies were not willing to let their prey escape that easily. Just when he thought their ordeal was over, Thurzo spotted three pterodactyls behind them, giving chase. Two of the riders wielded spears, while the third was armed only with the claws on her hands and feet.

One spear was flung towards them, grazing Thurzo's shoulder and barely missing the pterodactyl's wing on its way down.

"They're following us! Can you shake them off?"

Oria took a deep breath and grasped the reins of her steed tightly. "No, but I can turn us around... prepare yourself to use that spear."

She nudged the pterodactyl to make a sharp turn, and Thurzo had to hold on tightly to stay in his seat.

"The one with the spear first," said Thurzo, and Oria nodded.

Oria steered the pterodactyl towards the spearwoman, and as soon as they were within reach, Thurzo struck at her chest. She made to parry his attack, but it was merely a feint – he angled his spear downward and stabbed her pterodactyl in the neck.

An angered shriek came out of her throat as her slain reptile sailed downward. She jumped off its back and tried to tackle Thurzo, but he rammed his spear into her chest before she was upon him. The jagged tip penetrated into her chest, and with the spear still stuck in her flesh she fell into the depths.

The other two harpies passed them by, too far away to reach them with their claws.

The opponents brought some distance between them before sharply turning again. They were heading towards each other like knights in an aerial joust. The two pursuing harpies flew in a tight formation, their pterodactyls so close to each other the tips of their wings almost touched.

The two harpies went for a straight collision course, ready to gang up on Oria's pterodactyl and tear it to pieces with their claws. But at the last moment, Oria nudged her steed to soar upwards, passing over their heads.

It was a tight manoeuvre, only narrowly avoiding a collision. The heads of the two harpies were just at the right height for Oria's feet to reach them. She stretched out her legs and kicked at them, knocking them off their pterodactyls. They fell to their deaths screaming, and their reptilian steeds continued their flight without riders.

"Now we're rid of them," said Oria, letting out a breath of relief. "Time to hunt."

Thurzo tore the left sleeve off Oria's shirt and replied, "Time to bandage your wound, first. You are already weak from hunger. I don't need you weak from blood loss, too."

*

They had been flying for almost an hour; the adrenaline of battle had long subsided, and Oria became painfully aware of her hunger again. She barely managed to keep herself from biting into the pterodactyl. She felt its muscles move between her thighs whenever it flapped its wings, delicious firm flesh, lean and nourishing. She dug her claws into the trousers on her thighs, tearing holes into the fabric in frustration. Her claws craved to dig into flesh instead, to tear out a juicy chunk of meat and shove it down her throat.

Thurzo scanned the area for dread-lizards. Oria had steered the pterodactyl towards the dwelling place of the mighty reptiles. Unlike the spacious plateaus the harpies dwelled in, this area of the Karthan Range was far more treacherous. The ground was rocky and uneven, the cliffs taller and steeper. A wrong step here meant certain death.

He spotted one of the beasts lounging on a precipice below, enjoying the sun on its scaly skin. It was a massive creature. Its light brown scales blended in well with the ochre-hued sandstone of the mountains, but the long protruding spines of yellowed bone on its back gave it away. They curved inward, ending in a hooked spike. Though impressive, they were not the deadliest weapon of the squat, four-legged lizard: the tip of its tail was a mighty club of hardened bone plates, massive enough to crush skulls with a single swing.

"There!" exclaimed Thurzo, pointing his finger at the creature. "A dread-lizard!"

Oria could no longer control her urges. As soon as she saw it, she leapt off her pterodactyl and fell upon the huge lizard. Her well-aimed jump avoided the creature's back-spikes and she landed on its flank. With her claws holding on tightly, she opened her mouth and buried her teeth inside the lizard's sun-warmed flesh. The creature woke from its dozing and thrashed about wildly, trying to throw the assailant off its back. But Oria's claws were wedged deep in its skin and she stubbornly held on, ripping out one piece of flesh after the other to sate her growling stomach.

Thurzo scrambled forward on the pterodactyl and took the reins. He had never ridden such a creature, but he had been on a horse many times before; he hoped it would obey the same commands.

With gentle tugging of the reins and subtle movements of his thighs he guided the pterodactyl towards the scene of battle. Slowly it descended – too slowly for Thurzo's taste. He muttered a curse and, like Oria, jumped off his flying steed to assault the dread-lizard from above.

His feet hit the lizard in the flank, driving the air out of its lungs. He could see Oria biting and clawing into its flesh on the other side through the gaps in its long, bony spines.

He grasped one of the spines with both hands. It was

about as thick as a man's forearm and rough to the touch. He pushed his legs against the lizard's body with all his strength and pulled at the spine. His muscles strained against the thick bone and the lizard's thrashing became much more agitated. Its body shook to and fro like a slithering snake's, and Oria was finally thrown off its back. She hit the hard stony ground and rolled away, coming to rest only inches from the edge of the precipice. A large chunk of the lizard's torn-out flesh was still between her claws and she chewed at it with abandon. So absorbed was she in the act of feeding, she was not even aware of the dangerous drop looming next to her.

Thurzo, too, was thrown off the lizard's back – with the thick, bony spine still in his grasp. The force of the throw, combined with the strength of his mighty arms, put enough strain on the spine that it finally broke. The lizard howled in agony and scurried off, its clawed feet clattering against the stone.

Thurzo leaned against the spine as against a quarterstaff and took a deep breath. He watched the lizard vanish into the mouth of a dark cave, likely its lair. It left a trail of blood behind it, seeping from the deep wounds Oria's teeth had inflicted upon it. Its tracks were easy to follow.

He left the lizard for later and went to check on Oria. She was still chewing on her chunk of meat, oblivious to the world around her. He grabbed her by the leg and dragged her away from the edge.

"Oria. How do you feel?"

She finished the last of her meat and a smile appeared on her bloodstained lips.

"I never had such a delicious meal in my life." She looked Thurzo in the eyes and her smile vanished. "You must think me a monster now, how savagely I fell upon the lizard…"

Thurzo shook his head. "Never have I seen more humanity than in you. Even ravaged by hunger, you held onto your principles and fought your urges – until adequate prey was in sight. A monster would have feasted upon me… or even upon her fellow harpies during our escape. But you did not."

"I almost succumbed… so many times, I thought about sinking my teeth into your flesh. So many times."

"Yet they remained mere thoughts."

He offered her a hand and she grasped it. She allowed him to pull her up, and once she was on her feet, she closed her arms around him in a tight embrace. They remained like this for a long moment; her touch said more than words ever could.

After a while she released her embrace and stepped back. Thurzo nodded toward the cave entrance.

Together, they followed the trail of blood left behind by the mighty dread-lizard. Despite its grave wounds, they proceeded with caution. On the precipice, they had taken it by surprise; now it was in its own lair, where surprise was on its side.

Inside the cave, Oria felt the jagged edges of shattered bones underneath her bare soles with every step she took. They belonged to the dread-lizard's prey, cracked open to suck out the marrow.

The light grew dimmer as they penetrated deeper into the cave. The stench of rotting flesh and lizard dung assaulted their nostrils. It made Thurzo feel light-headed, and he cupped a hand over his mouth and nose to keep it out.

Oria's hand grabbed him by the shoulder and pulled him out of the charging dread-lizard's way. It rushed out of a dark corner of the cave, snapping at the two hunters with its mighty jaw. Its sharp teeth missed Thurzo's knee by mere inches.

Oria stepped forward and kicked at the lizard's face. Her claw-like toenails hit it in the eye, blinding it on one side.

The lizard roared with rage and turned its massive body around with surprising speed. The thick bony club of its tail hit Oria in the thigh. She was flung through the cave by the powerful blow and landed in a heap of old, dusty bones. They shattered under her weight, and sharp little bone shards ripped her clothing and sliced into her flesh.

The lizard scrambled towards her, the barbarian on its blind side now all but forgotten.

Thurzo swung the thick spine like a battleaxe, bringing it down onto the lizard's head as it charged past him. Its hooked spike broke through the lizard's skull and spilled its brains onto the already filthy cave floor.

The dread-lizard was dead, slain by its own weapon.

Thurzo dropped the spine and helped Oria to her feet. She groaned with pain, holding her thigh where the dread-lizard's tail had hit her.

"Can you walk?" he asked.

She took a step forward and winced. "Badly... but it will do."

"Then let us get what I came for, and then leave. I don't want to stay here longer than necessary."

Oria nodded and limped towards the once-mighty lizard's corpse. She helped Thurzo break a sharp tooth out of its jaw, which he used as an improvised butcher's knife. While he was carving a path to the lizard's heart, she gorged herself upon its still-warm flesh until she could eat no more. After days of starvation at the hands of her sisters, this tough raw meat was like a feast of gods.

Thurzo retrieved the dread-lizard's heart and tied up the arteries with a piece of string to keep the blood inside its chambers. Then, he wrapped it in a sheet of cloth and stuffed it into the leather pouch at his belt.

He sheathed the knife-like tooth in his belt and said, "I have what I came for. Let's get out of here."

Oria nodded and limped towards him. He offered his arm to support her, and she gratefully took it. Together, they made for the exit. The sunlight welcomed them with its warm brightness as they approached the mouth of the cave.

Outside, they were greeted by a pack of dread-lizards hissing and snarling. Thurzo counted half a dozen, but more scurried out from their lairs to join their brethren.

Thurzo pulled the tooth from his belt and said, "And so our journey ends. It will be an honour to die by your side, Oria of the harpies."

"Thurzo, wait – they're not attacking. They don't want to fight."

More than half a dozen lizards surrounded them in a semi-circular formation, their forked tongues flitting out to taste the air. The stench of death from the slain lizard's lair was thick in the air.

Then, they started beating their tails against the ground in the rhythm of a drumbeat.

Oria noticed that they were slightly smaller than the massive specimen slain by her and Thurzo's hands. It only took her a moment to realize what was going on.

"Thurzo, they are celebrating us as their new leaders. The one we killed, it was the alpha lizard… and through its death we have earned the right to lead the pack."

Thurzo eyed the lizards with a sceptic glance. Oria's observation seemed sound: they were pack animals, and every pack required a leader. But he was still wary of the mighty lizards and their bone-crushing tails.

He cautiously approached the lizard in front of him, and all of a sudden the whole pack ceased their drumming and fell onto their bellies, spreading their limbs outward and lying flat on the ground.

Thurzo sheathed the dagger-tooth in his belt and mounted the submissive lizard. He sat down just behind its neck, where the first of its large spines emerged from its back.

The lizard accepted him as rider without complaint.

"All hail Thurzo, king of the lizards!" Oria shouted with a bright laugh upon her lips. "Looks like we have found ourselves an army!"

"They shall carry us out of the mountains," said Thurzo. He experimented with different signals to get his mount moving: jabbing his heels into its side, guiding it with movements of his thighs, tapping its neck with the flat of his hand.

It took steed and rider a while to get used to each other, but once he had figured it out, the lizard was as easy to ride as a horse.

Oria took her own mount and, under Thurzo's instructions, guided it with her hands and feet. They rode southward, back the way they had come from. The rest of the dread-lizards followed behind, escorting their new leaders.

Only a fool would dare accost them now.

*

The shrill calls of pterodactyls echoed through the mountains as they passed the plateaus of the harpies. They circled overhead, mounted by harpies on the hunt. One voice carried above the shrieks of the animals.

"I can smell you, Oria!" shouted Marra, mad with rage. "I can smell your wounds! I can smell your weakness!"

Thurzo glanced up and counted a score of them. "They won't dare attack. Not while we have the dread-lizards with us."

"They won't," said Oria, pointing at Marra's pterodactyl, "but she will."

"Come and face me, traitor!" Marra challenged Oria. "I will tear out your lungs and devour them as you watch!"

But she did not wait for Oria to meet her challenge. She fell upon her in a rapid descent, an enraged scream on her lips.

Her pterodactyl impaled itself on the sharp spines of Oria's mount. Marra was catapulted off her steed and hit the ground with her hip. She quickly got to her feet and charged at Oria, leaping at her from the side.

Oria was thrown off her dread-lizard, and the two harpies rolled over the ground, an angry ball of intertwined limbs struggling to bring their claws to bear.

Marra snarled and screamed at Oria, her eyelids wide open, empty sockets staring at her without sight. She snapped at Oria's face and her sharp teeth grazed her brow, drawing blood.

"You took my eyes, traitor," hissed Marra, "now I shall have yours!"

She went for another bite, but suddenly an arm locked itself around her neck and pulled her away.

Thurzo lifted the enraged harpy over his head and smashed her against the ground. The bones in her right arm shattered with a sickening crunch as her shoulder met hard stone.

Quickly, she scrambled away and got to her feet. She raised her left hand to the sky and shouted, "Harpies!

Sisters! Come to my aid and slay the human!" She sniffed the air and spat on the ground. "Or are you afraid of his pets? I smell them all around me... cowards! I do not dread the lizards!"

She turned around and jumped onto the head of the dread-lizard that sneaked up behind her. She latched onto it and raked her claws all over its neck, scratching deep wounds into its flesh.

The pterodactyls above shrieked as they descended upon the dread-lizards. Some impaled themselves on their long spines, while others were batted out of the air by their club-like tails.

The harpies jumped off their battered steeds and continued the fight on the ground. There were more than a score of them, and they used their superior numbers to surround the lizards and attack their vulnerable flanks. Bones shattered under the thick clubs of the dread-lizards' tails, but one by one the giant reptiles succumbed to the relentless assault of spears and claws upon their bodies.

Thurzo drew his dagger-tooth and entered the fray, stabbing it into a harpy's neck from behind. When they turned their attention towards him he went on the defensive, distracting them for long enough to allow the dread-lizards an unopposed swing at their bones..

It was a deadly dance that ebbed and flowed, offense followed by defence, a raging maelstrom of thundering tails and rending claws..

Only Oria stood still amidst the chaos. She could barely walk with her wounded thigh, let alone fight.

Marra, her claws stained red with lizard blood, emerged from the melee and approached her with calm, determined steps.

"I can smell your weakness, Oria. You have always had

that stench about you. It is unmistakeable. You've always been like a human... never a true harpy."

Oria stood still and waited for the blind harpy's approach. She with her shattered leg against Marra with her shattered arm and sightless eyes. A duel of cripples.

"No, I never was a true harpy. But you are mistaken – it is not a weakness," she said.

With a hiss, Marra leapt at her. Her claws raked across Oria's chest, tearing a large hole into her shirt and slicing deep into the soft flesh of her breasts.

Oria struck back, hitting Marra against her crippled shoulder. She hissed in pain and jumped back, dodging Oria's next strike on agile feet.

Oria's wounded thigh left her at a disadvantage. Despite her blindness, Marra was still a skilled fighter, fleet of foot and quick to react. But Oria's bad leg left her stationary, unable to dodge or manoeuvre. It was painful enough to keep standing upright, and one wrong step could collapse her leg and make her crumple to the ground.

Marra sensed her weakness and kicked at her knee. The impact took Oria by surprise, and her leg gave out from under her. She fell with her back onto the ground, and Marra leapt upon her before she could recover. The blind harpy laid herself onto Oria, pinning her down with the weight of her body.

Oria wrapped her arms around Marra and raked her claws across her back, but Marra seemed not to care. She lowered her face to hover so close before Oria's, she could smell the blind harpy's fetid breath.

"Claw at me as much as you want," Marra said with a mad cackle. "You are not a real harpy. You are like a human, weak and pathetic. And we harpies feast on humans. I shall savour your flesh, weakling."

No matter how many wounds Oria carved into Marra's back, she would not back off. And with her body still weakened from days without food, her strength was not enough to push the blind harpy off her body.

"Maybe you are right, Marra," she whispered. "Maybe those who eat the flesh of men are better."

Marra laughed in triumph as the whispered words reached her ears. In the final moment before her death, the wayward harpy had finally seen the light.

And then Oria sank her teeth into her throat and ripped it out.

Marra got to her feet and backed off, clutching her mauled throat. Her eyeless sockets stared at her in utter surprise. Even as her lungs filled with blood, she staggered backward and ran questing fingers along the gaping wound, unable to comprehend what had happened.

She collapsed and died with her eyelids wide open, an expression of shock forever frozen in her face.

Oria spat out the chunk of harpy flesh between her teeth and wiped her lips with the back of her hand. To bite into the flesh of her own kind – it was utterly revolting to her, and she struggled hard to keep herself from retching.

But it had been the one thing Marra never expected from her.

She looked up and beheld the raging battle. Several dread-lizards lay dead, but so did many harpies. Thurzo wrestled with one of them, his hands locked around her throat while she drove her claws into his sides. Two others flanked him and were about to attack his unprotected back when Oria shouted, "Cease! Your leader is dead."

The surviving harpies froze. Their eyes went to Marra's corpse, lying in a pool of her own blood. Hesitantly, they retreated from the remaining dread-lizards and gathered around their fallen leader.

Thurzo let go of the harpy he wrestled, and she meekly joined her sisters.

"I killed her, so now it is my right to command you. Crawl back into your caves and let us pass."

"Oria! You cannot leave us!" wailed one of the harpies. "You have taken the right from Marra! Who will lead us if not you?"

"If it is my leadership you wish, then follow this: never eat of the flesh of men again. Hunt the lizards on the peaks and the mammals in the valley, but not men. That is all."

Without another glance at the kneeling harpies, Oria mounted a surviving dread-lizard and spurred it on.

Thurzo followed atop his own, and the few remaining lizards followed.

The loud wailings of the leaderless harpies echoed through the mountains and followed them all the way down into the valley below.

\*

Once they reached the lush forest south of the Karthan Range, they dressed their wounds with leaves and strips of cloth torn from their clothes. There wasn't much left to cover their battered bodies – their garments had been reduced to tattered rags, and their skin would show many scars once their wounds healed.

Of the dread-lizards, there were only four left: their two mounts and two more. But it was for the better, as they were wild and ravenous. Countless creatures of the woodland fell to their mighty jaws.

Their path led them past the town Thurzo had picked

Oria up in. They spotted three armoured men patrolling the outskirts, and Thurzo showed Oria a broad grin.

"They arrested you for stealing a chicken... I wonder, would they do the same to a mightier thief?"

"A mightier thief? What do you mean?"

Thurzo dismounted from his dread-lizard and slapped its flank. With shouts and gestures, he pointed out the herd of fat cows grazing on an enclosed pasture, and the dread-lizards marched off on nimble feet to feast on domesticated prey.

He held back the one Oria was mounted on and seated himself upon it, sitting down behind her.

Oria laughed and shook her head. "Unleashing dread-lizards upon your fellow men? You must like them as much as I like my harpy sisters."

"I am not a friend of those who call themselves civilized," Thurzo chuckled. "A lesson in humility will do them good."

They watched the three lizards break into wooden barns and tear up entire cows with their mighty jaws. The three guards tried to scare them off with shouts, too afraid to approach the mighty beasts. Such was the nature of the civilized: harsh against the weak, but afraid to face the strong.

Harpies and men were not that different, after all, Thurzo concluded.

When they grew bored of the spectacle, they resumed their journey towards Thurzo's home, where his father waited for his medicine. He knew his son would return; Thurzo had never failed him before.

But that he would return with a wife whose strength was greater than that of any woman among the free tribes was a surprise even to Thurzo himself. She was not even of the race of man, yet her bravery rivalled that of its greatest heroes.

Sometimes, the bravest souls were found where no man dwelt.

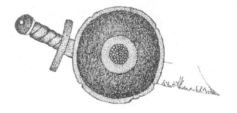

# CITY AT THE MOUTH OF CHAOS

A tale of Elfloq, the Voidal and other
Creatures of the Night

## *Adrian Cole*

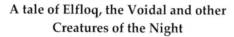

*Those gods whose knowledge is fuelled by sound reason and
diplomatic restraint know well enough that ambition is a sword
with two edges. Certainly it can lead to great and worthy
achievements, either among the gods themselves, or in the ranks of
the lesser beings who look up in aspiration. However, ambition can
also lead to dire calamity, the fall of entire dimensions. In such
situations, it is often the case that once begun, the manic race for
glory can be as unstoppable as a landslide.*

Salecco, a scribe of very modest designs

Somewhere, deep in the stone entrails of the living, evolving
city, the sprawling, convoluted entity Monumentis
Vulgarian, whose many limbs, thoughts and dreams
permeated every nook and cranny of that abominable
structure, focused his attention on the diabolic majesty of his
Grand Plan. Shudders of contentment rippled throughout
the monstrous self-styled god. This realm and those around
it were slaves to his power, buckling under his will, in total
thraldom, obedient and helpless to resist. Most of the
aspiring god-beings of the omniverse would have revelled
in such stature, gloating over the domination it bestowed,

117

the obeisance of so many slaves. Monumentis Vulgarian, however, desired greater things. He had tasted the joys of power, and now hungered for more, an unprecedented banquet, indeed feast upon feast, to appease an appetite that would consume worlds.

Monumentis's mind, dark and labyrinthine, horribly unchecked, drooled and boiled with thoughts of conquest. He had festered for countless ages, for what was time to a god? Dreams were once enough to satisfy him in his sluggish half-sleep, couched luxuriously in the depths of his endless city. Perhaps he would have remained enraptured by his contemplation of greater godhood for countless eons to come. There was much pleasure to be gained from such an effortless pursuit. And yet, one small ripple in a pond can expand and become a little tide, a wave, even a storm.

One such ripple dropped into the murkiest recesses of Monumentis's mind-pond. Its ripples grew until the god felt them—and stirred.

*

Elfloq rubbed his eyes and tried to focus. The darkness around him was not so utter that he couldn't discern anything. He could feel stone beneath him, though not smooth and neatly cut: it seemed to him to be more in the nature of, well, a vegetable. This place was likely a building of sorts, for its geometrical shape suggested as much. Not a prison, for there was an opening, with an almost starless vault beyond it. He had left the astral, that endless region that slides between the dimensions of the omniverse like a thin sea, and had fetched up here on a world he could not properly recall. In fact, his memory had almost completely deserted him. He'd been dreaming, and those dreams had been monstrous things, filling his head to bursting. Perhaps he'd reacted to their nightmarish quality by tumbling back out into one of the many dimensions before his sanity had been ripped from him.

He sat up in the cold chamber. It was empty, not much better than a cave. He knew who and what he was. A familiar, a small being bound over in service to a master, on whom he depended for his own survival. As for the nature of that master – well, for the moment that was also lost to him, stolen perhaps by devious enemies, of which there were many. Had he been sent here on a mission? Embarrassingly, he couldn't recall that either. This was going to make matters awkward.

There was a door, a narrow, squashed affair, but it was locked and Elfloq, being of slight stature, lacked the muscle to barge it open. Opposite the door was a floor-level balcony, which the diminutive figure investigated gingerly. He peered out at night's darkness. There were stars out in the vault beyond, though very few of them, suggesting that he was somewhere at the remotest point of this dimension. Looking downward he felt himself swoon at what was revealed in a greenish, diseased light, for the drop seemed eternal, a falling away of a cliff face into unfathomable depths. The wall itself was alive with an entanglement of foliage, branches, roots, creepers and every kind of vegetable organism conceivable, some of it drifting in the air like vast fronds of seaweed, other strands wriggling and writhing like knots of bloated worms, but worms of such dimensions! Far down in the abyss there were the most terrible of writhings, as though the foliage fought an incessant battle with whatever sprouted upward from the unfathomable deeps. Things screeched out in the night, creatures disturbed by the horrific contest and the ripping and tearing of mighty boughs.

Windows, similar to the one in which Elfloq stood, peppered the wall, and from some of them light spilled, wan and pale, daubing the gnarled growths around them. Whatever flitted or flapped out in the skies passed spasmodically through shafts of light, revealing elements of their shapes, from which Elfloq shied away in horror.

How could such deformed beings fly? Turning his neck cautiously, he looked first to one side of him and then the other. The view this afforded him was no better than the bizarre conglomeration of growths below, although the frenetic activity of battle was absent.

He craned his neck and looked upwards. There was no moon in these skies, and the sheer wall that ran up and up to infinity was partially revealed by more, occasional windows, or orifices into the stone that resembled bore-holes, possibly the work of living creatures, though none were visible. Elfloq considered this a blessing. Whoever or whatever had either constructed or adapted this wall of walls would almost certainly not be creatures whose company he would enjoy.

Knowing that he would be unable to free himself from the quasi-stone chamber within, he decided to fly outside it and attempt a little exploration. Spreading his wings, he hovered outside, cleared his head of the final shreds of his haunted sleep and rose. He could not go far, though. Something barred his way, an invisible membrane, gossamer thin. Further aerial investigation revealed that he was locked in place in a kind of bubble, whose only exit was the window of the cave. Reluctantly he went back inside. For the moment he was confined, a prisoner. Once again he began to wrack his brains in an effort to remember how he had come to such a disturbing pass.

*

Id Abrazaan gazed into the tall glass orb. His globular features were not devoid of eyes – indeed he had several – and his mouth was not shaped for human expression, so he was not capable of smiling. He gave vent to his pleasures in life by emitting a series of sighs, which he did now repeatedly. It was thus evident to the other three sorcerers around him that his mood was somewhat ebullient. Id Bazaandar, Id Cazaakar and Id Daanzaar were relieved to know that the Grandmaster of the Living Passageways of God was in good humour. Especially so as this was clearly a result of the recent developments as revealed to the gathered company by the orb, here in the sepulchral chamber.

"Monumentis Vulgarian is pleased," said the Grandmaster, settling his cephalopodal bulk comfortably in the shallow bath. It was an invitation for his senior colleagues to follow suit, which they did with much relief. The atmosphere in the living structure of the city had been positively writhing with tension for some time recently.

"Our divine ruler has realized the initial phase of his latest magnificent working. You will recall there had been some extraordinary disturbances in the outer world, beyond the city. Alien creatures, beings from other dimensions, had pierced our skies and come here to the most sacred and secret part of the city, the Crimson Gate. Such intrusions are beyond rarity. This was blasphemy beyond all knowing! Unless it had been welcomed and encouraged by the Gods beyond the gate. Indeed, only gods, or a god, could have passed within."

"A ship, master? Was there not a ship?" said Id Bazaandar.

"Quite so. A curious, sentient being, a ship fit for a god,

or a renegade deity, which this intruder proved to be. The ship, named Evergreed, was banished by other gods long ago, and yet the renegade has the temerity to command it."

"Is it so, master," said Id Cazaakar, "that this ship passed within and later *emerged*? Unscathed? It scarcely seems possible that such a thing could transpire."

"That is indeed the case. Monumentis Vulgarian tracked this improbable voyage, to and fro, although its details, deep in the cloistered dimensions of the Gods, were hidden from him. Our glorious ruler did, however, find a way to prize a few secrets from intelligences cognizant of the incident. To whit, he abducted one of the crew members from the ship named Evergreed. A small familiar, seemingly of no consequence, and yet one which may yet prove to be the keystone in this illustrious new venture. This familiar was apt to fly about in the ether around the ship, rather than remain, sensibly, on board it, where it would have enjoyed a greater degree of sanctuary. Our ruler flipped it away effortlessly."

"I was aware that this creature had been imprisoned in a cell in the middle holdings," Id Daanzaar commented. "Are its companions aware of their loss?"

"I would assume so," replied the Grandmaster. "In fact, I think this obnoxious little waif of the astral has been brought here as bait."

His three companions sighed. "Ah, a trap. For the ship. Evergreed."

"You see," went on the Grandmaster, magnanimous in his dispensation of knowledge, "there are beings of rare power on that ship. Monumentis Vulgarian desires to absorb them and thus take into himself these powers. He will become puissant beyond imagination. He will come forth from his stone chrysalis, take flight and – who knows?

The omniverse will open up to him and he will call no one master. And we will be elevated to – well, who can say? The powers to be invested in us will be unique, vast certainly."

The air in the great chamber vibrated for long moments to the deep sighs of the gathered company.

\*

On board the great ship Evergreed, the company of four felt the endless vaults of darkness wrapping it like shrouds, blotting out its future path, or paths, whichever destiny had been chosen for each of them by inscrutable gods. The Voidal stood at the prow, gazing ahead, though the deeps between worlds gave little hint of what awaited him and his fellow travellers. Since leaving Holy Hedrazee and the Divine Askers, a place of revelation, prophecy and endless possibilities, the startling revelations imparted to him there by the Dark Gods had made him silent and solemn, separated now from his companions by his contemplation of those mysteries. Had they been no more than dreams? Wild, improbable visions, tipping him dangerously close to the borders of madness? And for the others, Scyllarza, the mistress of demons, Orgoom, the Blue Gelder and Elfloq, the familiar, the nightmare of the voyage to the threshold of those Gods and its outcome slowly receded, sinking deep down into the subconscious levels of their minds. Such things could not be forgotten, but they could be suppressed. For now, the Voidal's companions would best be served by clouded memories.

Elfloq? The Voidal turned, looking back down the wide deck of the monstrous craft. Where was the little familiar? The creature whose purpose in life had finally been uncovered for him – but no, the Voidal did not yet want to assimilate that sharp shard of knowledge. Or what must be done in light of it.

Elfloq had been wont to flit to and fro in the murk around Evergreed, nervous as a gnat, content to be a scout for the party. However, there was no sign of him now. Nor had there been for too long a while. Scyllarza, who had also been studying their ethereal surroundings, came close to the Voidal's side and he put an arm about her waist. The movement had become a natural thing now, and did not seem to invoke the wrath of powers intent on enjoying the tormenting of his emotions. Yet he remained cautious about spontaneity.

"Have you seen Elfloq?" he asked her.

"As well try to hold down the wind," she said, laughing softly. "And he seems the embodiment of fear."

"Ironically I spent much of our past time together attempting to persuade him he would serve himself better by finding another master, and urging him to begone and on with that search. Now that he is missing, I feel a deep unease."

"You think he is in danger?"

"Indubitably." The Voidal stared long and hard at the emptiness behind the stern of the great ship, as if by doing so he could bring into focus realms that were far away, the distances between him and them shrunk down to nothing. And he saw again that incomprehensibly vast wall, like the surface of a world, rising up from its churning, embattled deeps, up to alien stars, the wall in which the Crimson Gate gaped like a gigantic mouth, the city within it, and the fathomless depths beyond into which Evergreed had journeyed and later emerged.

Elfloq was there, the Voidal now realized. Somehow he had gone back, or worse, been taken back by some infernal force, trapped like a fly in a jar.

The dark man locked his concentration on the city, that living, writhing organism, balanced on the very lip of chaos, its arteries and vital parts those of something sentient and organic. A being, a god perhaps, with dreams and desires, inevitably centred on power. His power! *I have your familiar,* it told him. *Come and reclaim him and face me.*

The Voidal went down on to the deck, his companions watching him quietly, though neither spoke. They saw him climb down into the hold. There was to be a new course set. Evergreed, sluggish and half asleep, must be woken and given his instructions.

*

Evergreed, engorged and replete, drifted through the great vaults of the ether, the endless expanses of space between the life forms that comprised the Universe of Islands, directed here by his master, the dark man. Sated on the bizarre feast he had devoured at the Crimson Gate, Evergreed moved efficiently but with somnolent ease, his huge organic wings spread wide, beating in a graceful rhythm. He was guided now by the Voidal's instructions. The many islands floated by, some minute, little more than chunks of turf, trailing tendrils, others colossal, shifting across the horizon like continents. Legends had it that all would one day curve inwards to the Continent at the Heart of All Things, the immeasurable central life mass, as it reformed like an exploded star.

The Voidal had returned to the prow of his monstrous ship, leaving Scyllarza and Orgoom on the lower deck to contemplate the deep green vaults.

"The master knows this place," Orgoom said. As always, he looked uneasy, every shadow a threat. His blue-skinned body, half the height of the woman, gleamed like that of a demon in the peculiar light of this realm, though it was cold, as if far from its natural elements.

"There's much beauty here," she replied. "Yet I sense evil things, far out in those mysterious regions. Gods and demons both, perhaps."

"Why are we here, mistress?"

"If we are to disentangle Elfloq from his plight, we will need something, another instrument of power, perhaps."

"Will the Sword of Shadows not be enough?" Orgoom was hardly able to name the ebony-handled weapon that was strapped to the Voidal's back. He feared its power almost as much as he feared the dark man.

"He spoke to me of this. Whatever god lies in wait for us back at the city of the Crimson Gate, it knows of the Sword, perhaps even covets it. By inviting this conflict, that god must be confident of its own power. The master fears a trap, possibly laid by the Dark Gods. Even now it is not easy to trust them. He wishes to prepare for the coming contest thoroughly."

"Allies, mistress?"

"I think so. We go to visit a place where they may be found and recruited. On the Mercantile Island of Fortunis Major, where even the beggars and mendicants have things to exchange."

Orgoom's deep shade of blue glowed brightly, as though Scyllarza had touched a nerve. What if his master had decided to trade him for something more useful to his cause?

*

Several of the teeming Mercantile Islands drifted through the ether in a regular flotilla, the largest of them,

Fortunis Major, at their centre, the hub of all trade and the base of the presiding Guild of Merchants, the Highmost Order of Purveyors. Though the Guild had built several empires on the provision of every imaginable kind of food and sustenance throughout the Universe of Islands (and rumours abounded that the Guild dealt far beyond its boundaries) it had never been averse to trafficking in anything that could turn its hand to a tidy profit. Such was the power and influence of the Guild that everyone paid tax, in one form or another, to it, from the lords to the menials in the street. Forever busy, like a gigantic beehive, the Island buzzed with the constant comings and goings of fleets and single ships. As Evergreed neared it, it was evident that the activity around it was at its most feverish, although most of the ships were leaving, apparently in haste, as if deeply disturbed.

Fortunis Major had a principal city of the same name, perched atop lofty cliffs that formed one of the many sides of the vast island. Great quays had been chopped into these extraordinary vegetable outcrops to form a magnificent harbour, and it was into this haven that Evergreed now eased, gentle as a leaf on a calm sea. Countless eyes studied the grotesque ship, unique among the other craft that were tied up here, from small barges to deep ether galleons. It was testament to the shadowy reputation of the Voidal's ship that no one came too close, or showed themselves eager to do business with who or whatever sailed in such a notorious vessel.

It was, therefore, with some equanimity that the Voidal left Evergreed at the harbour, paid an extravagant mooring fee to the agent of the Guild, and took to the streets of the city with Orgoom and Scyllarza. There was no night in this green Universe, but deep down among the narrow confines of the city's alleys and byways, the shadows clotted and the sky seemed far away. Even here, however, there did seem to be an unusual amount of frenetic activity, as though whole sections of the population were collecting belongings and preparing for hasty flight.

The Voidal took his companions to a building that appeared to be either in the process of rebuilding after a major collapse of its walls and roof, or crumbling to an advanced stage of neglect and decay. The place was known as the Battered Abbey, and legend had it that it had once been the hub of a powerful religious sect, whose god had abandoned it and gone in search of newer universes. Such was the whim of gods. The Battered Abbey, meanwhile, had been acquired by an enterprising brotherhood of privateers, brigands and freebooters, and had become a hotbed of intrigue and treachery. The Guild had not seen fit to burn it to the ground or otherwise eliminate it, recognizing it as being far too valuable a source of information. If there was skulduggery at work, or dissident factors plotting harm to the Guild, someone in the Battered Abbey would know about it.

Inside, there was a great space, with many places to eat, drink and otherwise be merry. Travellers from across the Islands were always made welcome, even if their fortunes were so low that all they had to share was an extravagant tale or two. The Voidal smiled to himself. Elfloq would have revelled in such a place, thriving in its stories, its bartered treasures of knowledge. The dark man ignored the few stares he and his companions received and made for one of the quieter areas, where he had seen a small group. It was comprised of several men, by their attire evidently warriors. They saw his coming and stood in silence, like black-cloaked statues.

"We know you," said their leader, a tall, gaunt man, whose long sword was strapped to his back and whose black leather harness equalled the darkness of the Voidal's own clothing. "I am Mordruin of the Skaveen. It is not usual for us to be summoned. Usually our Navigator dispatches us to do our work."

And bloody work it was, the Voidal knew. These sombre fighters were in the charge of the strange ship, the *Scavenger*, which plied the seas of all the dimensions, its controller a mystery to all but a few. Many were the battles these immortal warriors fought, bringing balance and stability to the omniverse in its most chaotic regions. Even so, the Navigator had responded to the Voidal's call. The Skaveen were here. Mordruin was waiting, eyes locked on the Voidal's. They were like two beings cut from the same stone, fated perhaps to tread a shared path.

While the dark man sat with the warriors, Scyllarza and Orgoom kept their distance, hidden in the shadows. The Gelder was deeply uneasy as he always was in human company, certain that at any moment he would be challenged. "What men are these?" he asked his companion. "I smell much blood on them."

She frowned. "Dangerous company," she replied. "Our master crosses paths we would be advised not to tread." Whatever the Voidal had learned on their voyage beyond the Crimson Gate, he had only partially relayed to her, and her own memories were already smudged, like dreams drifting away. Yet she sensed a fresh unease in her lover, as if, for some reason, he felt a new vulnerability, whereas before he had been strong, terrifyingly so, a challenge to man and god alike. By opening himself to her, even if a little at a time, he had made himself more vulnerable, wary of bringing her into the shadows of his life's passage, she understood that. Yet their bond grew stronger, and she welcomed it.

Scyllarza felt a hand on her arm and turned to see the small, hunched man who had touched her. She favoured him with a scowl that made him wince.

"Your pardon, mistress," he said. He kept looking around him as though expecting a blow from anywhere to land on his stooped form at any moment. "I note you have recently entered the city. You must have come from beyond. May I ask what news?"

Scyllarza's frown deepened. "About what?"

"You've come from the deep places beyond the Mercantile Islands. Are you in flight?"

"From what?"

The little man gulped down whatever horror he felt. "Ah, surely you must know what is coming. You've seen the sailors and citizens fleeing."

Scyllarza's frown eased. She had been wondering, assuming that her dark lord had presaged the terror of the people. Those who knew what he was and what he was capable of often scuttled away in fear. "No, we're not in flight."

"Perhaps you should be, mistress. Very few will remain here in the hope that the horror will pass us by."

Scyllarza decided it was not the Voidal these people feared. "What horror?"

"The Gaping Dread, mistress. That which comes to engulf all that lies before it." The man turned away and moved off, as if he had said too much.

Orgoom, who had been listening to the bizarre conversation, studied the chamber with a new understanding. There was an air of apprehension about it, bordering on terror, and a number of groups were breaking up, people stumbling quickly away. The Gelder would have commented on this, but saw his master had now completed his conversation with the Skaveen, who waited in silence while the Voidal came back to Scyllarza and Orgoom. "I want you to go with them," he said.

Scyllarza frowned, surprised, while Orgoom shrank back in horror.

"You will be safer with them than with me," said the Voidal. "You must trust me in this. When I return to the Crimson Gate, there will be turmoil and my enemy will seek to weaken me through you. Go with the Skaveen, who will protect you during this conflict."

Orgoom was too shocked to speak, but Scyllarza shook her head. "My place is beside you, whatever the odds against us. You know that."

He would have protested, but saw the fire of determination in her eyes. *This is how we are now*, that gaze was telling him. *Set me aside whenever you are threatened and our bond will quickly weaken.*

"Very well. But you, little Gelder. You must go with them. They will need your guidance."

Orgoom shuddered.

"We go to find Elfloq. Will you aid me in this?"

Orgoom nodded, eyes again bulging with horror.

"Then go with Mordruin. Be his pilot in this venture."

Reluctantly the Gelder went to the Skaveen, who had apparently agreed to have him as a pilot, and however grotesque they may have thought him, they made no show of it and wasted no time in departing with him for their own ship.

Scyllarza shared her new unease about their situation with the Voidal. "What we have seen on this Island is an exodus," she said. "Driven by deep terror. Something threatens this place. They call it the Gaping Dread."

He nodded. "I know of it, as does Evergreed. He is anxious to join the exodus and quit this universe. He is almost hysterical. However, we have work here yet." He would say no more and Scyllarza knew when not to press him. Instead, they returned to their ship. She settled herself in the prow, while the dark man went below to give fresh instructions to Evergreed. It seemed to her that the great body of the ship, which she knew to be a living organism, held itself in a state of fear, or anticipation of something incalculably evil at the very least. Whatever discussion the ship was having with its master was not an easy one.

The Voidal returned to her. For once he looked tired, almost human in that, but he set his gaze at the surrounding emptiness, resolute. They waited in the prow as the ship shuddered anew and left its berth. Still more ships at the quay moved away with all haste.

"What is this Gaping Dread?" Scyllarza asked.

"To many it is a legend, or a forgotten god. Lost out in the infinite deeps of the ether beyond all Islands, drifting, chained by its own dreams. Now and then it wakes and when it does, everything flees, as a precaution."

"Have you seen it?"

He shook his head. "But I will. Evergreed will lead us to it."

Scyllarza gasped. The dark man was powerful beyond understanding, but this sounded almost foolhardy. She would have quizzed him further, but saw that his mind was closed as he watched the green deeps of the ether. Soon Evergreed had swung into his new course, heading away from Fortunis Major, in completely the opposite direction to all those who were leaving the Mercantile Islands. It had become even more evident, from the shuddering of the ship that Evergreed was appalled at having to steer his current course. He was moving as if fighting heavy waves in a mid-ocean storm, rising and falling through invisible but turgid spray.

Scyllarza felt something small and wet strike her bare lower arm. She wiped away the offending object, a translucent creature, not unlike a small jellyfish from an aquatic sea. More of these things streamed by like rain, as if Evergreed sailed into an oncoming tide of them. Other, larger shapes flew past above and below them, a storm shower of dizzying dimensions. As the voyage progressed, these things increased in size, and Scyllarza realized there were now small Islands, no bigger than the ship itself, passing them. Out in the distance on port and starboard, blurred by what had become a torrent of the tiniest creatures, bigger shapes swung by. It was yet another exodus, though the scale of it was vast. Everything fled and only Evergreed sailed against this colossal living tide.

Still the Voidal remained silent, standing high in the prow, watching the distant ether directly ahead of them. It was habitually green, lighter in shade in the vicinity, and darker in its depths. Now, however, the distance had become grey, a cosmic wall, like the coming of twilight, the march of thickening shadows, driving everything before it. Bigger Islands passed far overhead, trailing their countless roots that writhed and powered their movement. Scyllarza's eyes grew tired as she tried to assess the greyness beyond. It had assumed the dimensions of a vast moon, and its orbit would take it through the ether occupied by the Mercantile Islands and any others in their vicinity.

Evergreed at last braked his surge forward and hung, poised like a small pebble in the path of that oncoming gargantuan force. The Voidal drew from its scabbard, the Sword of Shadows. As he did so, something on the endless grey surface ahead changed. A vast split, all darkness, widened to reveal a gulf as measureless as space, endless miles across. It was lined with irregular shapes, pointed and dripping with roots or filaments, growths. Teeth! Scyllarza's mind screamed. It was a mouth, incalculably immense.

"The Gaping Dread," said the Voidal. "Swallowing everything before it. The god is awake, feeding hungrily after a sleep of centuries."

*And we sit directly in its path!* Scyllarza wanted to shriek. *Why in the name of all the gods have you brought us here?*

The dark man raised his blade and it shimmered, its own bleak powers shifting like living things, unfurling around the two figures. Evergreed swung around, altering his course, so that now he presented his stern to the oncoming shape. The Voidal crossed the ship's wide deck and climbed up into the stern, where he again raised the Sword of Shadows. It was like a beacon. And, Scyllarza realized with a fresh surge of utter horror, *a lure!*

Evergreed increased his speed back through the ether, although he had changed his course to move away from the Mercantile Islands. Scyllarza looked beyond the Voidal to see the black mouth of the Gaping Dread coming closer, its impossibly huge size becoming ever larger. Creatures large and small, including Islands, were being sucked into that maw, swallowed as the harvest of the sea is swallowed by a whale, only this was on a much vaster scale. Evergreed could never hope to outrun that monster and ultimately would be sucked up into it. Surely that could not be the Voidal's intention?

The darkness flowing from the Sword of Shadows increased until it became a thick cloud, suddenly enveloping the entire ship. A dim glow suffused it and Scyllarza could barely discern the shape of the Voidal, immobile as a statue.

It was as though deepest night had fallen, starless and devoid of sound. Evergreed still moved swiftly, but he seemed to have come into a space between dimensions, where nothing else existed. Scyllarza could feel the bitter cold of the place, and her chest tightened until she thought she might lose consciousness and collapse. She felt something out in the impenetrable darkness, the inexorable coming of the Gaping Dead perhaps, but she succumbed to oblivion before she could confirm it.

When she came to, Scyllarza was leaning on one of the ship's rails, her head slowly spinning, until the giddiness eased away and an insipid light washed the deck and, in the prow, the stationary Voidal. Fresh fears assailed her. Since their coming together, she had experienced a bone-deep joy at what she had shared with the dark man, but in this place that seemed under threat, the madness of the encounter with the Gaping Dread like a fresh chasm between them. She rose and went to him. To her relief he put an arm around her and pulled her to him, gently kissing her.

"Whatever course we take now will be dangerous. What I do next may seem demented, but our path lies ahead into madness. I would have had you wait on the *Scavenger* with the others."

"Together," she said. "If we are not so, are we not diminished?"

He had sheathed his great Sword of Shadows and its haft protruded above his back, the blade within its ebon scabbard. He seemed about to demur, but something in her eyes softened his usual steely gaze and he nodded, pointing directly ahead. "As you say. We have returned to the dimension of the Crimson Gate. Elfloq is trapped within its city."

Scyllarza saw again the huge wall, stretching across their path in the night sky, like the end of all things, rising

135

up beyond the limits of vision, and similarly downwards and to either side. The massed growths that sprung from its incalculably huge blocks yet fought their war, writhing and twisting like huge weeds stricken by hurricane winds, or deep-sea currents. As she studied it from an ever-decreasing distance, she saw shapes break away from the wall and speed towards Evergreed's bulk.

They were aerial creatures, bloated things with wide, flapping wings like sails, and claws like huge hooks. Their elongated heads were shark-like, over-filled with row upon row of teeth. These and other monsters like them had attempted to rip Evergreed from the air on the ship's first visit to this unique realm, and as they gathered, a veritable swarm of them now, Scyllarza made ready for conflict.

"They'll not attack us," said the Voidal with surprising confidence. "Their master waits for me. He wants me here, before him, and undamaged."

"Who is he?"

"Monumentis Vulgarian. A god, it seems. And obviously he feels the need for a little ostentatious display of power." The Voidal smiled.

Scyllarza's horror at sight of the circling winged aberrations eased. It was rare that her lover smiled at the world beyond them.

Evergreed, unlike his master, did not feel comfortable at the return to this realm, as was evident from the gradual reduction of his speed, as if he worked his laborious way through yet more storms and sluggish counter-tides. Twice the Voidal went below to speak to him, and Scyllarza knew there had been a debate, almost certainly heated. It must have ended, for the dark man returned and the ship slowly moved closer to the great wall and once more the huge, mouth-like opening appeared within it, the city of the Crimson Gate perched on its lip.

The ship glided gently down toward it, unhampered by the aerial terrors around it, as the Voidal had predicted. The outer walls of the city plunged down and merged with the wall, and in their wide gaps there was room enough for Evergreed to navigate further inward and berth at an open, deserted quay. The buildings beyond were misshapen, the homes of unknown creatures, certainly not human, possibly crustacean or insect-like, or a hybrid entanglement of both. Shadows moved about deep within the cave-like openings, and a rich, fetid stench wafted across the quay, but the ship was not molested.

Scyllarza stepped on to the quay and felt a pang of revulsion: it was as though she had put her feet down on living flesh that gently quivered. The Voidal paid it no heed and motioned for her to follow him as he made his way to the first of the openings that suggested a narrow street into the city. The place was lit from overhead, where a cavernous, red-hued ceiling hung over them like the curve of an impossibly large mouth. Entering the city was like being swallowed, Scyllarza reflected. She was conscious of more movement now, scuttling things and things that slid, so that she would have drawn her blade instinctively until the Voidal stayed her hand.

They wound through a maze of buildings – if such they were – squashed together like over-sized shellfish, rising up in clustered towers that dripped with thick fluids, the reek of which was almost intolerable. Within the numerous alleys and passageways, shadows hid any signs of life, although many sounds emerged, all reminiscent of the sea, redolent with a saline stench. Beyond the suffocating maze, an open area revealed itself, with wide steps leading to a squat building that was no more than a bulbous growth, its windows vents that suggested a kind of gill. Scyllarza felt repulsed by the place and started as a number of beings emerged sluggishly from the only doorway. They were as hybrid as the buildings, large cephalopods, with globular heads and several eyes, though they moved surprisingly quickly.

Scyllarza was surprised by a voice, that of the leading being, she assumed, whispered in her head, clearly as if it had been voiced by human vocal chords.

"I am Id Abrazaan, Grandmaster of the Living Passage-ways of the God. My master, Monumentis Vulgarian, welcomes you to his humble city."

"Take me to him," said the Voidal.

"I am so commanded by my master. However, there are a few procedures to perform before I can discharge my duty."

The Voidal tapped the haft of his blade. "Time is limited, Grandmaster. For all of us. I would advise the utmost haste."

The Grandmaster and his two companions briefly consulted one another, but decided to comply. They led the Voidal and Scyllarza up into the building behind them. Inside, it was far more vast than the visitors might have expected, cavernous and sepulchral, grown rather than hewn, its slick walls vibrating softly as if this were the inner part of an organ, suffused with the vital life fluids of the city. A roughly curved area rose up on its far side, lost in the deep red veins of the ceiling, where bones took the place of beams and arches.

Scyllarza gasped as that strange, palpitating wall rippled like flesh and began to warp itself into a face. Yet it was no human face, despite the protruding eyes, bulbous nose and wide gash of a mouth. Whoever or whatever it was, it hissed like a reptile, the eyes lidded, another shade of scarlet. The face contorted into a parody of a smile, and yet was redolent with dark, dangerous energy.

"Welcome, Voidal," said a voice that grated along the nerves of all those who stood before this being. The three cephalopods had withdrawn, shrunk down like huge molluscs at the entrance to the chamber. Their terror was a palpable force.

"Monumentis Vulgarian," said the dark man, himself apparently unmoved. "You have my familiar imprisoned in your city. I must ask you to release him immediately."

The god hissed with amusement. "Well, you waste no words, Voidal. Yes, I do have your little companion. Such a minute fly of a being, and yet – immensely valuable to you."

The Voidal scowled. What did this creature know?

"I am a god, you know," Monumentis told him. "In fact, I was one of the very Dark Gods who controlled you for so long. Thus I know your history, and all your secrets. I know what transpired in Holy Hedrazee when they released you. And of course, I know precisely why the little familiar is so important to you. If anything should happen to him, well, it would not bode well for you."

The Voidal waited. This creature, if it had indeed been one of the Dark Gods, would have ambitions of its own.

"Not all of those gods were in favour of releasing you. Personally, it is of no great matter to me. However, you do have something I desire. You carry with you the Sword of Shadows, which, among other things, embodies the Thirteen Seneschals, the incalculably powerful beings who have done the work of the Dark Gods for millennia. I desire that weapon."

The Voidal reached over his shoulder instinctively and touched the ebon haft of the blade. "It is not given to me to release it. I am commissioned to use it in fulfilment of a new destiny, warring on evil throughout the omniverse."

"Oh yes, I know. However, even the plans of the gods can change. I am sure you will undertake your valiant mission with every success – even without the sword. I can give you another. Less powerful, but sufficient for your purpose."

"Why should I relinquish the Sword of Shadows to you?"

"Because if you do not, your familiar, Elfloq by name, as I recall, will be eliminated. I will crush him between my fingers in front of you. You, of course, will be terribly diminished."

"Even so, I could use the blade to destroy you."

"Quite so. I have no doubt of that. I am gambling, am I not? Why? You may ask. Well, I have been here for time beyond human understanding. I could go on in a similar vein, if you'll excuse a wretched play on words. No! I'd rather gamble. I believe you want the familiar alive. You need all your strength and corporate powers if you are to go on. If not, you will almost certainly fall victim again to the whims of the Dark Gods. The rebels among them would again have you their pawn. Elfloq's death will give them that."

Something slipped silently out of the soft wall below the great face, forming itself into a long, gnarled arm, with a hand like the claw of a carrion bird. It reached out and opened those razor-sharp talons.

"Give me the sword," said the god.

The Voidal stepped back. "Bring the familiar here," he said coldly. "Be swift, or I will cut that hand from you."

Monumentis hissed, his anger simmering like fire. Yet he agreed. His commands sped through the city, like adrenaline pumped through his vast body. Somewhere they were heard. It was not long before two humanoid figures arrived, bringing with them another figure, half their size. The batrachian features of Elfloq were drawn into a grimace of fear, pain and embarrassment. He looked at his master apologetically.

"Release him to me," said the dark man. As he spoke, he unstrapped the weapon on his back.

"A sensible exchange," said the god. He reached out further with the claw, but the Voidal drew back.

"Elfloq," said the dark man. "Come to my side."

The familiar shrank from the two beings on either side of him and for a moment it seemed as though Monumentis would use his long arm to snatch him back.

"I will give you the sword," the Voidal told him. "Let my familiar go."

More moments passed in an agony of tension. Elfloq eased forward as though dipping his feet into fire. But his passage was unhindered. The god's eyes glared at him as if it might melt him. Elfloq scuttled the last few steps and got himself behind the Voidal, trying to make himself into as small a ball of flesh and bone as he could.

The Voidal stepped forward and put the scabbarded sword into the huge hand, the talons at once closing around it. Monumentis laughed softly and withdrew the long arm back into the wall, and with it the sword in its night-black scabbard.

"A sensible resolution," he said.

"I will leave you," the dark man said.

"By all means," said the god, though there was something vaguely ominous in his tone. "Board your ship and go about your business. Oh – I did promise you another weapon. There are many. Will you choose?"

The Voidal indicated Scyllarza. She had remained silent and immobile at his side throughout the exchange, her face cool, but in her eyes there was unease. "Scyllarza carries the binder of demons. It will be enough for us. As you have said, we are one."

"Yes, it is a fine weapon. I am sure it will serve you adequately. Go, then."

The Voidal led his companions out of the chamber, watching for any hint of betrayal, but the party was permitted to wind its way back through the living streets to where Evergreed waited. As the Voidal stepped aboard, he felt the ground beneath him give a sudden shudder. It was as though the city of the Crimson Gate had woken from a slumber, its walls and towers vibrant with a fresh emotion, a raw fury.

Scyllarza glanced back, where darkness was already uncoiling from the side streets. "He has realized!" she cried. Quickly she pulled her sword from its scabbard and tossed it to the Voidal.

Elfloq gulped in horror at the flashes of power in the blade. "That's not the demon binder. It's *your* sword, master."

"The Sword of Shadows, yes. Simple enough for it to disguise itself and garb Scyllarza's weapon in deception. Come, we must get away before the god unleashes his own sorcery."

Evergreed had been prepared for a swift flight from the city and moved with deception, grace and speed back out into the darkness beyond it. It was a darkness teeming with movement, for the servants of the god had already gathered. Scores of huge, flapping shapes milled about, like vultures above a wounded beast. Their bloated heads dipped, mouths agape, jagged teeth flashing in crimson light reflected from the city. The Voidal leapt again to Evergreed's prow. This time they would be attacked, and the onslaught would be as merciless as any blizzard.

"Go below!" he called back to Scyllarza and Elfloq. "I'll cut our way through these abominations."

Scyllarza would have remained, but without a weapon, she would have been helpless under the ferocious attack of the sky beasts. She and Elfloq did as bidden and went below deck. Meanwhile the Voidal began the work of defending Evergreed's progress, using the Sword of Shadows, cutting this way and that. Its terrible powers were unleashed, and beast after beast was blasted by fire, or disintegrated, or beset by madness, dying a dozen ways. They attacked in droves, crowded each other for the privilege of striking at the lone figure, but he struck back with a tireless energy. His right arm that held the sword pulsed with light and fire as though the gods worked through it, pouring incandescent power into it and through the blade, growing in puissance every time an assailant was blasted apart. It was as though he bestrode a storm, violent and passionate, rising to a crescendo, as irresistible as the onset of time itself.

Evergreed ploughed onward and upward into the darkness beyond the great wall. A few of the aerial monsters attempted to tear at his wings, but he beat them back with swift strokes, crushing and mangling the horrors. There were fresh sounds in the city, from which more creatures poured in a black cloud, quasi-human things, winged and clawed. Somewhere the stentorian voice of the god roared like a storm, its frustration and fury a searing, blasting wind. Evergreed shook to its rigors, but yet moved forward.

Far out in the darkness, the ship paused as the assaults on it eased. The Voidal swung back to the stern and watched as his enemies rearranged themselves into a solid wall, clearly intent on a combined attack, to be unleashed like a mountainous wave that must surely engulf the ship and its minimal crew.

"Give me the sword and live!" came the thunderous bellow of the god. "There is no escape for you."

Somewhere in the darkness, another ship moved, silent as a shadow, and the Voidal studied it. It eased across the vault, its shape and many oars distinctive. It was the *Scavenger*, with its crew of warriors, the Skaveen. Gradually it pulled alongside, and on its deck, the Voidal made out the figures of Mordruin and Orgoom among the watchers. The ship and Evergreed gently touched and rode the night together.

The Voidal called to Mordruin. "I have two more passengers for you." Behind him Scyllarza and Elfloq had returned to the deck and he waved them to him.

"Go with Mordruin," the dark man told them. "I will finish this business with Monumentis."

Elfloq needed no second bidding, being only too glad to avoid the next potential assault of the aerial army behind them. He opened his wings and flew across to the *Scavenger*, landing beside Orgoom.

Scyllarza shook her head. "No. I remain with you."

"You cannot. Not this time," he said, though his face was strained, with a hint of unaccustomed fear in his eyes. "I bring madness to this place. I will survive it, but you may not. I'll come to you when it's done. You must trust me." He kissed her.

It seemed that she might protest further, fighting an inner turmoil, until at last she relented and climbed across to the *Scavenger*, where Mordruin awaited. His silent companions watched solemnly, their own powers held in restraint, like war hounds awaiting a command.

The Voidal called again to Mordruin. "Go to the arranged place."

Mordruin nodded. There seemed to be a reluctance about him, too, as though he would rather have pitched himself and the Skaveen into this conflict, but whatever pact had been sealed between him and the dark man was not to be broken. The *Scavenger* pulled away from Evergreed and its invisible rowers took it swiftly away.

The Voidal watched it disappear into the remote distance. Behind him the shrieks and snarls of the hunting army rose in pitch as Monumentis prepared to fling them forward in a final, irresistible assault. Once more in the prow, the dark man raised the Sword of Shadows and held it high before him, like a beacon. Light speared from it out into the vastness ahead and Evergreed moved forward more swiftly, gathering pace, racing away from the pursuit.

"You'll not evade me, no matter how fast or how far you run!" said the voice of the god, ringing inside the Voidal's head.

The pursuit went on for a time, until something ahead took shape, like a fast-spreading fog, a grey wall. Curved and vast beyond imagining, it rose in all directions, a bleak mirror of the great wall that housed the city of the Crimson Gate. A small moon, its surface split by a fissure of incalculable size. The Voidal's sword had summoned it, bringing it through dimensions to this place, *luring* it.

The Gaping Dread.

Behind Evergreed, the oncoming massed army tore forward, and it was only as the great ship swerved aside, the Sword of Shadows winking out, that the packed creatures became aware of the oncoming force. That colossal horror opened its mouth wider and whatever energies poured from it acted like a whirlpool, sucking the oncoming aerial army into it. Howling and shrieking, they poured forward, claws, and teeth, and in some cases weapons, at the ready, as the Gaping Dread received the offering of the dark man.

Evergreed had swung well away from its dreadful pull, finding other currents in this dark realm, using them to drag him to safety. Eventually he turned and waited. The Voidal leaned on the rail and watched as the endless mass of creatures that had been pursuing him flowed into the great maw like flood water emptying into a drain. Such a concentration of power would be expected to cause havoc and untold damage to the oncoming body, but the flow had no more visible effect than that of a sequence of heavy waves smashing upon rocks. Somewhere in the screaming, shrieking chaos, the Voidal heard the protestations of the god and pictured Monumentis back in his city, ranting and raving with frustration as his servant army was swallowed.

The conflict did not end here, the dark man knew. The Gaping Dread had only begun its cosmic work. Inexorably it drove on towards the distant wall. Evergreed, though far from the great wall and the approaching Gaping Dread, was potentially in danger of being crushed between the two ultimate forces. The Voidal, however, commanded him to wait. He swung the Sword of Shadows above his head in a pattern that made the air burn, flames licking out and contorting into a woven pattern that twisted its way around the entire ship, encasing it in golden fire. From its puissant shelter, the dark man watched as the two forces struck.

A tremendous detonation thundered throughout this warped dimension, crimson light spearing in all directions, like the birth of a new star. The last image the Voidal saw was that of the Gaping Dread fastening its moon-wide mouth on the wall, whose own vast opening clamped on the surface of the intruder. It was as though two monstrous beasts snapped and bit at one another, teeth fastening on flesh, shaking and snarling. All around the fire shield the Voidal had erected, great gouts of stone and organic matter tumbled past as the ferocious conflict brought about the mutual destruction of the two bodies. The wall was collapsing, huge stones tumbling down into the bottomless void, ripping out tendrils and roots as they fell, while chunks of the moon-like assailant flaked off and burst, showering the darkness with thick dust.

Time stretched on as the battle raged, the two powers negating each other, ripping each other to pieces, destroying with no hope of victory, only annihilation. The Voidal waited, ignoring the endless procession of debris that now floated out into the remote dark, creating, perhaps, a new island universe. Eventually the last major pieces fell away or broke apart into dust clouds. All that remained was a long, disc-like mass of rock, a small, flattened moon, from which the remains of a city poked upwards, its towers and higher buildings broken and leaning, dripping with the life fluids of the god it had housed. The city of the Crimson Gate had survived, but was now no more than a place of ghosts and congealed blood.

The Voidal removed the protective fires from around the ship and had Evergreed take him once more to the city. He knew the gate itself could not be destroyed. There would always be a path to Holy Hedrazee and the power residing there. Somewhere among the pulped organs and heaped, shattered bones of the god, there was a flat area where the ship could moor itself. Deep within the chaos, a voice could barely be heard, filled with pain.

"Voidal!" it called. "You deceived me. Is there no end to your treachery!"

"You brought this upon yourself, Monumentis," replied the dark man, stepping on to the broken quay. "Your own lies and deceit earned you this fate." He wound his way through the destruction, among which lay the crushed remains of the god's acolytes, not one of whom had survived. He came at length to the place where Monumentis leaked the last of his energy.

Somewhere amid the carnage, a distorted face could be seen, partially melted into the wreckage. One huge eye had melted, its fluids clotted beneath its socket. The other retained the baleful anger of the fallen god. It fixed the dark man, though he was impervious to its hate or the curses that dribbled from the torn mouth.

"Spare me," said Monumentis. "Leave me here as a ruin, but spare me. I can no longer be a threat to you, or the other gods. Let me go back to my dreams."

The Voidal bent down and pulled something from the detritus. It was Scyllarza's sword that he'd used to trick the god.

"Your dark arts are stronger than ever," said the god contemptuously. "Have the Dark Gods freed you only to unleash a greater horror on the omniverse!"

The Voidal clipped the sword to his belt. "Where there is evil, I will root it out. Your ambition, your cause, was an ill one, Monumentis. Greed, lust for power, contempt for any but yourself. You would have set yourself up against humanity."

"Are you so free of ambition?"

"Perhaps not. Perhaps I should be merciful and allow you what you ask."

"Let me sleep, eternally. The Dark Gods know me. They will never allow me to rise again. My ruins will rest here at the Crimson Gate."

"Be sure of that. I will seal the gate, even from the gods."

The Voidal used the Sword of Shadows in another ritual, making good his words. Monumentis Vulgarian consequently slid deep down into the oblivion of eternity.

\*

Evergreed again maneuvered himself alongside the sleek *Scavenger*, ship of the Skaveen. As the Voidal boarded the latter, Scyllarza came to him and gripped him in both her arms, laughing.

"We saw. It was like a sun exploding. I could not believe you'd survive such a thing, but Elfloq knew."

The familiar hovered close at hand, a rare smile on his batrachian face. "You saved me, master."

The Voidal also smiled. "I have to confess, my life would not be the same without you. Nor you, Orgoom. We are all of us united." He took Scyllarza's sword from his belt and handed it to her.

Mordruin detached himself from a group of his black-clad warriors. "Well met," he said. "I would stay and celebrate with you, but my Skaveen and I are called away. We have many other wars to fight. I suspect, somehow, our paths may cross again."

The Voidal looked thoughtful, his smile dissolving into a look of concern. "Yes, you have your own destiny." He turned back to Elfloq. "Now, little familiar, you have often sworn to serve me, and indeed, you've risked your life many times to win a path back to my side."

"And would continue thus," said Elfloq.

"And I," said Orgoom.

"Very well. You both shall serve me. But know this, it will not be at my side, not yet. I have other work for you. You must serve Mordruin and his ship, for a time. He will need your particular skills. Do this and do it well, and the time will come when we shall be reunited. That much is inevitable." He laughed softly.

Elfloq and Orgoom both wore initial expressions of astonishment, disapproval, but quickly masked them. It was never sensible to argue with the dark man.

Scyllarza, whose arm yet encircled his waist, studied him. "I trust you'll not mete out the same future to me. I go with you, not with the Skaveen."

He studied her for a moment as though he would tell her otherwise. Instead he kissed her lightly. "If you must. The omniverse throngs with nightmares."

"You fear your enemies will use me against you, to weaken you. But I have already said, I will be your strength. We are one."

He nodded. It was one of many things the Dark Gods had already admitted to him.

Soon afterwards, Elfloq and Orgoom watched Ever-greed spread his immense wings and flap softly away, out into the deep darkness and through it to some other dimension.

"So you will be my scouts, little ones," said a voice beside them.

They stared up at Mordruin, and felt the gentle waves of strange energy that bathed him. Elfloq managed a smile. Well, he conceded, power is power, and this new master wields it, that is certain.

He bowed. "At your command."

Mordruin called orders to his Skaveen and their sleek ship pulled away on a new course, to some fresh conflict at the heart of chaos and whatever turbulent destiny was lying in wait.

# IN THE BELLY OF
# THE BEAST
## *Edward Ahern*

The evening before his departure, Ishtal the Old One provided last instructions. They knelt on the dirt floor within touch of each other, under Ishtal's lizard skin covering, and spoke in a dead tribal dialect.

"You clutch at feelings for Hastet's chattel and the urchin you two produced. The bitch sorceress will use that against you."

Malame held silent. The Old One spoke truth. He still harboured feelings for Charlong and the child he had never met. And knew that Hastet, a woman magus as remorseless as his own master, would use those emotions against him.

"The sag-dugged sow will violate our agreement if there is the slightest discrepancy in what you provide from the unnamed beast. Observe all its terms. The beast has destroyed and consumed every mage and adept who has gone against it. I have advanced you as best I know, but I fear that in the end you will have to use your aberrant wits.

"As to your procreation, as the shrew and I agreed, she has kept the girl child. Do not fumble the spells which will ensure a boy, for that will be mine."

The Old One stared at nothing for several seconds. "You have begun to inhale the winds of existence beyond our world, do not choke yourself on the fumes of this one."

Malame nodded. He'd renounced comfort and the company of both women and men to start to achieve this. He didn't rue his choice despite the deprivations that came with it.

As the Old One continued, Malame wondered about the rumours that his master and Hastet had, a century before, also been lovers. And knew enough to keep the question to himself.

Malame set out with the sunrise the next morning. Ishtal did not see him off. He rode for four days through wilderness and abandoned villages.

In the false dawn of the fifth day, as he was breaking camp, four warriors accosted him. Malame backed away and began to conjure. The two women and two men were lightly armoured and quick moving.

As they circled him, Malame's spell took hold, and they turned against each other. The smaller woman had snake-strike quickness and was the last left standing. But not unharmed. She bled vigorously from cuts on her spear arm and thigh. Malame decided against exerting another spell and waited outside of thrusting range while she bled out. Once she began to stagger, he stepped in and cut her throat.

He left them as they lay, saddled up, and rode off. Two days later he came to Hastet's compound. She remained as he remembered, sinewy, thin of body and hair, with rheumy eyes that seemed always to glare. She was dressed in an undyed wool shift whose thick, coarse fibres would give comfortable home to insects.

She faced him in the doorway of her stone-on-stone manse, studied him for several seconds, and gestured him inside. Malame noticed several alcoves with their own hearths. He and his magus were not used to such amenities. Both lived in a thatched hut and slept in leather strap cots perched on the tamped earth floor, warmth and cooking provided by a fire in the middle of the hut.

"Tell me of your journey, whelp. In detail."

He suppressed a smile. She was as deliberately unpleasant as the Old One.

Malame described his encounter. "I debated taking their heads as bona fides for you, but presumed that you'd be aware of their fate. They fought well, I suggest recompensing their families."

The skin tautened over her already gaunt face. "Do not presume, whoreson. They failed in your testing."

Hastet slightly closed her eyes. "The Old One appears to have adequately trained you. Cleanse yourself, you stink of ungroomed horse. Then we will eat." She waved at an iron-collared woman who escorted Malame toward an alcove.

The evening meal was grilled squirrel and roasted beets. Only Hastet was at the table with him. Malame briefly considered asking after Charlong and his child, Saccul, but knew Hastet relished keeping him in suspense.

She and Malame ate the rodents with their fingers, occasionally crunching up and swallowing a bone. She wasted no time on small talk.

"You have somehow survived your testing, so the Old One was not so senile as to mistrain you. However, you are not as talented as you presume, and my expectation is that you will die during your major tasking. Therefore, you will remain here for three days while you perform your other mission."

Malame tilted his head in silent question.

"You will deliver seed to Charlong for the next three nights, during her estrus."

"Ah, most puissant sorceress, Charlong's last words to me were of hatred and my death, perhaps instead…"

Hastet's stern expression hardened into scorn. "Your offspring is proving capable, more spawn are beneficial. Surely the vermin-ridden Old One has told you this."

"He did, and the task is not onerous, but I would first like to convince Charlong not to knife me after coitus."

Hastet's eyes sliced into him. "She will do as I bid her. Her hatred is not pertinent, the only prerequisite is a modicum of lust on your part."

"Have you also instructed her not to curse me?"

"Ah, well. She does have some discretion in these matters. Wash your hands. No one likes to be fondled with greasy fingers."

After eating with Hastet, Malame walked over to Charlong's quarters, a two-lobed hut made of logs and wattle. As Malame entered she and their daughter Saccul were kneeling, the heels of their feet touching their buttocks. They faced each other, animated faces showing understanding without passing words back and forth. Malame wondered if he would be able to do the same with a son, and immediately threw the thought aside as distracting. He assumed the same position two body lengths away and held silent until he was addressed.

Charlong turned her head toward him. "You betrayed me, Malame."

"I did."

"And took me from a home I can never go back to."

"I did."

Young Saccul, whose hair was the colour of banana flesh, glared at Malame with a look of either fear or anger. He didn't blame her.

"And sold me into slavery to this witch."

"Barter rather than sale, but true enough."

Malame had been absorbing every detail of Charlong. Her slender prettiness had filled out to a strong-featured beauty. The goetic presence that had been little more than a hint was full formed. The hut roiled with their psychic cross currents. The child sensed it and withdrew her own fledgling abilities under a veil. As he'd opened up his senses, Malame also realized that Hastet had been correct, Charlong was in estrus.

"Charlong, I see you know the spell of sharing."

She waved a dismissive hand. "Of course."

"Anything I say aloud you'll consider lie or deception. So I'll open up all my memories about you. Some of my thoughts will be ugly, some selfish. But all involved keeping you and our daughter alive. I cannot offer better verification."

"I'd rather you just mount me and leave, saying nothing."

"Please. Even as you continue to hate me, you'll have the details for every aspect of that hate."

Charlong stood, pushing herself up using only the tops of her feet. She walked over to Malame and stared at him. Then she knelt back down, their knees a finger-width from touching. "Open your mind."

Malame didn't hesitate. Charlong would only be able to experience his memories of her, but if she were angry enough she could deface them. "Very well."

He sub-audibly incanted and nodded to her that he was ready. Charlong entered immediately, riffling through the weeks of their encounter, pausing, not at their moments of intimacy, but at Malame's manipulations of her. Her exploration lasted the life of a short candle and just prior to removing herself she went to the moment of her bondage to Hastet and poured psychic acid onto it, leaving a welt of her hatred.

Malame shook himself as she exited. "That wasn't necessary. I already have abiding memory of your hate."

"What I am now understands why you forsook me. But my memories know only your abandonment."

"May I reach out to our child?"

Charlong nodded. Saccul seemed shocked that her mother had agreed. She'd been unable to follow their thoughts, but had felt their regret and anger. She showed – not fear – resentment perhaps.

"Must I?"

"He won't harm you. Go ahead."

Saccul nodded agreement.

Malame rose and went over to his child. "Saccul, I'm well pleased in how adept you are. I offer you a choice of gift, either gold or a spell you may use against someone who torments you."

The child looked toward her mother, who nodded. Her eyes crinkled in concentration. "Gold I can find. The spell is gone unless I take it."

Malame allowed himself a smile. He looked toward Charlong, who again nodded. "Use the spell of sharing, child, and I'll give you the wordings."

She shifted slightly, her lips moving in the incantation of opening, then looked up and nodded at Malame. He gently laid the spell like a jewelled egg in her consciousness and withdrew.

Saccul studied the spell for a moment in silence, then looked at Malame. "Can I change them into yet another animal?"

"Sadly no, only one change is possible, but they will no longer annoy you."

A smile creased across her face as she considered the possibilities, then it disappeared. "Will you fornicate with mamma now?"

"I believe so."

Their pairing was competent and callus. Twice he thought he'd felt embers of emotion from Charlong, which she immediately tamped down. He resigned himself to a loveless whoring, a procreative calisthenic.

After the brief encounter, Malame returned to his room, took off his shift, and lay on the cot in a foetal position. He lowered himself into his inner well, descending into darkness until reaching the orange fires of his being. He bathed himself in their searing flames, the lies and deceits of his day charring into ash that flaked away. His un-filmed vision reached further and more clearly than any other time, and he venerated the beauty of the revealed truths. He fell asleep.

*

Breakfast at dawn was gruel and fat back, attended by all three women. Malame shifted his gaze from one to the other – the three ages of witchery. The intercourse the night before was not brought up, and Malame assumed that Hastet had held secret witness.

Malame spent his days with Hastet and his evenings with Charlong. After their third time together, while still lying in bed, Malame leaned toward Charlong. "Thanks for not attempting my murder."

Her smile was pursed. "Hastet forbade my doing so. At least until after you've completed your tasking. Or have failed, in which case you'd already be dead."

Malame's smile was tentative. "You've looked inside me. There's no lie in my emotions. What you do with that knowledge is for you to decide."

"And you to be concerned about."

That next morning, while sopping up the gruel with a crust of black bread, Hastet glanced at Malame. "Repack for travel. Your horse is being made ready for your excursion into Blackthorn Forest."

He'd been looking at Charlong when Hastet said it, and watched quicksilver fear cross her face. These woods were baneful. He nodded to Charlong, who gave an almost imperceptible nod back.

Hastet and Malame left the stone cottage and he had to quicken his pace to keep up with the cane-stumping old woman. He held his horse while she addressed him.

"I cannot emend the Old One's orders and spells concerning the beast without putting your task at risk. But hear me, randy sniveller. Better to fail and be damned than to double deal me. If you do not uphold his oath to me, you and the Old One will undergo torments you barely conceive of."

"My oath holds true, venerable Hastet. You'll either receive what has been agreed or I won't be alive to be reproached. I hope for your guidance as well."

The old woman snorted, a small snot clot dropping to the ground. "It does not abide in our world, nor think as we do. It acts like a summer storm, capricious in its course. Its great powers are largely unknown, even to Itself. It is the madman in the temple, the berserker warmed to his carnage. When It does not ignore us, It rends us. Powerful sorcerers have cast their spells at It and died. I have no spell to give you that has not already failed. You must use that abnormal mind of yours and find the twisted path to slaying It and bringing back some of Its powers. The male you have just conceived will go to the Old One, and will replace you if you fail." She leered. "He may replace you in any case."

Malame nodded, bowed slightly to Hastet, and left. He picked his way through virgin forest for five days, eventually entering a small, open lea. He unsaddled the horse and slapped it away, giving it at least a small chance of survival. Then he turned, brushed aside branches, and sidled into the alders. Thirty yards in, the undergrowth gave way to dimly lit open spaces between the boles of huge trees. Massive roots gnarled over the ground, making his way forward as much a clamber as a walk.

His remaining water, dried meat and bread would last for two days. But he wouldn't be eating it. He would fast until achieving a mystical state that would hopefully help keep him alive. He sat on a trunk-side knurl and induce-vomited up what little remained in his stomach. Then he settled in for motionless meditation.

Within minutes the mosquitos also settled in. They were expected. Their rendered bleedings and itches pushed Malame well inside himself. Once semi-conscious he retrieved the Old One's chant.

> This thing can be done
> You are come to slay It
> I have killed Its kin
> I use Its skin as bed cloth
> You use Its power against Itself
> You are the source of Its death
> You are Its ordained killer
> You are the light which burns It
> the arrow which pierces It
> the rock which crushes It
> You are…

Toward dusk a black bear emerged from its lair and shuffled off after a spoor of carrion. It then scented Malame and slowed to consider fresher meat, closer in. It swerved in its lumbering course and moved toward him.

That lone facet of Malame still on watch perceived its approach. To leave his trance would destroy a day's effort, and he reacted in an adder-strike response. The bear stared down at its left front paw lying in the ground, then at the bleeding stump at the end of its leg. It bawled and limped off, blood trailing behind it. It tumbled down a ravine into a creek bed, where it bled out and died. Malame had held his trance.

Timber wolves found the bear in the pre-dawn hours, tore open the hide and began to feed. Malame, his hearing sensitized by a night of almost silence, heard but did nothing. The sated wolves would have no desire to fight for more food.

Tree feeding insects continuingly explored his body and rejected him as unsatisfactory. A wayward tick set up camp on his inner thigh. All ignored. Another day passed. On the third morning Malame staggered as he arose, joints screaming.

He was sideways to this world, half in it and half in an even more unforgiving place. He could die in either. He shook off the bugs, circled the tree several times to loosen his limbs, picked up his kit and moved further into the forest. He knew the spoor of the beast from the Old One's bed cover, and allowed his nose to lead him.

*

It dreamt. Not as men do, of things hated and desired. It dreamed of being a roaring wind that rent forests and towns, of being the unquenchable under-earth fire, of being airless darkness. And then It sensed – something.

The oblivious and briefly living were food, infrequently taken, but in great quantity. But something partially aware was approaching, a moron, a defective intelligence, yes, but at least capable of knowing of Its existence. It stirred.

Many man years had passed since the last conscious visitor, and It had played too roughly with the woman, ripping her apart much too soon. Softly, softly, It thought, and focused on the approaching young man.

It had not spoken aloud in an old man's life, and cleared Its throat with a cough that charred an acre and announced its presence. It held off forming and coiling and rehearsed the games It would play.

Malame carried a sword with powers and a dagger with poison but doubted either would be of any use. Might had failed others. Guile had failed. Spells had been deadly to the caster. He settled his essence, making of himself a still mountain pool, clear down to its bottom, the better to see Its reflection.

The mosquitos had flown away and the tick dropped from its perch. There were no sounds of animals. Other creatures weren't tolerated here. A whisper noise of crushed plants came from just behind him.

Malame turned around. There was nothing to be seen, but his goetic senses were almost torn loose. There are no smells in dreams, but are in visions, and the rank odour of still-rotting spirits filled him. A dirty grey shimmer blob held against the ground, wider and deeper than his inner eye could encompass.

The questioning was not in spoken language but must be recorded so. "So immature. Have the magi made the mistake of losing respect for me? Speak, slug."

Malame compelled his body to step up against Its shimmer, then abandoned his physical presence and twisted himself completely into his other. "You who know so much must know that the fear is unabated."

Its purr was sandstorm rasp. "Perhaps I will review your pathetic little life before consuming it. You are not yet a master, what had your magus hoped to achieve with your sacrifice?"

The clear water clarity of Malame's mind allowed for no lying. "We wish to share in a small portion of your vast powers."

An immense snout briefly materialized and snorted. "Prepare to be violated acolyte, and then eaten."

The Old One's melded chanting was in Malame's inner ear-

> Fight in spirit not in form
> If a lizard you are doomed
> If a wraith you may escape
> Become of It and hide.
> Absorb what you will steal
> Only It can hurt Itself.
> Ever moving, ever without aim.

"Or perhaps the reverse, oh marvellous one." Malame's transparency showed him that It was preparing to take form, to become fire lizard. His death would immediately follow. Malame's presence thrust itself into the translucence, and, wriggling, passed within. It screed, bursting the eardrums of Malame's discarded body.

Malame slithered furiously, without aim, for to have purpose would be to be found. He moved randomly, like an askaris roundworm, feeding on Its sensitive spirit tissue. And what he ate he retained, as knowledge offering to Hastet and Old One. Twice, three times, he randomly doubled back, gaining nothing, but forcing It to guess in all directions.

He paused too long at a ganglia of knowledge, and It found him and pounced. Malame wriggled sideways, but It seared open his flank and left him dripping psychic entity. Randomness brought him to a quadrant already stripped of concealment, and It reared up to strike, but lost traction in the vacuum of Its own absence.

It slashed through Its own being, knowing where Malame was but not where he would go. It severed Its own fibres in the chase, losing memory and power. Twice again It charred Malame's elongated being as It overshot, burns that also trenched Malame's body.

There was no measured time. The shimmer blob, not visible but present, quivered and shook as the two beings burrowed through It. Malame worm-slithered to no discernible purpose, gobbling ectoplasmic tissue and absorbing the knowledge it contained. It's presence shriveled but could not leave to feed. Malame's body also began to shrivel, voiding itself. His body would soon die.

It began to lurch, destroying more unintended parts. It tried to become the fire lizard and fight on as It's body, but that ability had been destroyed. Its thrashings weakened. Sensing the death, Malame asked his first and only question, and It was compelled to answer. At the end of the sixth day of measured time, It expired.

Malame rushed to discover more, but the blob was in rot, and that which he found was tainted. He slithered out of the decay, his flanks still burning from Its charring of his presence.

This presence had no eyes to see nor ears to hear with. He started writhing in increasing circles around the deflated remains of the blob until encountering his own body. As he re-entered, both halves screamed with the pain, but only the body could be heard.

An hour later he recovered the use of his senses and muscles. Vermin had eaten his food. He was able to call small animals in to him and drink their blood. A day later he began to consume their muscles and organs.

A day after that he was able to stagger up and totter his way out of the forest. And that night, Malame's mind clear, the Old One reached out to him.

"So it is done."

"So was it ordered."

"Your true tests will begin."

"You have instructed me."

"The vomitus shrew will try to trick you."

"I am prepared."

Malame continued on, eventually clearing the forest and stepping onto a two-rut trail. On his third day of walking, two mounted men accosted him. Malame performed ritual on their remains. Sunset was approaching and he considered dinner. The men were already dead and easier to butcher than a horse. But the goetic complications of eating man flesh were too time consuming. He sliced off the head of the weaker horse, cut open its back, carved out a steak for dinner, and butchered enough meat for the trip.

Four days later he had returned to Hastet.

"That raw scar on your neck, does it run down to your scrotum?"

"Merely to my belly."

"Are you come with knowledge or attempted excuse?"

"Knowledge. Some of which you demanded, some of which will over-amply replace that which was not obtained."

"You sport with your death. We shall see. Come with me."

Hastet led him into an inner, windowless chamber. The walls and ceiling were covered with tapestries embroidered with minor and major arcana.

"Your disease-riddled, decrepit master cannot sense us here. Tell me first of your actions, then of your treasures."

Malame recounted his actions, then described in detail the goetic capabilities he had absorbed during his random flight through It. Hastet listened in silence, memorizing as he spoke, then shrugged.

"I am bound by my oath to Ishtal to release you. You have fulfilled your quest. The man child is his after birthing. When you come to receive it, I expect you to repeat your connubial performance."

"That is parlay between you and my magus. And my condolences on losing your daughter to It."

Her eyes were hot. "You have yet to lose a child for our art. I have, more than one. And ask yourself if he who preceded you as chela was of the Old One's blood. And how he died. And who really fathered you. The most bitter sacrifices are in your future."

Hastet's expression altered. "Go to Charlong and your child. You leave tomorrow."

Malame bowed and left, then walked over to Charlong's hut. She and Saccul were again kneeling, but broke off when he entered.

"So the beast didn't kill you."

Malame's smile was wry. "I couldn't die without seeing you again. And talking with Saccul. May I kneel next to you both?"

Charlong nodded and he did, facing Saccul. "My child, you and your mother would not have known that I also practice necromancy."

The girl swung her head to look at her mother.

"Manipulation of the dead."

"The attempt on my life after I left the forest was a simple plot to catch me in a weakened state. I would be prevented from further inflictions on a loved one, perhaps a loved one who hated me. The attempt failed, and I had a nice little visit with two dead villagers. Future efforts should probably be better thought out."

Charlong had tensed as he was talking, then realized there would be no vengeance to protect against. Saccul's face reddened and she began soundlessly crying.

"There, there, my child, no harm done to me. We all have to remember that we are scorpions and must take care when we play together." Malame glanced at Charlong. "May I?" She nodded, and Malame shuffled over next to Saccul and hugged her, then whispered in her ear. "Next time you must remove the conscious memories from your agents."

A fractured smile cracked across her wet face. Malame stood up and turned to Charlong. "Will you come with me to my horse?"

She nodded and the two went out side by side. He leaned toward her.

"Incredibly talented child we have."

She whispered back. "And protective. Thank you for your forbearance."

"Hastet wants even more children."

"She's told me so."

"I can delay my return for a year or two if you wish."

"Delay will not lessen my pain, but at least until after the boy is weaned."

"Please don't try to kill me on my way back."

Charlong nodded. "Not this time."

They stood near but not close. Malame mounted his horse and left.

Except for a hailstorm the return ride was uneventful. Once back at the Old One's encampment, after food and a wash down, Malame knelt facing the Old One under the lizard skin blanket, speaking in the dead tribal language.

"You performed somewhat better than I feared."

For Ishtal this was high praise. "Thank you, my magus."

"And you were able to discover Its name?"

"As It died."

"And with that name you will be able to summon It from the dead?"

"Yes. I am of It now."

"And obtain further powers from It?"

"Assuming I demand the right answers."

"And learn how to counteract the spells you gave the wizened hag?"

"I believe so."

The Old One nodded. "Acceptable. Rest. In three days, you leave to cripple a simpering nobleman."

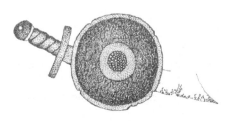

# THE TRACKS OF
# THE PI NERESKE
## *Wendy Nikel*

They came in the night and left nothing but footprints.

Though the snow had been floating down from the velvety sky for some time, Sashura arrived at the village before it could cover the tracks. Not a single candle blazed in the frosted-pane windows. Not a single mongrel rushed up to press its nose against her palm, to see if she'd brought a scrap of meat she'd be willing to share. The unnatural stillness would have set her on her guard even had it not been for the single set of footprints entering, the single set leaving.

*Pi Nereske.*

The thatch-roofed cottages were empty, as she knew they'd be, stripped bare of any morsel that could be consumed by the monsters: bread, grain, and cheese; horses, hounds, and cows; men, women, and children. The birds hadn't returned to the village eaves yet, so the fearful beasts couldn't have gotten far. It was too late for the inhabitants of this village, but if she hurried — and if the fates were kind — Sashura might be able to save others.

She shook the weariness from her shoulders as she repositioned her satchel. There were always others, always more to be saved. Hers was an endless task, a constant toil, but it was the life she'd chosen, a commitment she'd made before she was truly old enough to understand all that it'd entail.

She stuffed the villagers' weapons and tools into her bundle, muttering her thanks and vowing as she scavenged through the scattered remnants of their lives, "In exchange, I shall avenge your deaths."

In a cottage near the edge of the woods, not outwardly unlike the others, a shiver of hesitation met her as she crossed the threshold. The feeling of ill-ease couldn't be shaken.

Even before she saw the stacks of spell books, jars of potions, and amulets cluttering the shelves, the air's strange tension and lingering scent of magic indicated that this must have been the sorcerer's home. She'd heard of him in her travels and had thought him the typical, wizened old crackpot until an innkeeper at a nearby village had put her in her place.

"*Het*, Vasily Volkov is quite young, the son of a noble who has dedicated his life to healing and helping the poor," she'd said earnestly. "He saved my livelihood; I'd not have been able to stand here serving you had he not cured my bunions. Have a look."

Sashura had declined the offer.

Yet, here, something was amiss in the sorcerer's cottage — a wayward breath lingering in the air in the otherwise still and empty village. Sashura turned slowly, taking in every inch of the single room, searching for something, *anything* with life remaining in it. In the corner stood a cupboard, and it was this which her eyes finally came to rest upon. Its contents had been strewn across the floor as haphazardly as anything else, but the cupboard door was closed. Never in her years of stalking and slaying the forest's beasts had she ever encountered one courteous enough to close a cupboard door after its pillaging.

Drawing her sword, Sashura approached the cupboard on footsteps dulled by the soft leather of her boots. She bent, reached out, and flung the door wide.

At first, she thought the head of shaggy, golden hair belonged to a small, fluffy dog, quivering on the bottom of the cupboard. Then she saw the hands and knees that obscured its face — the face, not of an animal, but of a child.

"What are you doing in there?" It was a foolish question; she realized that as soon as it sprung from her lips. The boy obviously was hiding from the creatures. But why had they not killed him too?

The boy looked up, still hiding most of his face, but turning his bright amber eyes upon her. "You... you're not one of them."

Sashura sheathed her weapon and offered the boy a hand. As she drew him out of the cupboard, she looked him over. He slouched in fright but otherwise looked healthy, with clean clothing but dirt-encrusted fingernails. His too-long hair hid his face, and Sashura guessed his age to be about nine or ten years. She asked again, "What were you doing in there? How did they overlook you?"

Even the smallest child in this country knew that the Pi Nereske had a keener sense of smell than any living creature. Hiding from them meant certain death, for no matter how well concealed, the smell of flesh and blood would give even the cleverest man away. How then had this mere boy evaded them?

The boy fidgeted. His grubby fingers reached up to touch an amulet hanging from a chain around his neck.

Sashura leaned in and inhaled deeply. Nothing. She smelled neither the sweat that trickled down his scrawny neck nor the lye from his last bath — whenever that might have been. "An amulet that can block your scent? Where did you find such a magical object? Did you come in here and steal it from the sorcerer?"

"I didn't steal it. My brother Vasily gave it to me when

he heard those nightmares coming. He promised it would protect me." His voice still had the high pitch of youth, squeaking even higher with emotion.

Her curiosity satisfied, Sashura turned away and resumed her task of gathering supplies. "Well, that's a handy little trinket, and if I were you I'd keep it on you and run as fast as those little drumstick legs can carry you to the next village over."

"What are you going to do?"

"Me?" Sashura cinched her bag and threw it over her shoulder. "I intend to hunt them down."

"But then you must be the Huntress."

"So you've heard of me?"

"Oh, everyone around here has heard of you, how after the Old Creatures were freed from the Urn of Imprisonment, you made an oath not to rest until they were captured or killed, and how—"

"Yes, well, I intend to uphold that oath, so if you'll excuse me—" Sashura brushed past the boy, tamping down her irritation at his enthusiasm. This was her life, after all, not some fairy tale for children to tell one another while resting their heads on fluffed, white pillows. She wasn't some hero, just a girl who'd made a hasty oath in a moment of passionate rage.

"Well, then I'll accompany you."

"Not a chance, boy." She strode past him and out the door. "The Pi Nereske may have been fooled by that amulet of yours, but they're not so blind as to pass up a tender young morsel if it's delivered, unarmed, to their lair."

"You know where their lair is?" The boy jogged a bit to catch up with her. Sashura gritted her teeth. He was worse than a puppy. And just as liable to get himself killed.

"Not yet."

"You're following their tracks, then?" He pointed to the

single set of tracks. "It looks like they came from the south, heading north."

She bit her chapped lip, wishing she hadn't spoken. The boy wasn't as dull as she'd thought. "How does a child like you know how to read Pi Nereske tracks? How did you know that they wear their feet backward and walk in their partners' tracks? Most people would have thought they were the tracks of a single man heading south, but you knew otherwise. How?"

"My brother told me."

Of course. The sorcerer. He'd have had knowledge of all the forest's darkest and deadliest creatures. If only it'd been him who'd survived rather than his impish younger brother. He may have been of use. Sashura had neither the time nor skill to play nanny. If anything, the boy was a liability, a millstone around her neck. Although...

The amulet sparkled against his chest.

"You realize, boy, if you come, you must follow my instructions precisely. No arguments, no questions. You do what I say, hear?"

"Yes, ma'am."

"Don't call me ma'am. I am Sashura."

"Yes, Sashura."

"Good. You may begin by hauling this sack."

*

They travelled for two days, never stopping to rest for more than an hour or two. Sashura led the way through the knee-deep snow, the rabbit-skin lining of her boots keeping her warm. The boy stepped in her footsteps just as the Pi Nereske travel. He never complained, though the icy wind bit their ears and Sashura refused to slow her pace.

Sashura kept returning to the same strategy, despite her attempts to discount it as too risky, too dangerous. The Pi Nereske's tracks were becoming more difficult to track, but they couldn't be far. And what one thing would be guaranteed to draw them out? The scent of a young boy, lost and alone in the woods. If she wore the amulet, she'd be invisible to them. When they arrived to tear the boy to bits, she could swoop down and slay them. They'd never anticipate the attack.

The boy treaded three steps behind. The amulet swung with each step, hypnotic and alluring. Sashura pulled her gaze away from it.

She'd never doubted her own abilities, not since Volgonski, the greatest monster hunter in the country's history deemed her worthy to carry his sword. How she missed his kind eyes, his strong voice that always spoke words that were not only true, but *right*. He'd know what to do, whether the life of one small boy too high a cost to wager, if it freed the land of the foul beasts and brought her one step closer to her own freedom.

*

When they reached the Pi Nereske's lair, Sashura still hadn't made her decision. Shadows extended over the banks of a small creek, and the scent of pine — mixed with something sharp and sour — hung heavy in the air. Tangled blackberry bushes obscured the cave's entrance, but Sashura knew it was there by the drops of crimson blood on white, claw-marked snow where the creatures had torn through the shrubs, heedless of the thorns mangling their skin.

In the heat of the day, they'd be sleeping, but Sashura knew better than to let her guard down. Even in their slumber, the beasts could smell far better than any human.

The boy knelt in the clearing, gaze fixed upon something on the ground in front of him. Sashura tried to pull him away, but he resisted. Human remains. A cracked skull, a fractured bone, discarded at the edge of the trees. Whether these remains were intended as a warning or a boast, Sashura didn't know. Either way, they kept others from the Pi Nereske's lair.

"Those foul, loathsome beasts," The boy brushed his dingy sleeve across his face. "They did this to my brother, too, didn't they? Though all he'd ever done was to help others."

Sashura unsheathed her sword. The tears were the deciding factor. The boy may be brave enough to follow her thus far, but she couldn't use such a tender soul as bait. She looked about for a tree he could climb, a hollow in which he could hide, until her work of slaughter was done. "Come now—"

"I'll kill them or die trying!"

Something spiralled through the air toward Sashura, and — with reflexes as quick as a hawk's — she caught it. The amulet. The boy took off running toward the Pi Nereske's lair.

"Boy! Come back! Are you insane?"

The sorcerer's sibling spun around, brushing hair back to reveal a face that was softer, more feminine than Sashura had expected. "I'm a girl. My name is Nika. And I know what I'm doing. I'll draw them out, and you can cut them down!"

Sashura cursed the boy – that is, the girl's impulsiveness, even as she reluctantly admired her daring. Had she guessed Sashura's plan all along? Or had she devised the same strategy on her own? Is that why she'd allowed Sashura to believe her a boy, knowing that she'd never have allowed a girl to follow?

Rather than trying to catch up to the fleet-footed youth and causing a ruckus which would surely bring all the forest's dark beasts out in full force, Sashura draped the amulet over her own neck, whipped out a second sword, and stalked toward the lair. A large oak's trunk made a perfect hiding spot where she could see the girl's progress and keep out of the creatures' sight.

"Come on, you nasty, ugly dog-noses!" Nika called, waving her arms. "Can you smell my brother's revenge on my breath? Come taste my hatred! I dare you!"

From deep within the cave's darkest reaches, two sets of eyes glimmered. Two black-nosed snouts emerged, their nostrils flaring and twitching. Inch by inch, the creatures appeared: first their canine muzzles, then their canine ears, and then — just when one would expect to see padded paws step out from the darkness — they rose up on their feet, towering with man-like forms over the clearing.

*Run, child*, Sashura thought. But the girl seemed frozen at the sight of the enormous abominations, clothed in skins that were a patchwork of hair and fur.

They stepped out from behind the shrubs, not bothering now to walk in line, though they still wore their freakish feet backward, the toes pointed behind them and their knees bending inhumanly backwards. They snarled, and the wind carried the scent of their breath, making Sashura's stomach roil at the fetor of dried blood and rot.

*Come on, girl. Run!*

She couldn't wait any longer. The beasts were almost upon the girl. Sashura sidled from tree to tree until she was close enough to see the scraps of meat dangling from their teeth, the madness in their bloodshot eyes. Never before could she have gotten so close without them turning upon her, but the amulet swinging from her neck seemed to do its job. The beasts inched closer to the girl, circling around her, drool and foam collecting around the corners of their mouths.

The Pi Nereske looked ready to pounce, their leg muscles tight and muscular.

Sashura strode from behind the tree and with a swipe of her sword the nearest Pi Nereske crumpled to the ground. But before she could turn the blade upon the second, a third and fourth leapt from the cave.

"Take the amulet!" Sashura pulled it over her head and tossed it to Nika. "Take it and run!"

"Give me a sword!" Nika demanded as the token dropped at her feet.

Sashura snarled in frustration but lobbed one of her swords hilt-first in Nika's direction as she fended off a Pi Nereske with the other. It snapped at her with ragged, rotting teeth, and she spun, allowing her sword to slice through the air. From the corner of her eye, she could sense Nika jabbing and flailing with the other blade, making up for her lack of skill with her animalistic fervour. The Pi Nereske crouched just out of her reach, smirks on their canine faces. They knew she was an amateur, that she didn't really know how to wield the weapon she held. They'd be on her in a heartbeat if she let her guard down.

Sashura maneuvered to the girl's side, sliding beneath the outstretched arm of one Pi Nereske, snatching up the amulet, and then slashing at the creature reaching for Nika's throat. A deep, red gash opened on its human-like arm, and it hissed and howled, shrinking back in pain. The other two beasts circled around, and Sashura pulled the amulet over Nika's head, never taking her gaze from their wild, raging eyes.

"Go. You've done enough."

The girl didn't budge.

"You'll get yourself killed, just like your brother," Sashura said between gritted teeth. "Now run. Take your amulet and don't look back."

"There's a reason the Pi Nereske hunt in pairs." Nika pressed her back against Sashura's as the wounded beast circled around behind them. "Two hunters are better than one. They can watch each other's blind spots, see what the other can't see."

"You don't want this life," Sashura warned with a snarl.

"Neither do you. But someone must protect the land from these creatures."

Sashura pursed her lips at Nika's foolishness. If the girl had a kernel of sense, she'd run and hide. Though, if she had to be here, she might as well be watching Sashura's back. Together, they faced their foes, determined to show as little mercy as the demons had shown their families. Sashura slashed one, then another, until two lay dead and one mortally wounded, gasping through a ragged, red gash in its throat. When only one remained upright on its perversely angled legs, Sashura and Nika both faced it. Their breaths crystallized in the air before them. They had to end it soon; they would weary far more quickly than the unnatural creature, that master of hunters who never tired and never backed down from a fight.

The dog-face smiled. What did it know that they—?

Nika cried out. The fallen creature had crawled along the ground and latched its yellow claws to the soft flesh of her exposed ankle. In her moment of distraction, the other swiped at Sashura, striking her across the face. She stumbled and fell, her blade flying from her grasp and coming to rest just outside her reach. Frost bit at her bare hands as she scrambled backward, but just as her fingers twisted around the hilt, the heavy form of the Pi Nereske crushed her. She braced herself for its bite, her last thought focused on her hope that at least Nika — with the amulet around her neck — might stand a chance of escaping while the beast was busy feasting on her.

The bite never came. The body pinned her against the ground with suffocating weight. Sashura opened one eye, then another, blinking in surprise. Nika stood over her, staring, open-mouthed, and holding a blood-soaked blade.

"I... I killed it." Nika's voice wavered. Her sword clattered to the frozen ground. "I didn't think I could, but I did."

"Perhaps you were right." Sashura pushed the stinking corpse off her, struggling to catch her breath. "Perhaps two huntresses are better than one."

\*

Sashura taught Nika how to wipe her blade clean with snow and the creatures' rough tufts of fur. Together they set out toward the nearest village, the ears of the Pi Nereske tucked away in pouches at their belts as proof of their kills. Nika followed in Sashura's footsteps, leaving a single set of prints.

At dark, they reached the village. When the innkeeper rolled from her bed to still their knocking, Sashura announced, "We need a pint of ale, good meals for our bellies, and soft beds for myself—" she placed a hand on Nika's shoulder "—and my new apprentice."

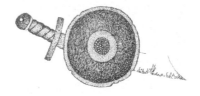

# SLAVES OF THE MONOLITH
## *Paul D. Batteiger*

They came down from the hills, through the forest-shrouded dark, and they brought fire and death into the valleys below. Black steel to rend flesh and spill blood upon the earth, fire to set house and village ablaze. They rode out of the dark under the moon, when the mists rose from the black soil and the nightbirds sang. And they vanished by dawn, back into the mysterious wilderness, leaving none behind but the dead.

We came after, from the hollows, following the river north to the place where smoke rose up into the morning mist. There were nine of us – all that would come from the villages and farms close by. Some of us had kin we feared for, while others answered the call of danger from some deep instinct. I was one. I was nineteen that year and yet unmarried. I was too big, they said, too tall and too wild to attract any man. I was restless in those days, and so when old Joran called for men to follow him to the place of killing I came. He did not refuse me, because there were so few who answered, and because he knew I was strong.

We were not warriors, most of us. Joran was, or he had been, though he was not young anymore. It was he who we followed and trusted. He led us through the forest paths along the river, keen-eyed. He wore his old armour and sword, bore his battered shield, and he had a new spear as I did, made in haste from an old point and a new haft that was not quite straight. I wanted to walk beside him, but I did not quite dare.

We smelled the smoke when we came close to the first village, and that was the first time I smelled burnt human flesh and bone. We were all afraid. I tried not to show it, but I wondered if they could see it. We came into the open, where the farmers had dug out their hard-cleared fields around the few buildings, and we saw it was all gone. The wood and thatch houses were all burnt down to black stains, the hard-raised barns and granaries scorched to the earth. On the ground I saw butchered remains – the flesh was black and split, the heads and arms severed and chopped apart. The smell was overpowering, and I was not the only one who retched.

Joran went alone into the ruin and knelt on the ash-dusted earth. He looked around him, as if the very soil might tell him what he wished to know. I wanted to learn from him, so I followed and stood beside him as he studied the destruction. Beyond the fields the black shroud of the ancient forest lay upon the hills like a stain, and when he looked up to the hills, so did I. We all knew from childhood to fear the forest, that something terrible lived there, or had once. We all knew that we should not hunt or herd or wander too far into those wilds. But I did not know why, nor did the rest of the young ones.

Joran pointed to the ground, and I saw bare footprints on the ash in among the blood and the blackened wood. "It's them," he said. "They have come again."

"It is bandits," said an older man named Targo. "They robbed and burned the village."

"No," Joran said. "They killed, and then burned. No one escaped, and they stole nothing." He stood and pointed west, to where another column of smoke rose up. "And there, another. There are not enough dead here for all those of the village. They took prisoners." He stabbed his spear into the earth and spat to one side. "They took them away into the forest."

"No," Targo said. "No one comes from the forest." He sounded afraid.

"They took them to the stone," Joran said. "It has begun again." He took his spear in his hand, shook the dirt from the iron head. "If we go, there is still a chance we may stop them before they reach it, we might save some of them and spare ourselves."

"We will die." Targo said.

"We may," Joran said. "But I will go. Who will go with me?"

I gripped my spear and thumped the haft against the blackened earth. "I will go."

*

All of us went. Once I said I would go, no man dared to be left behind. Who would refuse to go where a girl did not fear? They paled and spat and muttered oaths, but they all followed as Joran led us up the long slope of the ground away from the burnt village. We passed beyond the fields and then climbed the rocky slope toward the hills themselves. They seemed to watch us, timeless and ancient. The forest on them was thick and black as soot, and I wondered what secrets hid there. I wanted to ask Joran, but it was a hard climb, and all our breath was needed for it.

Before we entered the forest, we came upon the trail. The dry, late-autumn grasses were beaten down by the passage of many feet, and blood stained the ground. The path led upward into the hills, and there was no more talk of bandits. All the men grew silent as stones, and everyone clutched their weapons. I was glad to have a spear, for it served as a walking stick as well.

When we were almost to the trees Joran paused so we could rest, and he beckoned me closer. "Brona, if we are attacked stay on my left and guard me." He tapped his temple. "I cannot see as well on this side anymore. I don't want to be caught on my blind side."

I nodded, burning with questions I hesitated to ask. "I will."

"You are a big girl, and strong," he said. "Hold the spear in both hands, and aim for the gut." He patted his belly, hand slapping on the mail he wore. I wondered if the extra weight tired him. "Stab hard, then pull back at once, else they may climb the haft and trap it. If they are close, stab and then turn, from here." He showed me, bracing his own spear against his hip. "It will throw them off their feet."

I nodded again, proud that he spoke to me as an equal. I looked ahead to the dark trees. They seemed so much taller as we drew near them. "You think we will be attacked?"

"If they watch from the trees, they have seen us coming." He rubbed at his beard. "I think they will wait for us."

"Who are they?" I said, fearing the answer, fearing no answer.

"The people of the black stone," he said, his voice aged and fearful. "The servants of the monolith."

*

They attacked us as we entered the forest, just as the shadows of the trees closed overhead and the sky disappeared. We climbed a rocky defile lined with fallen leaves and jagged rocks, and they leaped from hiding and sprang down upon us. I saw pale faces and black eyes, the shine of the light on axes and swords. Battle-screams tore the air, and two of our number turned and fled at the sound.

I did not flee. I turned and braced up my spear in both hands as a man with a long black beard hurtled down the embankment upon me, an axe in his hands and his eyes like blank stones. He howled, teeth bared and white and long, and I caught him in the guts with my spearpoint and plunged it in. Blood shot out, spraying over me, and then he was impaled, and I could not get my weapon free. I shoved sideways and he tumbled away from me, axe falling from his hands. I bent and caught it up just as the whole world seemed to fracture into chaos.

There were screams and the sound of many blows all falling at once on armour and steel and flesh. A man sprang on me with shield and sword in his hands, and he struck at me, and I put the axe in his way and caught the blow, only for the force of it to dash the back of it against my forehead.

I stumbled back and fell among the rocks, and he leaped in to finish me, but then Joran was there, and he smashed his shield into the man, using all his weight, and flung him back. It was enough for me to get up. My blood ran into my face, and I blinked it away, and then I was angry.

Another man stumbled into me, raving and flourishing a bloodied sword, and I set both hands on the axe and chopped down with all my strength. The axe-blade sheared off his ear and then bit deep into his shoulder with a sickening sound. The black steel chopped through the bones and when I jerked it out of the wound, blood sprayed out in a torrent. I shoved the man aside and then the other swordsman was on me again. I smote my axe upon his shield with so much force it was split in half and my blade cut into his arm. He lost his footing on the rocks and fell, and I leaped on him with a cry.

He tried to bring his sword up, but I stepped on his arm and felt the bones snap, and then I split his face open with the axe, and then hit him again, and again. Blood gushed out and covered the rocks, splattered my face and I tasted it and spat it back out. I staggered back from him, and then it was quiet, and I wiped blood from my eyes and looked around.

In moments the gully had been transformed into a place of butchery. Two of our men had fled and I did not see them; three more were dead, one of them gagging his last and clutching at the spear through his body. The bodies of three of the invaders lay twisted in among them. I stood over two with blooded axe, and Joran had accounted for three. His spear was missing, and he stood breathing hard with his sword in hand. It had all been so fast.

I sat down hard on a stone, and we all breathed and blinked, shocked by it. All my life I had dreamed of battle, and now this was it. The smell of dead men was quick and foul, and the other two men – Targo and a farmboy named Ath – both bent and vomited. I felt dizzy, but I did not purge myself, and I was proud of that.

Joran cleaned his sword with hands that shook. He sheathed it, and then took up his spear. It was embedded in a dead man, and he had to rip it free. The corpse wheezed when he stepped on it. I saw all the raiders were of a similar look, with very white skin and blank eyes, like polished black stones. Their eyes were bruised-looking as well, shadowed. They looked like corpses, though their blood was plentiful, and hot. It steamed in the cool air.

"It's them," Targo said. "Curse all the gods, it's them."

"What are they?" I said. I looked at Ath, and he did not

know either. I could see that in his face. I looked at Joran. "You know what they are."

He climbed a way up the defile, away from the smell, and then sat down on a rock. He began to scoop up handfuls of dirt and used them to clean the blood from his spear-haft. I followed him, the others behind me, and I took a rag from my belt and tried to clean off my face. Joran looked very old then, with blood in his grey hair.

"They came in my father's time," he said, "before I was born. Down from the hills by night. They killed many and took the rest. We learned they killed women and children and the old – any who were not suitable warriors. They took only the fittest. They came by night, and never moved by day unless they were under the shelter of the forest." He looked up at the canopy above us. "They do not come forth into the light."

He cleaned blood from his spearpoint. "Some men followed, to see if they could find where they came from, who they were. Only one man returned. He told the story, and soon they saw it was true. They took their prisoners high in the hills, to a place where a great black stone rises up on the edge of a precipice, and there the power of the stone enslaves them, and makes them into what you see." He gestured down at the dead below us. "They are consumed, and made into madmen who live to hunt and to kill and ravage."

I looked down at the bodies, the smell still creeping after us, and I turned away. Did some of them look familiar? I could not say.

"It is why we have to find the prisoners, and free them. If we do not, they will come back, and we will not know them any longer. They will be enslaved by that dark power." He thrust his spear into the ground four or five times, twisting it so the soil cleaned the iron. "Three winters it took the last time. Three winters of killing and dying before the last of them was destroyed, and they came no more. If we do not strike, they will grow stronger."

"We can't stop them," Targo said. "We are just four, and they will be many. We have to go back and warn the other villages, gather more men."

"Go back then," Joran said. "I will go on alone if I must. I will find them before they reach the stone, and free the prisoners. If I do not, then tomorrow we will see them again." He stood up.

"I will go with you," I said.

He nodded. "Good. Go down and take weapons from the dead, and a shield, if there is an unbroken one. Then follow quickly." He looked up to the fading light. "Soon it will be dark."

*

I took a sword from the dead, and a long black shield. I hung the sword on my belt and took up my spear again. It was stained with blood, and I had to clean it as best I could. Targo did not want to come with us, and he spent a good amount of time convincing Ath to go with him, so by the time Joran and I went on, they both turned back and headed for their homes, promising us they would warn the people. I thought they were cowards, but I said nothing.

I followed Joran up into the hills, and now I was alert for anything, watching every shadow and behind every tree. The forest grew thicker, and the undergrowth more tangled, and it became more and more difficult to go on. I was sure we would be ambushed at every turn, but we saw and heard nothing. Even though it was just after mid-day, the trees blotted out the sky, and it was as if dusk covered the whole earth.

I looked for signs of others passing before us, but I saw nothing. I did not know how to read the trails, and I trusted that Joran did. I had much I wanted to ask him, but I needed all my breath for climbing, and so did he. I was much younger, so I did not tire as quickly, and before long I was beside him, helping him up the steep slopes.

We came to a place where giant stones grown green with moss leaned and slumped against one another, making a kind of arch, and Joran grunted and gestured ahead. "Be cautious here." I gripped my shield and my spear and followed him through, and we came out into a ravine that curved away out of sight ahead. The air was damp, and a small stream flowed down and through it. The rocks were covered in green, and in among them I saw many shapes of weapons or of skeletons. Crumbling skulls lay heaped to one side, and the hilts of swords thrust up from the moss and weeds.

"What is this place?" I said. I saw that many of the fallen weapons were of the same black steel as the sword I carried. "Is this where they come from?"

"No," Joran said. "This is where they ended. I never thought I would see this." He sat down on a heavy stone. "My father told me. They trapped the last of the raiders here and slaughtered them. He would not say how many men died. He only said it was the end."

"Where did they come from?" I asked. "This." I touched the black sword that hung at my side. "This is not like ordinary steel."

"No," he said. "I have always thought another race must have lived here, in these hills, in another age. A clan who worshiped the stone and forged that dark metal. This forest is filled with old ruins, if you seek for them. Signs of things raised by the hand of man in another age. Perhaps they raised the stone, or perhaps it was already here. Something older than man. I believe that." He sighed. "We cannot go much further."

I looked up to the trees as wind sighed through them. "Are we close to it?"

"Yes, I think we are. My father said this place was not far from the stone. He was the only man to ever look on it and return with his mind still his own. And he saw it from afar. He said it called to him, and some nights when the winds howled he woke from ill dreams with a cry on his lips. Perhaps it never ceased to call to him. He said it was a terrible thing, but would say no more than that." Joran looked up to the sky. "We should turn back."

"Turn back?" I was confused, and afraid, and disappointed, there was a bitter taste in my mouth.

"It is too late," he said. "We have not caught up to them, and we will not. We cannot reach them before dark, and the two of us cannot save their prisoners. We should go."

I heard a rattle of stones, and sticks breaking as under footfalls, and I turned to face up the hill, my spear ready. Joran stood up. "You must go now. Run."

I looked up and saw the forms of men darken the ridge above. Too many of them. Joran readied his spear and shield. "Run!"

I ran. I hated myself for it, but I ran back down the ravine as the sound of war-screams rent the air. My spear was too heavy, and I let it fall clattering to the stones. I splashed in the stream and nearly fell. I heard the sounds of battle behind me, the clash of sword and spear and bone. I heard Joran bellow his battle cry and it was like the sound of a beast. I was afraid of him then, even as I knew I left him to die.

I raced under the arch at the opening of the cut, and they fell upon me there, four of them. I saw a shadow and just had time to lift my shield and catch the sword-blow. It bit a piece from the rim, and I staggered. I almost fell on the rough footing, and had I fallen, they would have killed me.

But I caught myself, and then I felt anger inside me again, and my shame was there as well, and I drew my stolen sword with the fire in me to burn it away. Another one leaped down on me and I deflected his spear-stroke with my shield and then I smote him so murderously on the shoulder that my sword bit through his flesh and cleaved through to his heart. Black blood spurted into the air, and I screamed my own wrath.

Two of them closed on me with axes and then it was a flurry of strokes and counters. My sword rang and my shield was battered, and I had no time to think, only fight. I struck back with all my power, grunting and snarling, and one of them fell back with a severed arm. Blood painted the green stone, and I met the other one in another terrible exchange of blows. For a moment I forgot the fourth man, and so he almost took me from behind, but I caught the motion in the corner of my eye and turned at the last moment.

On instinct I smashed the edge of my shield against his face and blood splattered out of him. I felt his bones crush under the blow. The other one almost cleft my skull with his axe but I ducked back and then rushed in, smashed my shield into him so hard it broke in two. We went down to the rocky ground together. I rolled off him and then lunged, driving my sword downward into his eye. He caught the wide black blade and tried to hold it back, but I shoved it through his grip until it cut his fingers off and my blade plunged through his skull with a crunching sound.

I left my sword embedded in bone, staggered up and flung away my broken shield. I grabbed up an axe and then laid about me with unreasoning fury, chopping the fallen into pieces until they were hacked apart and motionless, and I stood over them covered in blood, my breath like a bellows.

All was quiet, and I looked up the ravine but saw nothing, heard nothing. Axe in hand I ran back to where I had left Joran, sick inside. I knew I would find his dead body, and it made my anger rise even higher. I felt such shame that I left him. A moment of fear and it burned me like scalding water. I gripped the axe in both my hands, ready to kill and die.

I came to the place, and the rocks were painted with blood. I saw there were six of the raiders butchered on the ground, cut to pieces, but there was no sign of Joran. I looked and I found his broken shield, his spear thrust through a dead man, and under another body I found his sword, painted with blood and notched from battle, but still straight and light when I took it in my hands. I tore cloth from the dead and cleaned the steel, looked at it and then upward into the hills. They had taken him, I knew that. They were taking him to the stone, and there they would make him one of them. I would see him again, but he would not be himself, he would have been burned away by that dark power.

I looked back down the hill, toward my home, and then I took Joran's sword in a strong grip and climbed after him. I would not turn back.

*

There was a trail of blood, and I followed it through the growing darkness. When the sun passed behind the hills, it cast a sudden shadow over everything, and I felt cold. Mist began to seep from the earth, rising around me like smoke from a netherworld. I huddled in my cloak as I climbed, wishing I could make a fire, but I knew I would not dare stop in the hills, not now. I started at every small sound, sure I was about to be attacked. I gripped Joran's sword and held it ready, waiting for the sound of war cries, but none came.

It grew darker still, and then I could scarcely see to walk, and I wondered if I could go on. But then I heard the sounds, and I knew I was close to what I sought, and my heart beat faster within me. I heard a low sound, steady, repeating, like wind, or waves. Then I knew it for voices raised in a chant, and felt afraid.

I climbed until I crested a rise, and I found myself looking across a shallow vale to where the hillside rose up almost sheer, a great dark cliff studded with ancient stones jagged as knives, and halfway up there was a flat place, and upon it grew a sort of heath covered in blackened grass and stunted growths. It looked as if part of the hillside had collapsed, sending down a spill of churned earth and broken trees, and had thereby exposed something hidden beneath. Now it stood open, like an altar, and at the centre reared the stone.

As soon as I saw it, I felt my breath catch like a hook in my chest. It looked like the shadow of a man, or a beast. It was hard to make out details, for it was black and reflected almost no light. Around the base of it gathered a multitude – at least a hundred men – and their torchlight did almost nothing to illuminate the great monolith. They chanted, circling it in a slow shuffle, stomping their feet and shouting invocations in words I could not understand. The sight of it made my blood cold.

I looked at the dark monolith and felt the jaws of it close on my mind, pulling at me. It had a presence, a will of its own. It wanted me to come and embrace it. I felt the power inside it, held over from long ages, the dim epoch when it was raised into the sky to watch over the deep valleys and the shadowed woodlands.

I looked down then, and I saw a line of prisoners bound neck to neck by ancient chains, led past towering bone-fires, up the slope toward the stone, and my resolve knotted inside me like a fist. I turned away from that dark power and swore to destroy it. I looked down at all of them, the slaves of the monolith, and I felt despair, because how could I stop them alone? There were too many to kill. Even our original number would have been hopelessly outnumbered. I did not even see how I could slip down and free Joran or some of the others. The fires were bright, and the stone… the stone knew I was close.

I stood for a moment, feeling the night wind rise, and I looked up at the hillside that reared behind the stone, dark and heavy with exposed rock and mortal points, and I saw then how I might undo what the monolith had done, and I smiled.

*

The night closed in as I climbed. It was not easy to follow the rim of the valley in the dark, climbing among the rocks and the trees. I crawled over the remnants of ancient walls, and other pieces of black stone worked by human hands, and so I began to think that Joran was right, that indeed some ancient race had dwelled here, and this had been the centre of their power. But I could not imagine the monolith as something made by human hands. I felt its presence in my mind, I felt its power, and I could not long look away from it. It was like a scar upon the world that my gaze felt compelled to return to. I felt that it had always been here, perhaps buried under the earth until human hands or simple ill fortune unveiled it.

I drew closer to the stone, and the ground rose, becoming rougher. The slope grew steeper, and I had to thrust Joran's sword into my belt and climb with both hands. The rock was hard and cold and jagged, and before long my hands were cut and bleeding. I was hungry as I had never been in my life, and afraid, and very far from home. But I would not turn away.

The chanting rose to a crescendo below me, and then I heard the screaming begin. I looked down and saw the whole vale there beneath me, lit by fires and now, also, by a grim radiance that crawled like mist over the monolith itself. The slaves chanted and shook their swords and spears at the sky, and I saw that one by one they forced the captives forward, and pressed their hands against the black stone, and then they screamed.

I saw them, one after another. Forced to touch that unclean monument, they shrieked, twisting and contorting as if they were on fire, and I saw their struggles weaken, and then they slumped to the earth, and they lay for the time it takes to draw three breaths, and then they rose, pale and hollow, and they raised their hands and joined the chanting. And then the next one was brought. I looked, though I did not want to, and I saw Joran in the line of prisoners, his face bloodied and bruised as they marched him closer and closer to the stone. Soon it would be his voice screaming out as his soul was burned away.

I climbed higher up the rocky face that loomed behind the stone. It was hard going, but not so hard as it looked. The stone was cut by many ledges and passages, and even caves that led into the rock. The ghastly phosphor gleam that rose from the monolith flickered all around me, in among the stones, and I saw that here were sealed tunnels, and others that had burst open from within, and I saw there an entire crypt that had broken and tumbled open and that skeletons lay crushed in the rocks. I saw they were decked as kings in their forgotten tombs. They lay in their black steel finery, clutching their swords and spears and axes against the afterlife that was denied them. They lay like tyrants, interred ready to rise and go to war.

The chanting grew, and I saw the glow rise, and something ghostly moved from a fallen skull and coiled away through the air, and I understood it then. This race, long-dead, fallen into ruin and forgotten, their war-lords buried here above their black idol, waited ever for one to come. Once mortal eyes beheld the stone, they were drawn to it, and when they touched it, their essence was seared away and the ageless ghost of one of these long-fallen warriors took their place, their body. Thus the dead race awaited a new flesh to come and give them life again. It would go on, age after age, so long as the monolith endured.

Then I heard the rattle of stone below me, and I looked, and saw a line of warriors climbing in my wake, and fear knotted in my guts. I turned and climbed for the precipice above. I was close now. I dragged myself, exhausted and bleeding, over the rocks that thrust up like spearpoints.

I found a loose stone, long as my arm, and I pried it loose, cast it down at my pursuers. It struck one, and he fell with a scream, plunging out of sight. I heard angry bellows from below, and the chanting faltered. I looked and saw the whole of the slaves coursing for the cliffside, beginning to climb it like angry ants. Now, at last, they woke to their danger. I turned away and climbed faster, until I reached the top.

Now I stood at the base of the great boulder I had seen from below, that I had marked to be the hammer of my vengeance. I set my back against it and drew Joran's sword from my belt, and as the war-cries of my enemies rose from beneath me alongside the screams of the doomed, I stood at bay. A dozen warriors closed on me, howling, and I called upon every ancestor who ever raised a sword, and I fought as though I were twenty men.

The pinnacle was treacherous, and narrow, and when they came against me I struck at them with terrible, two-handed blows that sheared through flesh and bone and sent the pieces plunging over the edge. I cut them down and they fell against one another, dragged each other screaming over the precipice. I laughed at them then, and I think perhaps I saw a flicker of fear in their black eyes, or imagined that I did.

I cut down three, then five, while I took several wounds, and stood bleeding at bay there against the stone. They rushed me together and I killed two more. They seized me, dragged me down and tried to stab me, but I fought with them. Joran had called me the strongest, and I proved him right. I grabbed one by the neck and smashed his head against a rock, and then another stabbed down with his sword, and I grabbed the guard and plunged the point into the crack where the great boulder was set in the cliff.

I kicked them away, sent more of them hurtling down into the darkness, and then I had a moment of freedom, the rest of them were coming, screaming up the cliff to reach me. I set both hands on the long sword and wrenched at it. The black steel would not break, I knew that, and so I used all my strength, screaming as blood started from my wounds.

I wrenched at the sword, feeling the fell steel bend, and bend, until I was certain my arms would give way, and my bones snap. I waited to feel a blade pierce me, sure they would strike me down in another breath. And then the great boulder shifted, and cracked free of the cliff, and the release of the strain flung me back, and I nearly fell with it. Instead, I clung to the jagged rocks as I watched it fall.

It struck the cliff below me, shattering the rocks, smashing screaming warriors to pieces, and then a great part of the cliff collapsed and slid downward. It gathered more, and more. The tombs crumpled and the hillside fell in on itself, and as I clung to my perch, I watched the entirety of the hillside plunge downward in a sudden roaring torrent. I saw the mass of prisoners wiped away, and I knew Joran was among them, but this was the only way for me to save him. Better death than what waited at the touch of the stone.

I howled my victory, but I could not even hear myself over the immensity of the sound. I saw the monolith standing there, glowing and pulsating and malevolent, and then the rockslide smashed into it like a wave of earth and crushed bone. I saw the dark thing uprooted, and overturned, and then the whole valley was buried in dust and smoke, and there was silence again under the night.

*

I do not remember very much of my return. I stumbled through the hills, bleeding and shivering and starving. I remember when I emerged into the light as the sun came up. I remember crossing the empty fields as mist rose from the earth, and then I remember I fell as a crowd reached me. I heard voices, and questions, but I could not answer them.

I did my work that day, for the destroyers did not come again. The years passed, and I travelled away from my homeland. I wandered over many lands, and fought in wars and saw things no one from my home ever dreamed of. It was only when I grew aged that I returned to the places of my youth, and found them softer and greener than I remembered, the sun warmer. The hills were no longer a place of terrors, and few even remembered the dark times.

Sometimes, in the night, I wake from dreams I cannot recall, and I stand and look up into the hills, to the black canopy of the ancient trees, and I wonder if it is still there, buried yet unsleeping. The monolith beneath the earth, awaiting another age, when men will uncover it, and find its power undimmed.

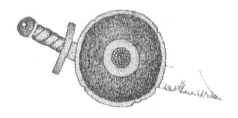

# THE GREEN WOOD
## *David Dubrow*

Grimacing at the ache in his shoulder, a pain so fierce that he feared a plague quill had pierced his lorica armour, Lior swung his spatha in a downward cut. The long, broad-bladed sword splintered the shaft of the pike that thrust at his side, and the dirt-grimed pikeman took the edge across his jaw, severing it. Shrieking, adding to the battle din, the man staggered back, clutching the crimson ruin of his face. Lior spurred his horse to trample him into the mire of blood and dirt.

Sweat streamed into Lior's eyes, narrowed to slits against the glare of the sun. Byzantium's 9th Cohort had struggled and strained and fought for every yard of earth since dawn, and now, at long last, he spied the crest of the hill past ranks of armoured Gauls. If Byzantium reached the high ground, the battle would be all but won.

Renewed by the possibility of victory, Lior flicked the reins to charge forward. His exhausted horse reared, and its iron-shod hooves shattered the skulls of the enemy on its way down.

"Sticking our necks out a bit, aren't we, sir?" shouted a voice behind him.

Lior grinned. "Perhaps a hair."

Optio Albian rode up to his left. Not as tall as Lior, but twice as broad, with skin the colour of brick and a jaw that jutted aggressively past his helm's cheek-guards. "We're too far ahead!"

"They'll catch up!" Panting, Lior leaned cross-body to drive his sword's point into the upper chest of a pikeman fumbling after a missed thrust.

"D'you see anyone else?" Albian hacked arms and heads with the workmanlike chops of a butcher. His entire right side was bathed in dust-caked blood from shoulder to sandal, and the horse beneath him rolled its battle-mad eyes, barely controlled by the pressure of his knees.

"When we reach the hilltop they'll flock to us."

"Not if we –" Albian paused. "DOWN!"

Without hesitation, Lior threw himself forward, along the neck of his horse.

A cloud of quills hissed overhead, followed by a chorus of outraged bellows behind. Cruel and honourless, the Nervii tribe of Gauls often covered their missiles with latrine filth on the assumption that even if their enemies survived an initial clash, they would later be struck down with disease. In Nervii hands, mere nuisance projectiles like thrown quills could be deadly.

Straightening, Albian pulled the last javelin from his saddle case and hurled it. The iron point punched through the quill-thrower's breastplate from front to back, driving the man into his fellows.

A glance over his shoulder told Lior that the 9th wasn't faring too poorly. Any quills they hadn't avoided had bounced harmlessly off of their round shields. Their sword-arms rose and fell with vigour, and if they remained strong, it wouldn't be long before they shattered the Gallic line to take the hilltop—

The sound of a horn shivered the air, two quick blasts, followed by a longer third. It repeated.

Lior blinked astonishment. "Did I hear that right?"

"Fall back," Albian shouted. "Centurion, we have to fall back!"

Growling a curse, knowing that arguing was futile, Lior hauled left to cut his way through.

*

Lior handed the reins to a junior cornet, headed to the water barrel, and accepted a ladle from the old campaigner manning it with a nod of thanks. He'd have liked to pour it down the back of his neck, but this far from the river the camp's water was only permitted for a man's insides, not his outside. Albian emerged from the mass of soldiers and horses to do the same, adding muttered thanks to Volturnus, God of Rivers, before drinking.

As they left the makeshift corral, the grassy stink of dung gave way to the odour of blood and decay wafting from the nearby physic's tent, where sisters in the undyed linen robes of Aesculapius seared stumps, sewed gashes, and lanced infections. Nearby, a young woman dumped a basketful of brown-stained bandages into a cauldron of boiling water outside the tent.

"No jokes about soup," Lior muttered.

"Wasn't about to, sir," Albian replied, and scowled as Lior turned left instead of the expected right, hurrying past the clangour of the blacksmith's pavilion. There, sweating men ground new edges on notched swords and hammered hot shoes onto restive horses.

"Sir," Albian said, "the Legatus isn't a cheery fellow at the best of times, and making him wait's not going to improve his mood."

"Won't take but a moment."

Shaking his head, Albian followed him to the 9th Cohort's camp, a broad square of tents arranged in strict lines. Here, the remains of the 9th sat talking, gnawing field rations, or trying to doze in the heat. Some spent time cleaning their weapons and digging bits of dried viscera from their armour, but few had the energy for even those meagre efforts.

When one man began to struggle to his feet, Lior lifted a hand. "As you were." Frowning, he peered across the camp at a figure curled up in a threadbare red cloak daubed with yellow handprints and distorted astrological symbols. None of the soldiers sat within ten feet of him.

"He ain't moved, Centurion," a Legionary offered, gripping a chunk of hardtack like he was trying to crush a rock. "Still dead."

At Lior's shoulder, Albian uttered a disgusted grunt.

Lior nodded, cleared his throat, and waited for all eyes to focus on him. "You fought well," he said in a clear, ringing voice. "The 9th was in the van the whole battle, and still we have fewer casualties than any other Cohort. It's because of you. You are the finest soldiers—the finest *men* in Byzantium. I am honoured beyond measure to serve in the 9th, and to prove it, I'm requisitioning double pay for all of you, from my personal holdings."

He grinned at the ragged cheer that went up, performed a quick salute, and half-turned to leave when Tesserarius Gnacio, sporting new dressings across both biceps, called out, "Sir, is it true we're surrendering? I heard we pulled back because we're surrendering to the filthy Nervii. Tomorrow, like."

Lior opened his mouth to bark an angry reply, something about the womanish nature of gossip, but stopped short at a nudge from Albian. After a deep breath, he put a smile on his face. "Surrender? To Gaul? The 9th never surrenders, Tesserarius. You know that. We win. We'll take the field again, and we will win." With a sharp nod, he stalked off.

Once out of earshot, Albian said, "Giving them twice pay's a kind gesture."

"They deserve more. Twice damn little's still not much."

"It's why I called it a gesture, sir."

Lior paused to let an empty wagon trundle by, pulled by a pair of swaybacked mares. "What do you think of what Gnacio said?"

Hunching his shoulders, Albian cast glances left and right. "Rumour's been going 'round, yeah. Wish I could discount it. We'll see soon enough."

The Legatus's tent was a high, round affair, guarded by two soldiers holding spears. The man on the left nodded when they drew near, and held open the flap to permit them entry.

Even with protection from the sun it wasn't much cooler inside. Oil lamps sat on large, iron-banded chests, with a plain soldier's cot in the corner and folding canvas stools arranged around a table bearing a wine jug and cups. Legatus Maecius, his bald head gleaming, looked up from the sand table and fixed them with his good eye, the other having been put out decades before by a Gallaecian archer's arrow. His seamed face pulled into a frown as he watched the two men remove their helms and salute.

"Centurion. Optio," he said, by way of greeting. "You're late. Come in."

"Apologies, sir," Lior murmured, approaching the sand table. As he did, his shoulder collided with something, and Albian stumbled, muttering a curse.

"I should have made myself seen sooner," said the figure they'd bumped into, blinking into visibility.

Freakishly tall, swathed in a plain black mantle, he towered over them, wearing a smile on his hairless face that resembled nothing so much as a rictus grin. His black hair fell to his shoulders in greasy waves.

Albian drew back, lifting his hands.

"Never seen a magus before, soldier?" Maecius asked, glowering.

Straightening, Albian said, "I apologize, sir. It's just that my experience with magi is, ah, limited, sir. Considering the 9th's excuse for one."

Lior frowned. "That's uncharitable, Optio. Orrick's a fine magus. A master of his craft." The corner of his mouth twitched, fighting to keep from smiling.

"A master? Yeah. Of skiving."

"He says every great magus spends most of his time dead. Keeps the physical world from polluting him."

"Polluting him? Have you stood downwind of –"

"Enough!" Maecius barked, and both men snapped to attention. "If the 9th didn't –"

The tent flap opened, and an armoured man stepped in, pausing at the entry to glower at everyone in turn. Bearded, dark of hair and skin, his lorica was streaked with soot as though he had just walked through fire, and hanging from his belt were a short-hafted axe and an officer's long sword.

"Kneel for your Emperor," the man growled, and wisps of smoke hissed from between his teeth.

Noting that even the Legatus's gaunt magus made obeisance, Lior dropped to a knee.

Emperor Solus entered, gesturing for the men to rise. A purple cloak on one shoulder and a thin gold diadem on his grey brow were the only concessions to royalty he wore in the field; without them, in his soldier's lorica, he would otherwise look much like the grizzled veterans who were too old to swing a sword, but still served in camp.

"Maecius," he said, approaching the sand table. He plucked up an infantry figurine marked *8C*, frowned, and put it back. "These are the men you suggested? The tall one's hair is too light. He doesn't have any Gaul in him, does he?"

Armor creaking, the emperor's guard moved to stand just behind Lior and Albian. He gave off the heat and fume of an open furnace.

After a tiny nod from the Legatus, Lior said, "Your Majesty, my line stretches back seventeen generations, to the court of King Raemus himself. Your servant is a pure Byzantine, through and through."

Solus snorted. "Knows enough to not say no to an emperor."

Lior bowed his head.

"Maecius," said Solus, "what we say must not leave this tent."

Spreading his huge hands out to the sides, the Legatus's magus uttered a guttural phrase deep in his throat. Pressing upon them like water, the air in the tent thickened perceptibly. The burned metal stink of the emperor's guard grew, and the noise from outside diminished to the barest of whispers. With a return of his skull-like smile, the magus moved off to the side. "Privacy is guaranteed, Majesty," he murmured.

Solus folded his arms, locking eyes with Lior until the 9th's Centurion lowered his gaze. "Though we are your Emperor, our power is far from absolute. Two of Byzantium's Noble Houses tire of battle. They tire of empire. They chafe under your Emperor's rule. They would yield this land to the filthy Gauls, to the savage Picts and Saxons and debased Etruscans. They would see Byzantium fall, to be carved into fiefdoms. Every petty noble a king."

Lior shared a glance with Albian, who swallowed.

Behind him, the Emperor's guard exhaled in a low growl. A haze of smoke fouled the heavy air. Sweat prickled out on Lior's back.

"Yes," Solus said, eyes narrowing to slits. "Already, House Allectum and House Sylla have withdrawn their support. We fight on the margins just to maintain our borders. You have seen this."

After nods from Maecius, Lior, and Albian, the Emperor said, "Without House Allectum, we may yet crush the Nervii Gauls. But without House Sylla, we will surely be defeated. Pleasantly, we have something that Consul Figlio of Sylla wants very much."

The Emperor's mouth twisted bitterly. "Our only daughter, the Princess Lucia. Figlio of Sylla has never wed, but now, in his last years, he very much desires a legitimate son and heir. So to save our empire, I will..." His jaw jutted. "*We* will offer her hand in marriage to Consul Figlio. House Sylla will then cleave itself to our line, as it has desired for generations, and will throw its considerable weight of gold behind us."

Solus grasped Lior's shoulder with a grip so firm he felt it through his armour. "But first, Figlio, he desires to..." His dark eyes glared upward, and his grip tightened. "He desires to...see the Princess. To *know* her. Before reaffirming his oath to Byzantium. We demanded of Maecius two men of the Cohorts to serve as the Princess's honour guard for this, her...*betrothal* to Figlio. That is why you are here. Her mother the Empress refuses to participate. Byzantium is worth nothing when her pride is at stake. We would go ourselves, but we must remain here to mend the fractured alliance between the throne and the Noble Houses. Perhaps House Allectum can be persuaded to recall its loyalty, with enough land. Perhaps Byzantium can be preserved a while longer."

Squeezed between the Emperor and his smouldering guard, Lior bowed his head. "It will be as you say, Majesty."

"It will," the Emperor said, and released Lior's shoulder. "Ride, Centurion. You will find the Princess on the Livian Way, between Ravenna and the Green Wood. Look for a white coach and a man in blue. Wash the Gallic filth from yourself in the river, mount your horse, and ride. Ride, and with this...*joining* save our empire." With a curt nod at Maecius, Solus swept past Lior to leave the tent, preceded by his guard.

The near-viscous atmosphere fell to the ground at a gesture from the magus, and the faint sounds of the camp outside returned.

Lior took a deep breath of the cleared air. Next to him, Albian scrubbed a hand across his wet forehead.

"You have your orders," said Legatus Maecius, eyes on the sand table rather than them. "Go."

*

"It's still foolish, is what it is," Albian said, shaking his head.

Lior looked over his shoulder. The magus Undone Orrick swayed from side to side with each step of his horse, a piebald grey mare. Despite complaining about bringing him along, Albian had done a good job tying the dead man to the saddle; throughout the long ride, Orrick hadn't fallen once. The cowl of his red, yellow-daubed cloak remained over his face, hiding it from view.

"He's not doing any good at camp," Lior said. "And besides, he might serve as the Princess's dowry."

Albian drew back, blinking. "A *dowry*? You give that thing to the Consul and he'll call off the betrothal."

"Good news for the Princess, then." Lior put his heels to his horse to trot ahead. "I see them past that hill. If it is them."

The Livian Way, Byzantium's longest thoroughfare, stretched from the western border through the capitol of Ravenna, and to the edge of the Green Wood. Paved in grey stone, with regular inns for weary travellers, the Empire maintained it with the help of regular taxes and tolls. Here, along the rolling hills of the eastern province, it was less-travelled; the last wayfarers they had seen were a pair of wagons hauling bales of hay from one farm to the next. Grazing sheep and goats dotted the fields on either side, casting shadows in the grass.

"Likely them, yeah," Albian said, riding up. "Most men never even see the Emperor, let alone meet him. Now I'll meet the Princess, too."

"At this rate you'll be dancing with the Witch-Empress of Aegyptus by suppertime tomorrow."

Flanked by six mounted men in light mail, Princess Lucia's cortege consisted of a huge, white-enamelled coach pulled by four black mares, their trappings chased with gold; a smaller wagon behind, its heaped contents covered by a tarp; and a stocky, dark-haired man in blue robes riding beside the coach's open window, chatting with someone within. When Lior began to descend the hill, the rearmost guard peered up at him, squinting against the sun, and said something that caused the company to come to a halt.

The blue-clad man wheeled his horse around and, followed by two guards, moved to the base of the hill to wait for Lior's approach.

"Well met," Lior said as he rode up. "I am Lior Cassium, Centurion of Byzantium's 9th Cohort. The man at my shoulder is Optio Albian of the 9th, and the fellow behind is the 9th's magus, Undone Orrick. I take it this is Princess Lucia's coach?"

A shadow passed across the youthful face of the man in blue, but he nodded. "Well met, Centurion. We were told of your coming by a sorcerous messenger that made the Princess's nurse faint dead away." His lips curled in a wry smile. "I am Vesnian, of House Ionius. His Majesty has tasked me with…facilitating the Princess's betrothal."

Lior nodded again, in commiserating fashion. "Very well. If the Princess doesn't object, I will take point, and Optio Albian will bring up the rear. If there's aught else about honour-guarding, I pray you will teach us, my lord."

Chuckling low in his throat, Vesnian replied, "Being visible and alert are, I fear, all you must do. Still, if –"

Behind him, the coach's door opened, and Princess Lucia stepped out, followed by a lady-in-waiting shading her with a silken parasol. "Vesnian, is this my honour guard? They're quite late."

Lior watched her draw near, and found himself sitting up straighter.

Her smooth, flawless skin had the nacreous quality of mother-of-pearl, darkening to rose-pink at the buds of her lips. Tall she was, made more so by her chestnut coif, its braids held in place by ivory combs, with ringlets framing her delicate, heart-shaped face. Matching the clear green of her wide-set eyes, her silken gown clung to her slender body in a way that hinted at indecency, but was offset by a translucent jade shawl, shot through with golden thread. A small silver fibula pin on her shoulder bore the cornucopia symbol of the goddess Bona Dea.

Vesnian dismounted, and the doleful half-smile on his face eased somewhat. "Yes, Highness. This is Lior, Centurion of the 9th Cohort. And his Optio, Albian. They came straight from the battlefield for this signal honour."

Awestruck, Lior remained in the saddle until Albian kicked his stirrup while dismounting. He hopped down and made an attempt at a bow. "Your Royal Highness," he managed.

The look Princess Lucia gave him mingled frank appraisal and cool humour. "Though you could use a proper bath and a scraping, I am pleased, and not just because you are not Volnus, my father's dreadful shadow. You do not stink like a smithy or scowl like a thundercloud."

"I will avoid both, Your Highness."

Lucia's answering smile caused his face to redden. The lady-in-waiting, still shading her with the parasol, murmured something into her ear.

"Yes," Lucia said. "We were told by a wind-sprite, rather rudely, that there would be three men of the Cohorts. You are rather a small honour guard, and I am jealous of what is mine. Where is my third man?"

Albian stepped forward. "Ah, if it pleases your Royal Highness, I might say that our third man, such as he is, is actually, well, not amongst the quick, as one might say, and can't be relied on to perform such duties as –"

"Nonsense," said Undone Orrick, riding up. He pulled back his red cowl to reveal a dark, lined face, sparsely bearded, and stringy grey hair entwined with beads and pieces of bone. "I am ready. To be relied upon."

"That's a first," Albian said, frowning up at him.

Orrick lifted his chin. "I see and hear everything you say and do around me, you know. Even while I am dead."

"Good."

"Enough of that," Lior said, lifting a hand. He turned to the princess and bowed his head. "Deepest apologies for the tardiness, Your Highness. And the bickering. But we are here now, and under your command."

Lucia smiled once more. "As you say, Lior of the Cohorts." She graced him with another long, lingering look. "Vesnian," she said, without taking her eyes off Lior, "I shall ride alongside my new guard-captain until we reach the Green Wood. How long?"

Sighing, Vesnian gave Lior a sidelong glance. "We will arrive by sundown, barring further delay."

"Then we will not tarry a moment longer," Lucia said, and held out her hand. "Come, then, Lior of the Cohorts. My guard-captain."

*

As the shadows lengthened, the princess proved herself a witty conversationalist, as much listener as talker. About her upcoming betrothal to the Consul of House Sylla she offered little save a dryly humorous account of the joyless haste with which her Royal Mother, the Empress Camilia, had hurried her from the palace. Lucia had always known that her fate was to be married to a Noble House that would someday bolster her father's power. "Still," she said, "my lifelong prayers to the Good Goddess, offered with perfect faith, proved fruitless. I am to be betrothed to a man who was grey before my birth."

Under her skilful questioning, Lior found himself telling her things that he hadn't even said to Albian: his father's anger over him joining the Cohorts; the ugliness of his first campaign, putting down the Thucer uprising in Parma; his five sisters, all of whom had married farmers, except for the oldest, who married a miller. He made special effort to keep his talk light; the closer they got to the edge of the Green Wood, the quieter the princess became. That this clever, beautiful girl was to be offered like a camp-follower to Consul Figlio ate at him, and if he could keep her mind away from it with stories and jokes, he would gladly play the jester.

Downcast, Vesnian rode in the coach alongside, watching them from the open window while the princess's ladies-in-waiting murmured to each other, vacillating between excitement over the betrothal ceremony and distress at the rustic surroundings.

Behind the coach by the luggage wagon, Orrick fell into a doze in the saddle, indifferent to Albian's glowering.

At the edge of a forest of cedar, the Livian Way narrowed into a road through the trees. Stars glittered in the east as the sun descended. The princess re-entered her coach, and the cortege drew closer together as they passed into the Green Wood, where House Sylla marked the border of its demesnes.

Though the road was straight and well-kept, and the trees sparse enough to see through them, Lior felt unsettled. The day's warmth had fled, leaving a damp chill more suited for late autumn than a midsummer evening. Rodentine shadows scuttled in the high branches, and the chitter of insects threatened to drown out the wagon's creaking, the dull clop of horse hooves on the cobbles. Vesnian, mounted once more, kept his eyes upon the road ahead, while Orrick squinted into the forest with the keen glare of a raptor. In the rear, Albian grasped the reins in one hand and a javelin in the other, plainly suspicious.

Soon, a yellow-orange glow bled past the trees, and they entered a clearing. Surrounded by a low, whitewashed wall, the manse of Consul Figlio was enormous, with a tall-columned portico and a hedge-lined pathway leading to the front gate, guarded by a spearman. As they drew closer, the guard pushed the gate open, bowed, and stood aside to let them enter.

Built in the traditional style, much of the U-shaped villa was dark but for the central structure, with a brick firepit out front and flickering lamps glimpsed through shuttered windows. Several people stood silhouetted by the fire, with a tall, if stooped figure in front.

Vesnian murmured, "That's the Consul. I've met him twice. Stay by the Princess." He signalled for the cortege to halt.

Led by Vesnian, with Lior a respectful step behind, Princess Lucia approached the firepit.

"Consul Figlio of House Sylla, Lord of the Green Wood," Vesnian said, "His Majesty, the Emperor Solus, has granted me the honour of presenting Her Royal Highness, the Princess Lucia." He bowed with smooth grace and proffered a slender wooden scroll case, embossed with the Emperor's seal.

In his youth, Figlio must have been a tall man, broad of shoulder, but age had robbed him of posture, and he leaned upon a wooden cane shod with silver. His cream-coloured robes, embroidered with scarlet stitching, hung loosely upon him, his hair had receded to a grey fringe, and the sinewy hand that gripped his cane was covered with dark spots. He made no move to accept the scroll case, but his creased face pouched into a smile that failed to reach his shadowed eyes.

"Tarquin," Figlio said, "make certain the terms are acceptable."

The man at his shoulder, armoured in the northern style, all rivets and hammered metal plates, grabbed the case from Vesnian's hand and broke the seal, letting the pieces crumble to the flagstones. Dark of hair, his face scarred by pockmarks, he pulled out the scroll and squinted at it with eyes that didn't reflect the firelight.

Princess Lucia kept her head high, though colour bloomed in her cheeks.

Frowning, Vesnian stepped back.

The nobles behind Figlio, dressed much like him in robes of white and red, hid smiles behind their hands. Attended by slaves in grey mantles, they dripped with gold and jewels at wrist and neck.

As the silence continued, broken only by the insectile buzzing of the forest and the crackle of the firepit, Lior's unease grew. The humiliation of the Princess was troubling enough, but the Consul and his family had the look of intimates sharing a vicious, if private joke.

"It is as you agreed, my lord," Tarquin said, and slipped the scroll behind his breastplate.

Figlio's smile widened to show his teeth. He approached the princess, cane thudding upon the walk, and licked his lips. "Princess Lucia," he said, his breaths thin and laboured, "while I regret the circumstances that have brought you to my manse with such haste, I rejoice that we are to be wed." Even with his bent back, he loomed over her. "Will you do me the honour of celebrating our betrothal here, in the Green Wood?"

Smiling back at Figlio, eyes shining, Lucia linked arms with him. "The honour is mine, my lord Consul. Long has it been my dream to be wed, and to such a storied and ancient family as yours. Yes, please, let us celebrate, and thank the gods for our good fortune," she said, and her voice was a song.

"The sooner our nuptials, the happier I shall be." Figlio

said, patted her hand, and led her into the manse, followed by his retinue. The back of his head bore a red, S-shaped scar.

Stepping forward, Lior almost collided with the armoured Tarquin, who blocked the way.

"Do you keep your distance," Tarquin said, his eyes as flat as slate. "The Consul and his betrothed would have some privacy."

Lior's hand dropped to the hilt of his sword. "You do not –"

"We shall," Vesnian cried, moving to slip between them. "We shall permit all appropriate privacy between the Princess and the Consul. We encourage it, in truth. And yet the Princess's guard-captain has a duty to perform, commanded by Emperor Solus himself. And that is to see to her safety."

Tarquin levelled his lightless gaze on Vesnian, shrugged a shoulder, and turned to enter the manse.

*

In the manse's hall, the smells of baking bread, of spiced wine and herbed sheep's cheese and roast lamb filled Lior's nostrils. Albian's empty stomach sang a visceral tune, but the Optio remained stoically at attention, eyes lingering on the trays of food that slaves placed on the long, low tables. Consul Figlio and his family – cousins, nieces, nephews, and by-blows – lounged on couches by the hearth at the far end, laughing as they ate. The wine had been mixed, but not yet drunk; the betrothal celebration would not start in earnest until Princess Lucia presented herself.

Vesnian, seated near the Consul, replied to something a matronly-looking noblewoman asked, to general laughter.

Their amusement failed to lighten his mien. Heavy armour creaking at the straps, Tarquin paced restlessly among the couches, hand resting on the pommel of his brass-hilted sword. His flat eyes rarely slid away from Lior, except when speaking in low tones to Figlio or some other noble.

"He keeps staring at you like that, and I reckon we'll be celebrating two betrothals," Albian muttered.

"Imagine his longing when we quit this place, and not soon enough," Lior said. "Do you see, though: Tarquin watches me, but they all watch Tarquin. Even the slaves look to him. Not at the Consul, their lord."

"They've got eyes like sharks. The lot of them. Dead. Empty."

Orrick emerged from the shadowed corner by the guest chamber door. "Speak less," he intoned. "A silent man is never overheard."

Albian snorted. "I like that. Made it up yourself?"

"No."

To forestall Albian's reply, Lior leaned close to say, "You are right, of course." He lowered his voice to a whisper. "Still, have you *seen* anything?"

"Seen anything," murmured Orrick, and shook his head. The firelight glinted on the beads in his hair. "The ethers are clouded. Opaque."

"Opaque." Albian rolled his eyes toward the roof beams. "Useless as teats on a boar hog."

"You misunderstand," Orrick said, lifting his upper lip. "Typical. I say the ethers are clouded. They are. I have not been so blinded since the Wenjiao Coven attempted to resurrect Apollo, conjuring the remaining pieces of the dead god's shattered heart. They failed. Every magus and child under six within seventy-seven leagues died of brain haemorrhage, and the ethers across the Earth were blackened for eighteen full moons. The Consul's manse is immersed in evil at least as great."

Lior blinked at him. "You might have told us this before."

"I had not –"

"This is cack," Albian hissed. "Centurion, all we need do is keep watch on the Princess tonight, take her back to Ravenna tomorrow, and get to camp. I'd rather be on the battlefield dodging plague quills than –"

Grasping the man's shoulder, Lior leaned close. "Go," he whispered. "Tell the Princess's men-at-arms to make ready to leave. Tarquin has gone, and the nobles watch us now, as cats with mice. Once the celebration is ended, we will ask the Princess to return to Ravenna with all haste."

Albian swallowed, nodded, and headed for the side door.

All eating had stopped, and the Consul and his family watched Albian leave with amused smiles. Among them, Vesnian frowned and made to stand, but the matronly woman he had been speaking with leaned up, grasped his wrist, and pulled him down with a murmured word.

Orrick turned his back to the nobles, pulling a tiny copper knife from his sleeve. "I will attempt a working," he whispered, "but –"

The Princess stepped out of the guest chamber clad in a gown of whitest silk, fastened at the shoulder with her silver Bona Dea brooch. Her chestnut hair cascaded down her back in soft waves, and a silver chain hung around her slender waist, set with three glittering rubies. She offered a faint smile to Orrick, inclined her head at Lior's hasty bow, and drifted past them to the hearth, where Figlio struggled to his feet with the help of his slaves. Lucia's two ladies-in-waiting followed in her wake, each in lavender mantles of similar style: her nurse, a sturdy woman in late middle age, and her body slave, a young blonde girl skilled in the arts of kohl and comb.

After accepting the Consul's kiss with a smile, Lucia took the wine cup offered her and waited as the other nobles rose from their couches. Vesnian, face pale, was first to stand, and sought Lior's eyes from across the hall.

Chanting under his breath, Orrick made a small incision on his forearm. Blood welled up, and he used the knifepoint to paint scarlet runes in the middle of his palm.

Lior approached the Princess, hand on his sword's hilt.

The Consul lifted his cup. "To the long-awaited joining of our two Houses," he called in his breathless voice. "To the children we will make, and the dynasty we will found!"

As the nobles drank, cheering, Lior paused. Despite the odd looks and Orrick's stories of clouded ethers, what was there to fear? If he interfered he would be crucified—

Albian slipped inside and hurried to him, face grim. "They're gone, sir. Both the men-at-arms and the drivers. The horses, the coach, they're in the stables, but the men are gone."

"And Tarquin still absent." Lior glanced at Orrick, who continued to chant under his breath, body swaying. "Stay here." He noted with approval that Albian had slung a quiver of javelins over his shoulder, and moved to Lucia, surrounded by nobles.

"Centurion," the Consul said. "Young Vesnian spoke highly of you."

Both the nobles and slaves turned to watch him, and even as they smiled, their eyes were dead and flat, and he fought to suppress a shiver. Lucia leaned closer, as though seeking protection.

Lior bowed his head. "My Lord Vesnian is kind,

Consul. I must ask, however, that –"

"Please," said the matronly noble next to Vesnian. "Drink with us." She offered Lior her wine cup. "You are with us now, or soon will be."

Frowning, Lior said, "My lady, I –"

The side door burst open, and Tarquin stalked in, followed by the Princess's men-at-arms. All had naked swords and lifeless eyes. "Hold them," he commanded, and Lucia's men ran at Albian.

Lior thrust Lucia behind him and went to draw his sword, only to find himself borne down by the nobles, who leapt on him with terrible strength. Struggling, cursing, he crashed to the floor. His free hand smashed into a ribcage, eliciting a groan, and before he could punch again, a slave knelt on his arm, pinning it. Past the robed bodies he caught a glimpse of Albian being stomped to the floor, and Orrick kneeling at sword's point. Vesnian lay nearby, held down by a grinning noblewoman who placed the tines of an eating-skewer under his eyeball.

"How dare you?" Lucia shouted at Tarquin. Her nurse stood protectively over her, face white. "What madness is this?"

In three steps Tarquin was at her side. He struck the nurse away with the back of his gauntleted hand, grasped Lucia by her white throat, and turned her toward Consul Figlio, who stood with a straight back and a cold smile. "Show her, Figlio. Show her what we dare."

The Consul moved to crouch by Vesnian, who shook in terror.

"What…did we offer offense?" Vesnian asked in a hoarse whisper. "Please, I apologize if we have. Please."

Hissing breaths between his teeth, Lior strained against the nobles holding him down.

A low, wet, gurgling sound issued from the Consul's throat, and, leaning over him, he vomited a torrent of writhing black maggots onto Vesnian's upturned face. They gushed out of him in clots and strings, splattering into the young noble's eyes, his nose, his mouth.

Vesnian uttered a high, throat-tearing shriek. The woman holding him moved away, an expectant smile on her lips. Squirming, the maggots burrowed into his flesh, melting into grey sludge where they were flung to the mosaic floor in his flailing and clawing. In time, his screams tapered to a ragged croak. A final convulsion bowed his back, setting his heels to drumming on the floor, and then he collapsed, unmoving.

Lucia slumped against Tarquin in a dead faint.

Wiping his mouth with the back of his hand, the Consul straightened to his full height.

"I will take her to his tomb," Tarquin said, gathering Lucia into his arms. "Infect the others." On his way out, he gave Lior a small, humourless smile.

One of the men-at-arms kicked Orrick in the kidneys, sending him sprawling. "Stop your muttering, old man."

It took the other five to hold Albian down, who cursed every last one of them, their wives, and their ancestry in a stream of obscenities that few men of the Cohorts would be able to match.

Lior redoubled his efforts to free himself, to no avail; the nobles did not give. A pair of sturdy thighs trapped his head. Figlio's glistening face swam before him, grey spittle dripping onto his cheeks.

The Consul gagged once more. A surge of maggots boiled up from his throat, writhing and black.

*No, gods damn you, no—*

Suddenly, the floor rippled in waves, as though the mosaic, depicting a trireme sailing toward the setting sun, had turned into seawater. The Consul tumbled backward, and the pressure of limbs pinning Lior to the heaving tiles slackened in a chorus of surprised shouts. Lior wrenched himself away, scrambling to get to his feet.

Screams erupted. Two of the men holding Albian plunged completely through the roiling floor, disappearing into the tesserae, and the others threw themselves off of him, seeking steadier ground. Furniture toppled in the rippling waves, spilling food and wine. The Scylla guards who ran in from outside were deluged by the tides, disappearing in moments.

Orrick knelt in a small circle of stability at the centre of the maelstrom, pressing his rune-painted hand to the floor. Clouds of steam hissed from under his palm.

He glared up at Lior from across the hall. "My strength wanes," he gritted from between clenched teeth.

No stranger to the heave and roll of the sea from the recent campaign against the Tattered Sails corsairs, Lior regained his footing, drew his spatha, looked for Albian, who had raised himself to one knee, face bloodied. Something grabbed Lior's shoulder, and without thinking he spun and slashed, slicing off a slave's hand at the wrist. Screaming, grasping the fountaining stump, the man turned to flee, but Lior finished him with a thrust. Though the nobles and their slaves were unnaturally strong, they were armed with only fists, and proved easy foes on the bucking floor. Blood gushed as Lior slashed limbs and reaped heads, and by the time he reached Albian, he was drenched with red.

The Optio, swollen lips peeled back in a snarl, held off the remaining men-at-arms with his gladius in one hand and a javelin in the other as they tried to cut down the hoarsely-chanting Orrick. One of the Princess's guardsmen was stuck half-in, half-out of the mosaic, pressing a hand to a spurting wound in his neck.

Lior fell upon them before they knew he was close, hacking one man's head from his shoulders and driving his sword through the chest of another, the man's mail tearing like papyrus. The third guardsman turned, distracted, and took the point of Albian's javelin under the chin. Eyes rolling to the whites, he stiffened, toppling like a felled tree.

Orrick's chant ended in a mutter. The steam from under his rune-painted palm ceased, and the mosaic floor hardened to stone, though still contorted in waves and swells.

Sharing a grim nod, Albian and Lior turned to take in what was left of the hall.

Two figures stood amid the wreckage of corpses and broken furniture: the stocky Vesnian, who watched them with eyes as dead as Tarquin's, and Consul Figlio, clenching and unclenching his fists.

Figlio bared his teeth. "Even were you to leave unchanged," he said with a smile, "you will be hunted men for all time. Murdering a Consul and his family in his own home."

"The Princess will tell a different story," Lior replied. "I know not what black magic has been worked upon you, but –"

"The Princess is already one of us," Figlio said. "Unless Tarquin is ravishing her amid the slime and rot of Beremoch's tomb."

Lior started forward. "You –"

With a low grunt of effort, Albian hurled a javelin at the Consul. It flew straight and hard and true, but Vesnian leapt in front of it, taking the iron point through the throat. Choking, he fell.

The Consul leaned back with raised hands as Lior drew close enough to press the point of his sword against his chest. The old man's chin ran with greyish spittle.

"Where is this tomb?" Lior asked. "Who is Beremoch?"

"You mispronounce his name," Figlio replied.

"Tell me!"

From behind, Orrick shouted, "Stay back! He –"

Figlio spat a viscid gush of black maggots at Lior's face.

Lior dove to the side, slashing across the Consul's abdomen. Glistening pink loops of intestine spilled from the wound, bathed in tiny larvae, and the Consul staggered, clutching at his entrails. He fell face down to the rippled floor.

Orrick backed away from the spreading puddle, pulling an unprotesting Albian with him. "Did they touch you?"

"No," Albian said. "I don't think –"

"I was not speaking to you," said Orrick.

Albian yanked himself away from the magus, scowling.

After a glance down at himself, Lior shook his head. "No," he said, and wiped the Consul's blood from his spatha. "Know you of this Beremoch? Or his tomb?"

"He knew, no doubt," Orrick said, pointing at Figlio with his chin. "But –"

"Look!" Lior cried. The reddish, S-shaped scar on the back of Figlio's bald head pulsed, swelling, and a bead of dark blood dripped from the bottom curl.

Orrick grabbed up a fallen sword. "Move well back," he said, approaching the Consul. "'Tis a trepanation mark, and recent." He lifted the blade high in both hands and struck down, severing Figlio's head from his body. Blood leaked from the neck, and the scar throbbed, tearing further.

A thick black feeler, like the leg of an enormous cockroach, poked its way out. Wasting no time, the magus pulled a leathern bag from his cloak, slipped it over Figlio's head, and tied it shut with a rawhide thong.

Albian turned away. "I've never been more thankful for an empty belly."

Though Orrick held the bag at arm's length, it thrashed feebly, buzzing.

"What can you tell us?" Lior asked, eyes on the bag.

Orrick turned in a slow circle, step by step. "Little. My former master practiced trepanation in the Witch-Empress Ankhet's court, but never shared the art with me. The sisters of Aesculapius perform such surgeries in rare cases today, but not so sloppily." He waved the wriggling bag left and right, watching it. "Someone — perhaps Tarquin — cut away a section of the Consul's skull and placed something terrible into his brain."

After a long look at him, face white, Lior said, "And Tarquin means to do the same to the Princess." He headed for the side door. "We must find them. I will go east, deeper into the woods. Albian, you go west. Find me if —"

"No need," Orrick said, and shook the bag. "The creature inside strains to the southeast, no matter which way I turn. It seeks to return home, I think. We will use it as a lodestone, and it will guide us to Beremoch's tomb."

Albian swallowed with an audible click. "Lovely."

*

Crouched in the saddle, reins in one hand and a pitch-soaked torch in the other, Lior thanked the gods that he'd forgotten to fasten his helm's chin-strap, else he'd right now be on the forest floor with a broken neck. His horse wouldn't run headlong into any tree trunks, but low-hanging branches were the least of its concerns, unlike its rider. Shoulders hunched, Albian thundered behind on his roan warhorse, peering out from under the rim of his helmet.

Orrick, holding aloft the leathern bag containing Figlio's head, led them according to which way the thing inside pulled. In the moonless night, the yellow handprints on his ragged scarlet cloak reflected just enough starlight for Lior to follow him by.

*Tarquin is ravishing her amid the slime and rot of Beremoch's tomb.*

Lior silently told Orrick to ride faster.

Over the roar of galloping hooves, a high, insectile buzzing made itself heard, setting Lior's teeth on edge. He'd noticed the noise on their journey to the manse, but this was much louder, aggressive. Hostile. Bees typically slumbered after sundown —

Small, hissing shapes shot at him in the dark, exploding against his lorica where they didn't cling to his face and hands. Shouting curses against the pain of their stingers, he swung his torch to wave them off. Smoke burned his eyes, his lungs. He ducked his head, praying that the air would clear.

The buzzing grew deeper, louder, a vibration that rattled his bones. To his left, dimly glimpsed between the cedars, rose a massive swarm of black wasps the size of sparrows. As one, the insects raced toward them.

He couldn't tell if Albian remained behind or had been flung off his horse in the chaos. When Orrick glanced over his shoulder at the pursuing swarm, it occurred to Lior to bring his horse to a halt, hold off the things with iron and fire as long as his strength held out. It would be a horrible death, but his oath to Byzantium demanded sacrifice, when required. They didn't need him; a magus and an Optio of the Cohorts should be able to rescue—

"They seek the Consul's head!" shouted Orrick. "Ride southeast, toward the star Sirius! I will draw them off!" Without waiting for a reply, he angled to the west, and in moments was lost in the trees.

When the swarm of malformed wasps arrowed away in pursuit of the magus, Lior felt relief, and then shame. As Centurion, it had been properly his task to lead, not Orrick's.

The trees grew sparser, and those that remained were pale, stunted things, their trunks contorted in irregular humps. Sirius glittered above, the brightest spot in the southeast corner of the sky. Hoofbeats thudded behind him: Albian, his lorica stained black by insect ichor. Foam dripped from his horse's mouth. Its dark coat gleamed with lather.

They broke through the tree line onto a rocky plain studded with man-high cairns that time had eroded into mounds of tumbled stone. Clouds crept in from the east, obscuring the stars.

Faced with a labyrinth of unmarked graves, Lior slowed his horse to a walk.

"Southeast's that way, sir," Albian said, pointing as he rode up alongside.

"Just so." Lior handed him the torch, wiped sweat from his face, and shook his head. "Damn me for letting Orrick carry the Consul's head. He insisted, and I didn't argue."

"He'll be all right, sir. It's not the first time he's been dead."

Straightening in the saddle to peer over the tops of the cairns, Lior frowned. "See you anything, like the door to a tomb?"

"The 9th's magus isn't often wrong. If we keep to the southeast like he said, we may find it," Albian said.

Lior scowled up at the cloud-shrouded sky and set off again, picking his way around the ragged mounds of stone. Every moment that passed was another opportunity for Tarquin to perform some kind of disgusting surgery on the Emperor's daughter, but if they went faster, they might miss the tomb's entrance in the dark. Biting back a curse, he urged his horse into a trot.

Had they already passed this mound? The top that resembled a face in profile looked familiar. He'd get a better view by climbing one of these mounds and—

"Left!" Albian shouted. "I see something."

Slowing, Lior scanned the narrow paths between cairns until he spied it: Princess Lucia's Bona Dea fibula, tossed onto the side of a mound. He circled the heap of rocks, heart thundering in his chest, only to find nothing. No door, no entrance, no—

A faint nickering, to his right.

He moved around the rightmost cairn to a small clearing.

A massive black horse, flanks wet and head lolling, stood by a scattering of rocks. At the edge of the pile, near a hole in the ground, lay a huge, round slab of stone, engraved with symbols that had been marred by a chisel.

Albian dismounted and brought the guttering torch near the slab. "He's stronger than I thought."

Lior slipped to the ground, bent, and dragged his fingertips along the slab's ruined markings. "Holy symbols. Jupiter, Diana, even dead Apollo." He reached for the torch and moved it closer to the hole. Rough stairs had been cut into the stone, descending into blackness. "Hurry," he said, and entered the tunnel.

The air turned fetid, unpleasantly warm. Despite the tunnel's width, Lior found himself hunching his shoulders to avoid scraping against the walls as they descended. Recollections of the Thucer Clan disaster twisted his guts: crouching underground, his life measured in seconds.

Like the slab, the tunnel was carved with holy symbols, though similarly spoiled. A sloppy hand had scrawled the name BEREMOCH in dripping, brownish letters throughout.

Tilting his head away from the torch, Albian muttered, "Whoever this Beremoch is, them what built his tomb definitely didn't want him getting out."

"Tarquin will have much to answer for," Lior replied.

A flickering reddish glow lit the tunnel from below.

Lior drew his sword.

Wisps of foul-smelling smoke thickened the air, putting cinders into his throat.

The scrape of stone on stone, followed by a guttural laugh.

A high, despairing shriek.

With a curse, Lior leapt carelessly down the rest of the stairs, taking them two at a time. Albian at his heels, he burst through a round doorway into a vaulted stone chamber.

Square, its walls covered in now-familiar holy symbols marred by chisel and filth, the brazier-lit tomb was dominated by the screaming Lucia, bound to a huge granite catafalque in the centre. Betrothal gown torn open, eyes wide with horror, her bloody wrists and ankles pulled against the ropes. The smashed remains of a sarcophagus leaned against the far wall.

Standing over her, his left hand dripping with black maggots, loomed Tarquin. Pale, pockmarked face sweating in the tomb's heat, he glared at the newcomers with lifeless eyes. The braziers' red-orange flames reflected demonic shapes across the riveted plates of his heavy armour, and at his boots lay a withered grey corpse. Body dwarfish and hunched, the ancient thing had a swollen, bulbous head, its crown sawn off and black larvae wriggling from the remains of its skull.

"Cease," Tarquin said to the screaming princess, and struck her across the face with his clean, if gauntleted right hand. Stunned, she fell silent.

"Your Consul is dead, Tarquin," Lior said, dashing forward. "And you –"

Tarquin held his maggot-covered hand close to Lucia's face, turning it so that the black, viscid slime dripped near her cheeks. "No closer. You or your pet."

Lior stopped short, just out of sword's reach. Next to him, Albian froze, javelin over his shoulder.

"Tarquin is dead," Tarquin said, and his mouth shifted into a dreadful smile. "His soul became mine when he heeded my whispers in the Green Wood. He died weeks ago when he opened his own skull to let me in." Without taking his eyes from Lior, he lifted an iron trepanation drill from the catafalque, crusted with clumps of dried blood and hair. "His screams were a delight."

He tossed the drill away, where it clattered into a burning brazier. "You say you slew the Consul? You killed a shell. I was in him, too. As I am in his family. And slaves. And many others, high and low."

"Be you Tarquin or some *thing*, you will not defile the Princess," Lior said, tensing.

"You have no power," Tarquin spat, and lowered his hand to hover a bare inch over Lucia's mouth. "I am not one of your soldiers to be commanded. We ascend, my brothers and I. While the One calls his wayward godlings back to the Throne, we ascend. We have power. You do not. Why else could I make myself heard again? To live again? The time of mortal kingdoms—of Byzantium and Aegyptus and Aztlan—is over. We ascend, and you will fall –"

At the barest of nods from Lior, Albian cast his javelin. It was a clumsy throw, one that Tarquin easily ducked, but it distracted him long enough for Lior to launch himself at the man in a hard shove that sent him stumbling away from the bound princess.

Lior had time to cut Lucia's ropes before Tarquin spun to face him, sword drawn. The man's white face betrayed neither anger nor dismay, and rather than attack Lior, he swung at Lucia's unprotected arm.

Lior's attempt to block it drove his sword against the corner of the catafalque, notching the edge. He struck Tarquin's face with the pommel, snapping his head back, and shoved him again to gain distance. "Get her out of here!" he barked at Albian.

Nose sheeting blood, Tarquin launched a flurry of blows, forehand and backhand. What he lacked in finesse he more than made up for in speed and strength, and he drove Lior backward, step by step, toward a brazier seething with foul smoke. Eyes streaming, Lior caught a glimpse of Albian disappearing up the steps, Lucia over his shoulder in an undignified over-the-shoulder carry.

Tarquin pressed his advantage, hacking again and again. Each blow numbed Lior's arm further. Half-blinded, pushed against the edge of the flaming brazier, agony seared his back. His strikes, when they hit, glanced harmlessly off the man's heavy greaves and riveted cuirass. Desperately, he ground his blade against Tarquin's so the notch in his sword caught the edge, turning the man's wrist.

Lior's blade broke under the pressure, but it gave him the opening to dive past. As he hit the floor, his hand touched something, and his fingers closed around it:

Albian's javelin. Shouting, Tarquin spun to face him, slashing in a decapitating arc. With Lior an inch out of sword's reach, the blade whistled past, turning Tarquin halfway around.

It was the opening Lior needed. Taking the javelin in both hands, he drove forward, putting his entire body weight into a thrust at Tarquin's armpit. The point went home, punching through both mail and body in an explosion of scarlet. Armour clattering, Tarquin collapsed against the brazier, slid off, and fell to the stone floor.

Stepping back, arming moisture from his eyes, Lior watched the man try to stand. All that moved were his arms, and they failed to help him rise. The javelin must have severed his spine.

"Byzantium," Tarquin grated, "is already mine." His upper chest heaved.

Remembering what the Consul had tried to do in extremis, Lior lashed out with a hobnailed sandal, toppling the brazier onto the man before he could vomit a torrent of maggots. Tarquin thrashed and screamed, covered in in burning coals.

The air grew heavy with smoke. Coughing, Lior bent to pick up Tarquin's sword: a soldier's weapon, heavy like the man's armour, with a cruciform brass hilt and a pommel in the shape of a snarling dog's head. It would do until he returned to camp. Moving quickly, he kicked over the other braziers, making sure to set the ancient dwarf-thing's corpse ablaze before pounding up the steps toward cleaner air.

"Albian! Do you –"

Albian lay in a massive pool of blood on the stony ground next to the bodies of two horses: Tarquin's and his own. Both Lior's horse and the princess were gone. Dropping his sword, he moved to check on Albian, and noticed that while the horses' throats were cut, the Optio didn't have a wound on him. The blood on the ground wasn't his. A pulse beat in his neck. He still lived, but where was the princess?

Lungs still clogged from the nauseating smoke in the tomb, Lior scrambled up the closest cairn. The rough stones scraped his fingers bloody. Far off, a blur in the night's dark, he spied a mounted figure in white disappearing into the Green Wood.

It had to be Lucia. Intimations of betrayal gnawed at the back of his mind, but he shut his eyes against them and stood and coughed until his breathing evened out.

By the time he climbed down, Albian was sitting up, rubbing his throat.

The Optio tried to speak, coughed, and tried again. "Why's the ground all wet?" he croaked.

"It's horse blood." Lior held out a hand to help him up.

"Lovely." Albian got to his feet and swayed there. "She—the princess, sir—when I went to put her down, she wrapped her arms 'round my throat and wouldn't let go." His thick-fingered hands clenched into fists. "At first I thought she was scared. But then I could barely breathe, and I didn't want to hurt her, and I tried to pull her off, but I couldn't." He stuck out his jaw. "A girl not even half my weight was stronger'n I was."

Once again he rubbed his throat. "Things started going dark. Darker than now, I mean. Last thing I saw before I went out was her eyes. They…they were like Tarquin's, sir. Like a shark's."

Leading them away from the smoke pouring from the tomb's entrance, Lior said, "Well, Optio, she didn't know how hard it is to strangle a man of the Cohorts. Easier to choke a lion."

A reluctant half-smile jerked Albian's mouth. "That's right, sir. But she—I guess…"

"Yes," Lior said, and moved to undo the dead roan's harness. "It seems this Beremoch creature can get inside other places than the head. We were too late to save her. Tarquin was toying with me in our fight. Giving her time to flee." He pulled the travel pack free and handed it to Albian. "The stories she will tell her father the Emperor won't be flattering to either of us."

Albian stared at him in horror. "Gods, no."

"Yes."

"But…I've been a man of the Cohorts my entire life. What—I mean, how…"

Lior stooped to pick up his new sword. "Returning home would be unwise." He lifted it, squinting at the edge in the dim light of the cloud-swathed stars. "Perhaps mercenary work would suit us."

Albian's face grew mulish, then resigned. "Perhaps, sir. In any event, I'm not going back through the Green Wood."

"West it is, then."

"Yes, sir."

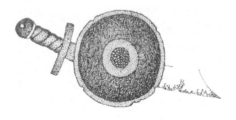

# DEMONIC
## *Phil Emery*

Shadows padded through the sweltering mass of frond and vine like soft predators. During the days these were disregarded by the hardened company of warriors as they marched deeper into the jungle. But in the still and sweltering nights the shadows became sounds – snarls and chitterings and eerie calls. It was in the darkness that tempers and imaginations frayed and even those not on watch struggled to sleep.

Except for Zain.

Zain was younger than most but as hardened as any. Shadows did not discomfort him. He carried his own. If sleep came he allowed it. If not he turned onto his back and gazed at the moon and shaped both inward and outward darkness into poetry. For Zain was as much poet as swordsman.

\*

Sebalo was more restive. Moisture pulsed nervously from his skin. He stared through the trees at the swollen moon, named Fesbur in the Kelvion tongue, glowing like pustular silver, and listened. The Kesnarat region of Balesh was no place for a squad of clean-killing Kelvion warriors. Sebalo's company had travelled down the coast but had no option other than to pass through the Balesh jungle to return the first princess of Jadar to her realm on Balesh's northern edge. Until one night she'd vanished together with several of his comrades.

Deserters, the commander had cursed, but Sebalo was less sure. Kesnarat was haunted by tales. There were temples, it was said, built by a lost race to worship equally lost gods, desecrated, it was said, by time and other forces. And there were legends of a dispossessed ghost tribe who fled their first more northerly homeland after unleashing a sorcerous evil which had turned it into a dead sea. They now supposedly hid in the Balesh jungle still in fear. And their fear had changed them. Not just in their hearts – their shapes had turned into fear, so vague stories told. Sebalo was not the only one to have heard leathern-winged whispers in the canopy.

Other sounds dripped down from the branches and lianas. He heard them now. Hot and slick and evil and deathly, they dropped onto and twisted around him as he lay shuddering. He seemed to hear 'he's dead' worming through his mind. But he wasn't. No, he wasn't, because he was standing now and he had a sword in his hand. Not as fine a sword as, say, Zain's, nor was he as fine a swordsman, yet he wasn't dead, because how could you ache with so much terror and not be living? And his comrades, they were living too, because they were hacking about them in the night at the same horror that was drowning Sebalo, all except the commander, who *was* dead, because Sebalo glimpsed something hideous swoop down from the blackness of the canopy and rip his head from his neck as he stood and loosed arrows into the jungle like a madman. Then, as Sebalo watched, the decapitating nightmare came at *him* and he sliced at it and it shrank back but then came at him again, and again he heard 'he's dead', and so he sliced at the words as nothingness swept over him.

\*

"He's dead." Commander Ebellon looked down at Sebalo's lifeless face, where the blood had ceased trickling feebly from nose and mouth and eyes. "The fever takes one more." Three now, of the fifteen strong squad that left Kelvion to stealthily return the princess to her land. Another five had deserted. Seven remained. "Zain – come with me," he snapped.

It was Ebellon's habit to take his second-in-command aside to consult, away from earshot of the rest of the squad. It had been so when the deserter Draymon had been his second. It remained so with Zain. The commander twitched as he spoke and paced in the nearby damp root-infested parody of a clearing. He was a brusque, brittle man. Even though he couldn't see his face in the gloom, Zain remembered that even Ebellon's eyes sometimes seemed to sweat.

Jadar and Kelvion were both minor powers, both with pretentions ("treasonous talk!" Ebellon hissed at Zain as he pointed this out). This giving the realms a bond of a kind. Jadar had Balesh at its southern skirts and so ready access to the wealth beneath its jungle wilderness. More northerly Kelvion had slaves to gather and technology to shape that wealth. Toying with politics, the queen of Jadar, wanting to exploit the relationship still further had sent her eldest daughter to talk with the king of Kelvion in secret. Not all her court would approve if they had known. "Perhaps they did know," breathed Ebellon. "Perhaps Draymon and the other deserters have abducted the princess at the behest and in the pay of a younger rival sister, rather than see her returned from her ambassadorship in Kelvion?"

A leathern rush spattered through the canopy above. Ebellon spasmed.

"Or perhaps it was the ghost tribe of Balesh," Zain offered levelly.

The moment's pause suggested Ebellon considered believing. Then he hawked. Spat. "No, no. Draymon has taken her. He knows Jadar and Balesh, supervised the mining here some time before, so would've had opportunities to develop relationships, find temptations in the gold raked out of this hellpit of a realm." Ebellon surged from the edge of the clearing back to Zain. His voice prickled with barely suppressed anger and despair. "For all we know he may already have killed the princess."

"If that were so," Zain reasoned, "we'd've woken to find her corpse in camp this morning rather than gone. More likely Draymon's taken her for ransom from the queen."

That pacified the commander a fraction and he paced away again, calmer. "A beautiful girl," he muttered, almost softly. "I've heard, do you know, as a poet you would know, if it's true that all the poetry of Jadar is love poetry – is that so?"

"Aye. They're called ghazal."

"Did you ever write a poem about her?"

"I don't write ghazals."

"You're an ashen-hearted bastard, Zain."

Another leathern spatter.

A glimpse of silhouetted wings against the moon.

Ebellon was gone.

The aftermath of the rush was almost a silence. Then Ebellon's scream soared above. The other soldiers were in the clearing as he screamed again and the jungle flared into clamour.

Zain drove in pursuit through the chitterings and screeches followed by the rest of the squad, guided only by yelps of moonlight, somehow holding on to the shrieks of the commander. Their jungle gear was only light wicker shields and bows and the swords with which they hacked away any hindering growth of frond or thorny liana and they moved swiftly.

The cries were hardly human when they dwindled to nothing.

But by then flickers of torchlight could be seen through the trees.

The soldiers emerged at the base of steps. Flames bloomed in cresset cages flanking a vast cascade of malachite treads narrowing to an open fronted building high above. One of the desecrated temples of Kesnarat. Five figures occupied the steps. Draymon stood near the top, as if he had just emerged. Below him the four who had deserted with him. Between leader and followers lay what remained of Ebellon. It was a shredded mess of a man, hardly a corpse. Draymon's followers, including Hekkiem, his lover, stood with sword and shield ready yet strangely hesitant. As if they had forgotten their use. They'd clearly witnessed what had discarded Ebellon on the steps and, from the trail of what blood remained, had disappeared into the temple. Their faces held the same hesitation as their bladearms, as if they no longer knew what to do with their sight. But Draymon only grinned, black-toothed, at Zain. His sword was also ready. As an affectation of arrogance he had once paid a Balesh shaman to fuse a shrunken skull to the hilt as a guard. And that too seemed to grin.

"The princess?" asked Zain.

Draymon gestured at the temple, his croaking agnail of a voice lounging at the back of his muscular throat. "She's inside." Then he shrugged away his shield and swept his sword in a mocking salute which meant that Zain's entrance had to be won.

Zain climbed slowly, discarding his own shield, leaving his squad with their swords also drawn but as equally hesitant as the deserters. Zain reached the latter and they parted as he passed them.

"My guardian fulfils its duties well," chuckled Draymon, nodding at Ebellon.

"He was in league with you, of course," said Zain.

"Of course, but how did you know?"

Zain took another step. "He was no tracker, but brought us here unerringly." He contemptuously flicked Ebellon's gory tatter with his blade as he stepped past. "One way or another. He knew where you were going." Draymon laughed and made the first sword stroke. Both deserters and soldiers watched. If any squadman was a match for Zain it was Draymon...

"Yes! Ebellon was in on the scheme, or – thought he was!"

"And you betrayed him."

"Who would've thought he had the courage to come afterrrrevenge? A fool who didn't – deserve! A part – oftheprize."

"Part of the ransom for the –"

"Princess. Yes, ransom of a kind. By my beard! More a sacrifice!"

"Ah – sacrifice, Draymon, sacrifice?"

Zain's question hung unanswered as if it were Draymon's final parry. His grunt was echoed by his lover's cry as his sword and knees dropped to the steps. She dove to his side and cradled him. "Is the princess still alive?" intoned his slayer.

Draymon lifted his dying hand to grope the stub of the wiry beard that Zain's blade had sheared moments before his ribcage. He coughed. "I would've made you the offer I made Ebellon," he mumbled softly. "But your oath of duty is... like your blade... straight edged..."

Without looking back Zain climbed to the temple entrance, only glancing as he did at the torches. But the slender metal stalks they were fixed upon were plainly fixed into the malachite beyond freeing.

Darkness awaited, then.

But not quite yet.

Moonlight flooded the spacious atrium, Fesbur's leprous shed bathing the flagstones. The same lapis-lazuli as the entrance, unsullied, undecayed, betokening an ancient, sanctified past. But as Zain had passed the threshold he'd sensed an intangible desecration beyond his poetry to describe. Some poets used costly paper or parchment to set their verses in ink, but Zain was a swordsman, a traveller in places where paper and quill were less precious than panoply and blade. He scribed his words in his head, tortured them or perhaps was tortured by them, invisibly.

What kind of temple was this? What kind of master had Draymon served?

There was no altar for a god in the atrium. Nothing but the smear of Ebellon's blood snaking along the lapis-lazuli floor. Zain followed it and passed through an inner portal almost without realizing and blackness closed around him like one of the sinister jungle plants he'd seen enfold insects.

However, the passageway was narrow, and no more guidance was needed. Zain had a shallow cut across his thigh from one of Draymon's rangy sword sweeps but what blood there was soaked into his breeks without adding to Ebellon's now-useless sanguinary vestige which would surely dribble out soon. Even his limp eased as he went blindly on.

Yet soon he realized that rather than peter out the trail continued. There was a slight slipperiness underneath his footfalls. And there was a familiar tang in nostril and mouth. Copper. Iron. Zain had tasted it in battle many times. And strangely both the slipperiness and the tang were growing. The knowledge prickled. Even if Ebellon had so much blood in him, most of it would surely have been left on the malachite outside.

Sometimes a light which was not torchlight flared ahead in the passage and in that moment he noticed that the temple walls had images. The images somehow recalled cave paintings he'd once seen when he had joined a force of Shastar knights tasked to extirpate a race of troglodyte cannibals in the Barg Spine mountains. But those faecal daubs had only engendered a leaden bolus of disgust in his gut. The apprehension these images engendered, akin to that at the temple's threshold, this was...

Eventually Zain's senses emerged into another impression. That the narrow penetralia and even the lapis-lazuli floor was gone, leaving only the blood trail, now as wide as the passage had been, stretching into a bridge? He halted. Warding premonition he edged to the very brink of the bridge. Looked down. Somewhere, on his way through the temple, his eyes had adjusted to the dark in a way that enabled him to distinguish between darknesses. What he saw below was a darkness that subtly *flowed*.

Then the light which was not torchlight flared again, brighter, and he saw the princess there, underneath the bridge in the *stream*, beautiful as Ebellon had said, not moving but motionlessly staring up, not stabbed or burnt or drowned but already sacrificed. Her eyes stared up, pleading into some horror beyond mystery which Zain had no wish to put into stanzas.

Only when he tore his eyes away could he see the thing on the bridge which awaited him. Its eyes glowed, the source of the moments of not-torchlight. Barbed cinnabar. (*baleful?*) (*baneful?*) Their glare hid what was behind them. It snarled, this thing which Draymon had served and thus served him. Zain almost smiled. Men worship gods, women, riches, why not demons? Zain wondered what kind of reward he had been promised, a promise that had swayed the four who had turned renegade with him. Perhaps simply wealth? The mines of Balesh yielded not just gold but iron and copper ore. But Zain remembered Draymon's twisted grin and suspected that his own reward would've been something more vile.

Then, in a leathern winged flurry, the demon attacked.

Zain's lip curled. 'Leathern' was inadequate – not skin, alive or dead. Nor were its 'wings' true pinions, more membranous fans of talon.

Zain's blade struggled as much as his thoughts. Draymon's bounding footwork, contrasting bizarrely with his more sophisticated bladeplay, was unpredictable enough but still human. Yet why should a demon move as a human, the cadence of onslaught not be different? So, what use a lifetime of sword technique?

How do you parry damnation?

How do you wound hell?

And how could the demonic be put into language? Though Zain had read all the great poets of the realms of the Tremaldikkan, he'd long been taunted by a legend of an esoteric school of poetry devoted to describing demons.

It snarled again. A batlike maw, an abyss going for the throat, widening and snapping (*pouncing?*), rushing, surging. And the stench. As if blood were (*vomit? venom?*) naphtha. Was it the fetor of the demon's breath or of the thing itself carried on the draught of its passing lunges? And those lunges were also abhuman, both swifter and almost 'translucent' if he could apply that word? It seemed fitting. But the gestating poem was an infuriating syncope of doubts in his head, mirroring his body's hurts. It was only in the aftermath of the creature's attacks that Zain could know if he'd been cut or gored or not. Sometimes not even then. He glanced at the back of the sword hand he could barely see. It burned. But from some kind of petty sore or a deeper injury? Did his parries work thorough some warrior's occult instinct or was he being mocked? Could any quillon thwart something demonic?

Could he even flee? The very manifesting of the thought chilled him, made him question who he was, but even this was rivalled by another question, a shard of terror – if this was indeed a bridge, what might be on the other side? From the day he'd first picked up a sword Zain had willingly ridden fear like a half-broken destrier, but this was a different breed. Yet he was doubly armed. Many warriors used the flames of berserker fury to conquer fear, but he had twin furies burning. Two kindred rages for perfection. Sword and poem.

The first was assuaged when his blade finally bit into the demon, a similar stroke to the one that had felled Draymon. The feel of the cut was more like bone than flesh, though unlike the texture of bone when his blade had sheered off Draymon's skull hiltguard. Nor was it the scrape of ribcage bone parting with the stroke that had felled him. And beyond the feel, the sound differed. No slathery (*slathering?*) sucking of steel into vital, more the sibilance of blade returning to scabbard. Not even that, no, something,

something, and then, as he stood over the monster, he had it! Its death-snarl, like all the other snarls, had the slithering ring of unsheathing...

Of course!

Some demons are *forged* things. Like swords.

The light from those glowing eyes had died with the rest of it and again darkness held full sway in the temple, but some instinct made Zain backstep.

Where the carcass had fallen there was a febrile stir of movement. Zain ran, and the twitching movement came after him. Only when he reached the moon-drenched atrium did he see what skittered behind. A spidery spate of demon sullage, a metallic glistening flood of carapaces.

The flood spilled out onto the steps. Zain pelted past Draymon's body, still cradled by his lover, who glared at him murderously, even as the devouring sullage swamped her, even as Hekkiem managed to shriek before the flood choked her gullet, "You're an ashen-hearted bastard, Zain!"

But Zain didn't hear as he plunged down into the rainforest, followed by the rest of his squad and the three remaining deserters, now deserting once again. Though unlike all of them he fled not from panic but elation.

Of course!

*Some demons are forged things – like swords – or poems.*

\*

Shadows padded through the sweltering mass of frond and vine like soft predators. In the days these were disregarded by the remnants of the troop. They were all deserters now; there was no returning to Jadar or Kelvion without the princess. As they straggled their way out of the jungle in the sweltering nights the shadows again became sounds, snarls and chitterings and eerie calls. But now in the darkness it was memories that frayed rather than imagination. And even those not on watch still struggled to sleep.

Except for Zain.

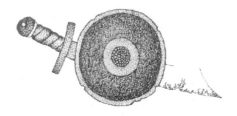

# THE WHIPS OF
# MALMAC
## *H. R. Laurence*

"Thief!"

Hardly an unusual cry in a port, and yet something in the voice caught Heodric's attention. Leaving the horse half-hitched to the wagon, he stepped out into the street beyond the alleyway. The sparse crowds paid no heed to the thief-cry, nor to the tall barbarian who stood alert and listening – it was nearing day's-end, and in the Pauper's Quarter one kept one's head down, or risked the throat that bore it.

"Thief!"

It was a harsh tone, like chain links slipping across one another. Heodric had not heard a voice like that since -

A slight noise somewhere above, almost drowned by crying gulls. The horse whickered. Heodric raised his eyes. In the Pauper's Quarter the buildings were built high and aimless, stacked like children's building blocks, and across and between them a slim whip-sharp figure was descending, leaping from awning to windowsill to ledge with staggering speed and confidence. Heodric was no mean climber, but the girl – there was no mistaking it, though she wore a man's breeches and jerkin – moved with a skill that astonished him, her dark hair flying proud behind her like a prince's banner.

She was followed. A hunched shape leapt after her, a good distance behind but gaining, finding purchase on surfaces where surely there was no grip to be had. The girl's movement was that of an athlete, body honed by years of practice. In the gait of the thing that followed her, Heodric saw sorcery. His jaw set. He didn't much care for sorcery.

Quick strides took him back to the wagon. His sword lay hidden beneath the straw rushes in the back: he swept them aside and propped it against the wagon with the hilt in easy reach, knowing that he was about to involve himself in business not his own, and accepting of the choice. The alley was all-but empty, save for broken mud-bricks, slop tossed from the rooms above, and a dry water barrel which he picked up and set in the back of the wagon. The walls above rose steep and sheer for some thirty feet before they became jagged outcrops of brick and beam, half-built or half-demolished. The girl came vaulting through them, and Heodric whistled.

She stopped and looked down at him, dark eyes narrowing. He motioned to the empty barrel. She made a choice of her own and came down, springing between the narrow walls of the alley with extraordinary speed until she landed on the back of his wagon. Their eyes met for a moment. She gave a quick, curt nod of thanks and hopped into the barrel as neatly as a carnival girl doing tricks.

Heodric slipped the lid into place over her and busied himself hitching the horse. The pursuer would be above him now, scouring the alleyway below for sign of its prey, and he fought the urge to look up. With luck, the beast would pass. He had no wish to draw attention if he could avoid it. There was a scrape of claw on brick, the dusty thud of a jump to the ground. No luck. He turned.

It had landed on all fours, but now it stood, hunched and horrid to look at. It was gnarled thing, all sallow skin and grey-brown hair, an unholy meld of man and dog with a long snouted face like the skull of something ancient. Its fangs were sharp. Its sickly yellow eyes glared at Heodric.

"Thief," it said, its voice the scrape of sword-iron. Heodric felt a tremor down his spine.

"Right enough," he said, keeping his voice calm. "I've thieved in my time. But *your* thief is gone –" he pointed down the alley, away from the wagon "– fled for the city wall."

"Liar," said the skull. One eye blazed at Heodric: the other had rolled horribly in its socket to light upon the barrel. "Liar. Thief."

Heodric snatched his sword up, for there was no point trading words with a beast that had only two of them. The monster sprang at him, and he drove strong to meet it upon his point. It turned in the air. His blow touched nothing, and the vile snout parted, and if Heodric had been a moment slower a mouthful of razors would have closed about his throat.

But Heodric was quick, for all his size. The foul jaws snapped shut on air, and when the creature came down in the dust the barbarian was behind it. He struck: it flung up an arm and to Heodric's amazement steel rang upon steel.

The beast stood. Its claws were twice as long as they had been, and not the talons of an animal but long shining daggers that jutted from the broken fingers of its paws, brought forth by horrid magick. It came at him again, fast and nimble, slashing with one claw and then the other; snapping with its jaws, a whirl of scything devilry.

Heodric had fought swordsmen and he had fought wild beasts: this daemon was halfway between the two and it took all of his skill to parry that first flurry of unpredictable blows. It drove him half the length of the alley before he could halt it, and even then it evaded his stroke with contemptuous ease. For a moment they parted, and Heodric drew breath.

The monster that faced him seemed to have no need of it. Heodric couldn't match its speed, nor its ferocity: if it maintained its torrent of blows it would only be a matter of time before he failed to dodge or parry one. But Heodric was a quick learner, and he had not wasted the first bout. The beast had a gait and rhythm of its own, the same as any man, and he was attuned to it now. When it came at him again he stumbled back, feigning retreat, and then as the beast closed upon him he moved quick and hard and put all of his power into the blows.

He took its arm and then its head. Two strokes. The body of the beast went thrashing to the dust of the street in a gout of blackish blood, and the severed head rolled its eyes to Heodric and blinked once, twice, and then was still and dead.

Heodric took a long breath.

"You can come out," he called. Silence. He walked back to the wagon. The barrel was empty.

"Did you think I'd sit there waiting?" came a lilting voice behind him. He turned: the girl sat on a ledge above the alley, a smile on her lips.

"I'm sorry, swordsman," she said. "I was gone the moment your back turned. I don't like trusting strangers."

She was dark and beautiful, and her mannish clothing sat tight upon a lithe figure. Heodric wiped black blood from his sword with a shred of the wagon's covering, and laid it back beneath the straw.

"You should have gone further," he said. "You've squandered a good start."

She waved a hand: for a moment a knife flickered there and then was gone.

"I don't like to let others fight for me, either," she said. "I thought I might stick it from behind while you held its attention. But you made good enough work alone."

She ran an appraising eye over Heodric: his long golden hair and the square cut of his jaw, the hard muscle of his bare arms. He flattered himself that maybe she thought he could make good work of other things.

"I also thought," she said, after a moment. "that a man with a wagon might be useful if I need to get through the city gates."

He smiled at that. She frowned and tossed something to him. He caught it. A golden ring set with a small blue stone.

"For your trouble with the beast," she said. "I'll not be in your debt."

Heodric studied the ring. He knew nothing of stones and their value, but he could tell the metalwork was very fine. It was good pay for hard work.

"How are you called, girl?" he asked. She drew herself up, tall and proud.

"Are you from so far away," she said, "that you've not heard of Zivia the Cat?"

He had heard of her – the Queen of Thieves, who could slip any crack and climb any wall, whose renown had spread all along the coast. From the stories she was a demi-goddess, a sorceress – and here was this pretty girl of little more than twenty summers, declaring her name.

"Whose ring was this, Zivia?" he asked. A small black bag bulged at her hip: he would wager it contained a small stolen fortune. The Queen of Thieves smirked at him.

"Why, who else but the fat toad in the harbour?"

Who else indeed. The newly-appointed Zyrentian Governor was in the midst of a tour of his province, sailing down the coast on his pleasure-barge and gracing every port and fishing village with the hefty expense of his presence. His ship, too vast for the harbour, had been resupplying for the past two days at the end of a new-built pier, and Port Usk was thick with soldiers to protect it.

"He's come ashore?" said Heodric. Zivia scoffed.

"Hardly! I swam out last night and paid a visit to his cabin. A full complement of soldiers aboard, a dozen guests, a brace of doxies in his bed – and not a soul of them knew until the morning."

Heodric looked back at the body of the beast in the alley.

"Something knows now," he said. "That thing was no port watchman."

"It was a pet of Malmac's," said Zivia, as casually as she might recall an old and foolish acquaintance of hers. Heodric marvelled at that. He had known scarred sell-swords to pale at the name of Malmac.

"The Wizard's here?"

"They'd not have tracked me without sorcery," said Zivia. "He's here. More reason to be gone soon."

Heodric patted the barrel. "Climb in," he said. "I'll carry you as far as I'm going."

She landed in the dust of the alley with the grace of an acrobat.

"Fine fellow!" she said. "It'll be worth your trouble."

*

When he entered Port Usk, Heodric had told the guards on the gate that he was a merchant's man there to collect cargo, and though his build and bearing showed him to be a warrior they had let him pass. He had a simple, friendly air, and his blue eyes were warm: barbarian though he was he seemed easy to trust. Perhaps they thought it not unlikely that a swordsman be sent to collect valuable goods, or perhaps they were overtasked and saw no good cause to challenge him. Perhaps, at some level, they had sensed that it might be dangerous to do so.

Had those same guards seen Heodric now their suspicions would have been confirmed. After three days his cart still carried no goods, except for the person of a wanted thief, and now all the warmth was gone from his aspect: he was grim and set, a man who had seen a risky path ahead of him and meant to take it whatever the cost.

He had brought his cart to the hills overlooking the bay, just within the city walls, only a short distance from the gate. Beside him, a tavern heaved with workers eager to spend their day's wage, but there was no thought of merrymaking in Heodric.

His gaze was set on the bay below, where in the late afternoon sun the Governor's barge sat like a floating palace on a golden sea. It was a huge, bloated craft, at least twice the height and width of the military triremes that escorted it. Hundreds of oars bristled from its fat sides like hairs on a boar's belly, and above the enclosed rowing decks was a second level the length of the whole vessel, born upon wooden supports carved in the form of kneeling slaves. The top deck was wide and open, decorated with flowering plants and flying flags, hanging lanterns and strings of ribbons, and at either end of the vessel rose terraced towers of cabins.

The horse snorted. Heodric patted its neck, the patient presence of the creature reassuring him against any unease he might have felt. He knocked once on the side of the wagon. Zivia emerged a moment later. Her pretty face clouded with confusion.

"But we've not left the town," she said. "Below is the very boat I stole from!"

"Yes," said Heodric. "I think they'll pay me very well for the thief, delivered alive."

She was quick: quicker than he'd expected. When he caught her wrist the knife was a half-inch from his throat.

"Beast!" she spat. "Is this how you treat a deal?"

"We had no deal," said Heodric gently, prizing the blade from her fingers. "I said I'd carry you as far as I went – and I'm going to that ship."

She hissed like the cat she was named for. A second blade appeared in her free hand: a sliver of iron as fine and sharp as a needle. He struck her once and the stiletto clattered away on the paving stones, followed a moment later by its unconscious mistress.

"Here," called a man, thickset and beefy, emerging from the tavern, his leather apron declaring him the owner. "None of that in my yard."

Heodric turned, and the taverner appraised his height and width and bearing, and quickly decided that perhaps this was no business of his after all. Heodric tossed him a coin.

"See my horse stabled, and the wagon kept safe," he said. "And bring me some rope."

Word spread quickly. By the time he reached the pier gawping onlookers were following him, and many more were waiting at the waterside, the whole throng of them buzzing with rumour. Heodric carried Zivia's bound form across his shoulders, and the bag of jewels swung from his free hand, and the crowd fell silent as they saw him.

There was no love for Governor or thief-taker in this place, and the quiet was sullen and full of threat. None challenged him openly. Heodric had left his sword in the wagon, beneath the straws there, but even unarmed there was no mistaking that he was dangerous. He walked tall, and met the gaze of those who glowered at him.

An iron gate controlled access to the pier. Heodric walked calmly up to it and told the guards there that he would speak with their master. They fingered their spears nervously. This was a calm province, but it had been conquered within memory, and any unexpected crowd still carried with it the threat of riot and sedition. Zivia groaned behind Heodric's back, beginning to stir into consciousness. The crowd murmured with discontent.

"I think you'd best let me in," said Heodric. "I have no weapon, but I can't speak for them."

It was growing dark by then and all along the wharf slaves were lighting hanging lamps against the dying light. The guards closed the gate behind him quickly. They took Zivia, and led Heodric out to where the massive barge was moored, its second deck just about level with the pier. A shuttered window had been thrown open, so that the two men who stood there could speak to him.

One was the Governor, just the fat toad Zivia had named him. A flabby young man with a gold chain of office about his neck and the affected boredom of great wealth, he ruled the whole coast, and between banquets and courtesans and other entertainments he occasionally gave the job his attention. Beside him, just as finely dressed but gaunt and thin and alert, was Malmac the Wizard, Minister of Punishments. The city guards and the secret police and the torturers all answered to him, and the word was that he had a special inclination to the latter.

The guards had Heodric stop, and one scurried up the gangplank to deliver the Governor the bag of jewels. He poured them out onto the deck and looked down at them.

Then he turned to Heodric, who stood tall with his hands clasped before him.

"This is good work, fellow," he said. "You'll be rewarded. This cat you caught has quite the reputation."

His lazy eyes rose; the guards were bringing Zivia along the pier at spear-point. If she was frightened, it didn't show. Her head was high and proud and she met the gaze of her captors with cool contempt. Only when her eyes lighted on Heodric was there a flicker of fury. The guards pushed her to her knees beside him.

"I hope you get a good price," she said softly, not looking at him. "But spend it soon. It won't be long before you wake with your throat cut."

The nearest guard clouted her into silence. Malmac the Wizard looked down with shrewd appraising eyes.

"I had a servant following this thief," he said. "It was on her scent from the morning. What became of that servant?"

"I killed the beast," said Heodric, simply. "I'd have been little enough of a man not to, seeing a horror like that seize a young girl. It wasn't until she offered me jewels for passage out of the city that I realised my error."

Zivia snorted, earning herself another clout from the guard. The Wizard nodded slowly.

"Errors can be righted, and new servants made," he said. "And yet I'm curious why a practical man like you didn't simply take what she carried and disappear."

"I thought of it," Heodric admitted. "But I grow tired of thieving. I've a mind to rise in this world, and" – he gestured at the great barge – "you clearly have coin to pay a man what he's worth. I caught your thief and I slew your monster: surely you could use me?"

"I've seen Malmac's pets," said the Governor. "If you truly killed the thing that's a story worth hearing."

He clapped the Wizard's bony shoulder. "Let's have the sell-sword aboard. He can tell us tall tales tonight and if we've no use for him he can go ashore at the next port – with a bag of gold for his trouble." He turned back to Heodric, and looked with a cruel leering smile at Zivia.

"Besides," he said. "He's given us some sport for tonight. Only fair that he should join us for it."

*

The Captain of Guards had Heodric stripped and searched in one of the holds below decks. They burned the jerkin and trousers he had worn in case poison or sorcery was worked into them, and gave him a simple tunic and breeches to wear. Both were a little too small to be comfortable.

The Captain was a tall stern man with a veteran's scars. Like many Zyrene soldiers he was of barbarian stock himself, and he seemed to trust Heodric little. He kept him in the hold a while, asking him questions of his business in Usk. Heodric answered them straight and honest, with a few exceptions, and after an hour or so they let him out onto the deck to join the promised festivities.

It was dark now, and lamps and oil lanterns cast flickering shadows from the plants and statues that dotted the wide wooden expanse of the deck. Near the stern tower a feasting circle had been arranged, where already a double-dozen of the Governor's courtiers lounged on cushioned couches. Heodric sat on his, provoking titters from the reclining dandies about him.

"Your first time in high company?" asked one. He smirked, his face white with chalk-powder. "No fear: we'll get you stretched out soon enough."

Heodric felt some temptation to stretch the man out himself, but before he could respond the Governor had seen him.

"Our hero of the hour!" he said. "Ready to celebrate, no doubt."

"Aye," said Heodric, though he thought little of his drinking companions.

"We'll travel overnight," said the Governor. "Usk is a dull place, don't you think? I hear there's a sweet little village down the coast, where the girls dive naked for pearls in the early dawn. We should arrive just in time: it'll be a pleasant diversion during breakfast."

He saw Heodric's lack of ease. "Why, did you leave something in Usk? Some tavern doxy?" He chuckled. "Put her out of your mind. We have ladies aboard who'll go mad for a big blonde brute like you."

Across the circle a pair of perfumed women giggled behind their veils. Heodric forced a smile.

"I left my sword," he said. "A good blade."

"What a fine thing!" cried the Governor. "The Barbarian whose only love is his blade. Tell us some stories, fellow."

And so Heodric told how he had left his tribe to soldier, and served both allies and enemies of the Zyrentian Emperor, and sold his sword for all sorts of causes. He left out the thieving, for he thought Malmac might not like it, but his stories of travel and battle went down well. Though no great storyteller, he gave his tales with a bluntness that seemed to amuse his audience.

"So terse!" a girl gasped to her paramour, after he told of the pit in Telos, and how he'd killed an ogre there. "I can't tell if he's a braggart or a shy flower."

"Tell us how you slew Malmac's beast," said the Governor. The Wizard was seated beside him, drinking only a little: an expression not quite a scowl drifted over his gaunt face for a moment. Heodric gave the story more or less as it had happened.

"A vicious thing, and a fine fighter it was," he said, nodding at Malmac. "In truth I had luck as well as skill."

The Wizard gave a thin smile.

"You're a modest rogue," he said. "And when I next conjure a servant I'll warn it of you."

The company laughed. The Wizard stood, and they quieted at once.

"A character is missing from this story," Malmac said. "Bring out the thief."

Zivia was led out from one of the many holds, struggling between two burly guards. They flung her down at the centre of the feasting circle. A murmur of cruel appreciation greeted her as she rose to her feet, for her thief's apparel was gone and in its place she wore only the scanty silks of a dancing-girl. A bronze collar bearing the Governor's mark had been set about her neck, and colourful bracelets clattered at her ankles. She glared defiance in the firelight, and Heodric fought the urge look away.

"Ordinarily, I'd flay a thief," drawled the Governor. "But with one this comely it seemed a waste. I thought we might have her dance for us."

Zivia flung back her head.

"I'll dance for no one, you fat fool," she said. "Give me a knife and I'll – ah!"

The crack of a whip across her back had cut her off – and yet she stood alone in the middle of the floor, no one within a spear's length of her. She gazed about in pain and confusion.

"Malmac has devised an amusement," said the Governor. "An innocent little merriment, to make you reconsider your wickedness." A chuckle arose from the audience. They clearly understood their host's taste for merriment.

The Wizard waved a bony hand, thick with rings and bracelets. From the shadows on the deck four sinuous shapes rose from the coils in which they had rested, and slithered forward to surround his lovely captive.

Snakes! thought Heodric, and from the way Zivia flinched she thought the same. But a moment later he saw he was mistaken. Not serpents or tentacles – four fine black whipcords twisted and writhed around Zivia, enchanted to move of their own accord. They rose high and snaked low, circling like cobras.

"Begin!" cried the Governor, and from somewhere in the depths of the barge a drum began to beat, and was joined in a moment by pipes and horns. Zivia gazed in horror as the thin cords rose above her, undulating to the primal rhythm of the music.

Malmac snapped his bony fingers, and the first of the whips slashed down and struck the deck. Zivia leapt: it had missed her bare foot by inches. The next blow came from behind her: she ducked to avoid it as a third stroke whistled past. Then all four of the whips were snapping and lashing at her, perfectly attuned with the music to make her leap and spin and twist in a grotesque parody of dance. The young thief needed all of her nimbleness to avoid the blows, and the fat Governor clapped his hands as he watched her.

"Malmac," he said. "This is superb. You've outdone yourself."

He turned to Heodric, leering. "She gives a fine show, don't you think?"

Heodric shrugged.

"We killed thieves in my village," he said. "Or took a hand, if they were very young."

"Wonderful!" said the Governor. "So primitive."

He stuffed an olive into his mouth, and spat the stone at his unwilling dancer. Zivia shouted curses at them, and the courtiers and functionaries drowned her voice out with taunts, and flung scraps to try and throw her balance. Even the serving-slaves were giggling as gleefully as their master. Heodric wondered at that. He was a practical man and he did what he felt served him best – but there was a deep cruel streak all through this civilised company.

More wine was brought out and while they laughed and drank and ate Malmac's whips kept Zivia dancing to their merciless rhythm. She had little breath to spare for curses now, and her nimble movement was beginning to look laboured. At last a hard blow caught her across the ankles and with a gasp of pain she tumbled to the deck. The whips rose, poised to strike at her bare back. Malmac raised his hand. Heodric saw that one of the rings upon it glowed white, and seemed to pulse with the movement of the whips.

"They would flay her now, if I let them," the Wizard said. It sounded to Heodric as though he was asking permission.

"A waste of a pretty sweetmeat!" laughed the Governor. "No, Malmac, I'll keep her – she owes me a little more merriment yet."

Malmac lowered his arm, his disappointment barely perceptible, and the whips tumbled like cut strings to the deck. Zivia rose to her knees, her breath heavy and painful. She glared at her captors, at her new owner, and with special hatred at Heodric.

"Bind her tight," said the Governor. "And take her to my cabin."

"You foul thing!" the girl spat as the guards hauled her up. "You -" the curse was stifled as she was bundled struggling into the cabin-tower at the boat's stern.

Something like shame was stabbing at Heodric, but he pressed it down. You know what you're about, he told himself. The Gods gave you this chance. He looked at Malmac, thin-lipped and bitter. While the company had been enjoying their entertainment, the Wizard hadn't smiled at Zivia's torment until the whip caught her. This one was the cruellest of all, he thought. He would need to be very careful around Malmac.

More wine was poured. Heodric drank. He thought they might start to pester him again with questions, but they were drunk and excited and more inclined to prod and poke than talk to him. A tattooed courtesan stroked his bicep and tittered, as the chalk-faced fool from earlier wondered aloud how an unwashed barbarian had such a marvellous head of hair. Heodric felt a deep absence of comfort in this company. A sword and an honest foe would have been a relief.

"Where do I sleep?" he asked.

"The night's young!" protested the Governor, and leered horribly. "And you needn't sleep."

He gestured to the next couch, where two of his slave-girls were casting long doe-eyed glances at Heodric and giggling. When Heodric looked at them they kissed each other, and beckoned him to join.

"I'm a little fuddled," said Heodric, slowly, for the prospect of joining the tawdry show made him feel sick. "And it's been quite a day. I think I will go to bed."

Ignoring a reproachful murmur from the courtiers, he stood, and stumbled, knocking a lamp. A couple of the guests yelped in alarm – but he steadied it and smiled ruefully at his oil-stained tunic.

"Barbarians," said the Governor to one of his flunkies, in what he thought was a low tone. "Always taking their wine too strong and too quick. Steward!" he called. "Show our hero to his berth."

The Captain took Heodric's arm as the steward hurried over.

"Listen, fellow," he said. "I've a dozen men on this deck alone. You've done his Lordship a service, but don't think to pilfer."

"What, and be put to dancing by your Wizard?" said Heodric, trying to stand straight. "I shan't steal from you, Captain, don't fear."

Candle-lanterns hung the whole length of the ship, and the steward led him swaying through pools of light across the dark deck, to the bow of the ship where tents were pitched for the servants to sleep. One of them was his, and he went inside and let the flaps fall after him, and lay down. He could hear the Governor giggle, the noise high and grating, and knew that his hosts would be celebrating for many hours yet.

There was no amount of gold, he thought, that could induce him to enjoy their company.

*

The barge pushed off as the watch-hour neared, with a great slow groan of timber and surf. And a short while after that Heodric sat up, quite sober, and took his blanket and his stripped-off tunic and slipped out of the tent. The barge was moving now, slow and ponderous, the hundreds of oars below a consistent thrum of noise as the lights of Port Usk grew distant. He had no time to delay.

The feast still continued. At the far end of the deck the slim silhouettes of dancing-girls whirled in the firelight, and the soldiers on watch were casting frequent glances in that direction, oblivious to the tall barbarian who slipped through the shadows on deck. Heodric took a candle from the nearest lantern, and slid over the side of the deck-rail. The water below was dark and fast and menacing, at the end of a long drop. But a man's length beneath the rail was the head of one of the kneeling statues, where he could stand quite comfortably.

With a spot of melted wax Heodric stuck the burning candle in place. About it, he wrapped his oil-soaked tunic, tied to the end of the blanket which he then draped over the rail so that it touched the canvas tent on deck. He thought he had the better part of an hour before the candle burned down far enough to ignite the rough fuse.

At last his real work could begin. The oars below hummed, and the sea air was salt and fresh and free of foolishness. He had a thousand handholds to choose from: barely an inch of the ship was unadorned with carved patterns, grotesque heads, spurious decorations. Hand over hand, he made swift passage around the barge to the stern, where the cabins rose highest. Faint music still rose from the deck, though there were fewer voices now.

He grunted a little as he hauled himself up the towering structure at the rear of the ship. The higher he went the smaller the handholds seemed to become, but no matter. Soon Heodric was hanging high above the sea outside the topmost cabin, where tiny delicate windows of stained glass adorned with the Governor's crest left him in no doubt that he had the right room.

He broke one, and went through it into an opulent mess of silk hangings and gold leaf. Half of the cabin was one huge bed, and upon it lay Zivia, tightly bound and gagged, the tousled sheets proof of fruitless struggle with her bonds. Her eyes widened as she saw Heodric. He pressed a finger to his lips.

The room was cluttered – so many things for one man – but after a moment of casting about he found a dagger on the wall. It was a rich man's toy, studded and inlaid with jewels, but sharp enough for simple work.

Zivia watched him with dark, angry eyes. He motioned to her to lie still, and stood in the shadows and waited. The music still played outside. Long moments passed. He wondered if his judgement had been right – and then he heard unsteady steps without.

The Governor came through the door. He leered down at the girl on the bed and opened his mouth, and Heodric put the blade through his chest. The drunken taunt on the Governor's lips became a bloody cough. He fell, and was still. Heodric cleaned the dagger on a corner of the silk sheets before he cut Zivia loose.

"You change your mind with the tide, barbarian," she spat, pulling the gag from her mouth.

"I've not changed my mind once," said Heodric, simply. "I was paid to kill him a month ago and I've followed this ship through five ports since. But the bastard never came ashore." He bent and took the signet ring from the dead man's finger, proof of his deed. "I'm a poor swimmer, and I needed a way to get aboard. You were a gift from the gods, little cat."

"From your gods, maybe," the girl said, sourly. "I'll be asking mine to flay you."

"Rather thank them for me," said Heodric. "How many thieves are given a chance to plunder the same room twice?"

Zivia paused, and looked about the rich trappings.

"Aye," she said. "There is that."

She sat up and tugged the collar about her throat. "Take this off me," she said. "I'll not have it said that his slave robbed him."

He couldn't refuse her that. A moment's work with the dagger, and the circlet was in two pieces on the floor. Zivia the Cat was free again, and she went about her work. She was well-called the Queen of Thieves, for she seemed to have a witch-sense for every nook and crack where something of value lurked. In a mere moments she had recovered every jewel she had stolen before, and more besides. The Governor's silk kerchiefs made for a good sack. As a last flourish she took the chain of office from his fat dead neck and fastened it about her slim waist like a belt.

"Let's be gone," she said. Heodric heard a cry from somewhere distant, the sounds of commotion. His fire had started, a little before he'd imagined it would.

"Aye," he said. "A good idea."

He eased open the cabin door and stepped onto the terrace deck without. Opposite him, smoke and flame rose from the foot of the bow tower and on the deck beneath a chain of frantic men passed buckets to quench it. He turned to the stairs that descended zigzag to the deck – just as the Captain and two guardsmen rounded a corner below, doubtless come to fetch their master. For a moment they stared, and then with a snarl the Captain went to draw the sword at his waist.

"I knew it! You damn dog –"

Zivia sprang over the rail onto the roof of the cabin below, and in a moment had disappeared leaping into the night. Farewell, cat! Heodric thought – and flung himself down the stairs. The Captain swung, and missed, and Heodric's dagger found his throat. The sword clattered away. Heodric thrust the dying man into the falchion-stroke of the first guardsman and dodged the spear-thrust of the second, striking back hard and deadly with the knife. In a moment there were three dead men on the stairway to the Governor's cabin.

Cries rose from the other end of the boat, but none close at hand, no running footsteps or clatter of weapons. Heodric left the dagger and took the Captain's sword. A better fit for him if he needed to fight his way out. He had no concern for the girl: she knew her strength, could doubtless swim to shore even with the golden chain about her waist. It was his own passage he worried about: he would have to find something to serve as a raft, and hope to strike out for land unnoticed while the boat's company fought the fire.

He descended. A handful of frantic half-clad courtiers passed him, fleeing their cabins, but none paid him any mind. The stairway disappeared into a low structure, just before the cabin-tower, and he entered with the sword before him, wary of lurking soldiers.

He found himself in a large dark room, ringed with couches and dim lamps and bowls of grapes and flowers on sculpted pedestals, some of them overturned by fleeing passengers. He stepped onto the richly polished floor, and realised a moment too late that he had sprung a trap. Whistling from the dark it came, and as he span to meet it a sharp pain lanced up his arm. Something bit into his sword hand and held it fast.

Heodric cursed. The whip had wrapped about his wrist and snapped taut, anchored somewhere in the shadows. As he reached to take the blade with his free hand a second lashed down, bloodying his arm and coiling about it and binding his wrists together. He stumbled and cast about for the nearest lamp, thinking to burn the things away – and then a third snakelike cord caught him about the throat and wrenched his head back to see Malmac the Wizard standing in the doorway, the glow of fire behind him.

"Fear not," said Malmac. He plucked a grape from the one of the bowls and bit it in half. "I mean to keep you alive a little while. I want to know who paid you."

Heodric snarled, and the whip about his throat tightened to cut his breath off. The Wizard finished his grape and spat a pip.

"A court rival of the Governor's, I suppose," he said. "No matter. You'll tell me."

He waved his hand, and the white-glowing ring which controlled the whips flickered with light. The bonds hauled down on Heodric, pulling the big man to his knees. He had broken many a rope before, but these thin cords were tough as steel, the magic woven into them easily proof against his muscle. The Wizard circled him.

"I suspected your purpose," he said. "But – a secret between us! - I thought I'd let you go about it. This land needs a strong hand, not a weak fool like him."

Heodric glared at him, the gaunt cruel figure hiding behind his sorcery. The whips cut tight into his arms: he could feel the fingers on his sword hilt becoming numb.

"Of course," said Malmac, "now that your deed is accomplished, it must be punished. Tell me who paid you, and I'll spare you long torment."

A shadow moved somewhere in the dark beyond the Wizard. Heodric's eyes didn't flicker, didn't betray a thing – but he saw her clear as day. Zivia, crouched and ready, the Governor's jewelled dagger in her hand.

"Damn you," he spat at Malmac, the words thick and painful through the strangling knot. Zivia was inching silently closer, and he knew that he had to keep the Wizard's eyes on him. "I stuck the fat pig for fun – and I'll stick you just the same."

Malmac smiled at the futile threat, but the smile soured as Heodric spat at him. He raised a hand to strike the bound barbarian – and then Zivia launched herself like a panther at its prey.

Something snapped across the room and caught her around the midriff, yanking her away from the Wizard. Heodric sagged in his bonds, his hope dying. Three cords bound him: he had forgotten the fourth. Malmac turned to Zivia, as she rose, groggy, reaching for her fallen dagger. He raised his hand and the whip snapped about the girl's neck like a leash.

"The naughty cat," he said. "Were the two of you in league from the start? No matter. Many ways to skin a cat, they say, but we can settle for just the one."

Zivia strained at the choking coil, her fingers inches from the hilt of her dagger.

"Cut me loose," she snarled. "And we'll see who skins who."

The Wizard smirked down at her.

"So the cat has claws," he said. "Does she want to play?"

He waved his hand. The bond at Zivia's neck slackened: without hesitating she snatched up her weapon and lunged for Malmac. The whip tautened just as she came within a swords-length of the sorcerer, stopping her dead. She slashed at it, furious, and it leapt away from her, only to scythe back and sweep her feet from beneath her and send her sprawling to the deck.

Heodric renewed his struggle. His face reddened as the coils about his neck tightened, every breath now a painful, rattling gasp. The whips at his wrists were no less tortuous: it took all his strength to cling to his sword. Malmac stood above him and ran a gnarled hand through his golden hair.

"A good place for you, on your knees," he said. "Don't exert yourself, fellow! We'll have plenty of time for exertion."

Heodric's eyes rolled, furious, helpless. The room was

swimming. He would lose consciousness soon. Malmac turned to Zivia, struggling to her feet as the last whip circled and snaked around her.

"This troublesome cat won't make much of a pet," he said. "I don't think we need to keep her."

With a cry of fury she struck at him again – and again the whip caught her at the last moment and pulled her away as the blade passed a hairsbreadth from Malmac's nose. He didn't even wince.

"Again, little cat? Maybe this time –"

At his motion the whip pulled away to give Zivia a free run. His hand hovered, poised. The glowing ring, Heodric thought. The key to his sorcery. If he could free himself for long enough to strike... Wheezing with pain, he strove with desperate strength to rise once again.

It was in vain. Malmac didn't even bother to glance at him. His eyes were on Zivia as she hesitated, knowing that the wizard was toying with her, knowing that she was almost as helpless as the kneeling barbarian. Malmac's thin lips rolled back from yellow teeth: he grinned at her despair.

Zivia met his gaze, and her eyes narrowed, and she made one last frantic lunge – not at the Wizard but at Heodric, a full foot closer. Malmac's eyes widened: his hand snapped up and the whip hauled Zivia off her feet – but not before her knife had slashed through the bonds at Heodric's wrists.

The barbarian grunted once and swung up his sword and Malmac screamed and span, his right wrist a bloody spurting stump. The severed hand clattered to the floor, thick with rings, blazing with white light.

The enchanted cords spasmed and slackened, and Heodric gasped as the bonds left his throat and he breathed again. The whips began thrashing wildly. With nothing now to control them they struck cracking sweeping blows blind across the cabin. Zivia ducked and leapt to avoid them: Heodric grunted as one caught him a glancing cut across his back. He let the bloody sword fall to the deck.

"You wretch!" gasped Malmac. "You dog –"

Heodric seized him and lifted him and threw him into the striking coils. The whips fell upon the Wizard like snakes in a pit. Blind and deaf and uncontrolled, they sought only a back to flay. Malmac shrieked. He tried to rise: the whips cracked the knuckles of his remaining hand and tore bloody rents in the fine robes on his back. They slashed his legs, tore his skin, blinded his eyes. The deck ran with blood. Zivia and Heodric fled, the Wizard's agonised cries echoing in their ears.

New cries met them. The front of the barge was a blazing hell, the whole bow tower already lost to the fire. Guards and sailors and oarsmen alike were fighting to control the flames, but it was clear that their efforts would be futile. No wonder their struggle with Malmac had gone unnoticed.

"You fired the whole ship?" said Zivia. Heodric shrugged.

"I don't know much about boats," he admitted. "I didn't think it would burn so quick."

Speaking hurt, and he touched his swollen throat tenderly. Zivia's blow had cut his wrist and blood flowed down his hands, but it was a shallow wound.

"You had no need to come back," he said. "You owed me no debt."

"I owe you a cut throat," she snapped. "I came back to kill the wizard, not to save your treacherous hide. No man whips the Queen of Thieves."

In the light of the burning ship she seemed as regal as any highborn woman Heodric had seen, for all that she wore the apparel of a dancing-girl. He cast about for their escape. One of the escort vessels had drawn alongside, and he could see slaves and courtiers plunging overboard to swim to it. But there would be no succour for them there. He turned instead to the distant shore, where the lights of Port Usk were still faintly visible. A large spar had fallen nearby: he pointed to it.

"Quick girl – we'll use it for a raft, and –"

"To hell with you," said Zivia, simply, and dived from the ship and struck out for shore. He was dumbstruck for a moment – and then he flung back his head and laughed.

"A swimming cat!" he cried. "One miracle after another!"

*

His strong arms drove him shoreward upon the spar, saltwater stinging the cuts upon his wrists and back. He hated water: thought a dozen times that he made no progress and would surely drown – but the gods were kind and the sea calm, and the lights of Port Usk grew closer. He made the beach within the city walls. A man came running down to him.

"Have you escaped the Governor's ship?" he cried.

"Not I," said Heodric, breathless, bare-chested, awash with blood and salt. "Just a little night swimming, to clear my head."

The man thought better of trying to stop him. There was an orange glow all over the horizon, and the burning barge was clearly visible, and the citizens of Port Usk stood along the shoreline to see it. He made his way through the small crowd, uphill. More people had gathered there, and more would come: the huge ship would burn for hours yet.

"Zivia the Cat," said one woman, with an awestruck tone. "She burned the ship rather than be taken."

Heodric smiled to hear it. The legend of the Queen of Thieves would have grown fivefold by the morrow. From the tavern stable he took his sword and his horse, and left the empty wagon, and rode. He meant to be far away by sunrise.

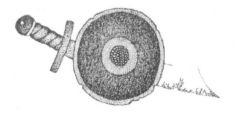

Volume 1

Volume 2

Volume 3

## *Volume 1: Great stories of swords and sorceries by*

Steve Lines, Steve Dilks, Susan Murrie Macdonald,
Geoff Hart, Gerri Leen, Eric Ian Steele, Chadwick Gunther,
and Adrian Cole
Illustrations by Jim Pitts

## *Volume 2: Great stories of swords and sorceries by*

Mike Chinn, Tais Teng, Martin Owton, Susan Murrie
Macdonald, Steve Dilks, Andrew Darlington, Pedro
Iniguez, Dev Agarwal, Phil Emery and Adrian Cole.
Illustrations by Jim Pitts

## *Volume 3 Great stories of swords and sorceries by*

Lorenzo D. Lopez, Tais Teng, Chadwick Ginther, Carson
Ray, Darin Hlavaz, Mike Chinn, Craig Herbertson, Rab
Foster, Jon Hansen and Adrian Cole.
Illustrations by Jim Pitts

# Rakehell

## A New Magazine of Swashbuckling Adventure

## Issue 1 sets sail July 1st

Featuring "The Mortuary Sword"
and five other thrilling yarns

## www.rakehellmagazine.com

# SO I'M WRITING A NOVEL...

is a
behind-the-scenes podcast,
following the journey
of writing
a SWORD & SORCERY novel
from earliest ideas
all the way through
to publication
and
promotion!

Feat. interviews with special guests
like
Howard Andrew Jones,
Ngo Vinh-Hoi of
The Appendix N Book Club,
and
Michael Curtis.

Find the show at
WWW.SOIMWRITINGANOVEL.COM
and
everywhere good podcasts
are found.

# WHETSTONE

**whetstonemag.blogspot.com**
## NEW SWORD AND SORCERY!

Printed in Great Britain
by Amazon